ANNA AND THE MOONLIGHT ROAD

BOOK TWO

The Metiks Fade Trilogy

Thomas Welsh

OWL HOLLOW PRESS

Owl Hollow Press, LLC, Springville, UT 84663

Anna and the Moonlight Road

Library of Congress Cataloging-in-Publication Data
Anna and the Moonlight Road / T. Welsh. — First edition.

Summary: Anna has battled her way back to reality, but she returns to find her friends scattered and her enemies have grown in strength and number. Her only hope for survival lies with new friends and a desperate plan to walk the Moonlight Road—a ghostly passage of frozen moonlight through worlds she can never touch—straight into the arms of the most dangerous Dreamer alive.

Cover design: Les Solot
Images: Depositphotos

ISBN 978-1-945654-51-0 (paperback)
ISBN 978-1-945654-52-7 (e-book)
LCCN 2019954552

Ewelina,

I think home is where you're surrounded by people you love,

People like your best friends.

And I think magic is real.

Magic is when someone changes your reality.

So I want to thank you for using your magic,

To change Scotland from a place my wife lived,

To a place she calls home.

prologue

The rain diluted the blood trail on the ground, creating abstract drip paintings that lasted for a few seconds before swirling away. Teej looked into the puddles and followed the trail, sure that Garret was above him but reluctant to tip his head back in the torrential rain.

Pausing for a moment, he walked across the concourse to the railing and looked out across the river at a massive ship breaking through the gloom. Its spotlights lit up the Foalmouth Bridge as the loaded tanker rose and fell on roiling waves, gliding slowly underneath. The sight allowed Teej to appreciate the massive scale of the structure under his feet. At almost three thousand feet long, it had taken him fifteen minutes to get halfway across the bridge. Buffeted by heavy winds and pelted with rain the whole way, he was sodden, cold and tired.

His raincoat was no match for the storm, and as he once more struggled to pull the zipper up to his neck, it caught his sweater again. Giving up, he leaned his hands on the railing, put his head down and let out a long, heavy sigh. A glass bottle smashed nearby. Teej flinched. Finally glancing up through the heavy drops of rain, he saw Garret.

"That could have hit me!" Teej shouted. His words were whisked off the bridge, across the river and out to the sea.

Teej put his hand to his forehead and squinted. Stooped and still, Garret was high above the deck, sitting in the superstructure on a thin platform between two of the suspension cables. He was maybe thirty feet above Teej. With his head bowed, his long, straggly hair was sopping wet and covered his face. His body hung limp and blood dripped from a wound on his head.

"Shit," said Teej with both concern and weary resignation. "How am I supposed to get up there?" he shouted into the wind.

"Climb," yelled Garret. He sounded grumpy.

Teej scanned the area, looking for a way up. Along one of the suspension cables next to the tower were little handholds used for maintenance, and they stuck out left and right alternately, each just large enough for a hand or a foot. Teej had made much more difficult ascents in the past, but climbing without a harness in high winds and rain was needlessly reckless. Still, there was no indication Garret would come down any time soon, so he would have to go up.

Walking across to the first rung, he grasped it firmly, let out one long, steady breath and started to climb. The ascent was difficult. Though the steelwork was solid, the whole bridge swayed in the storm. The metal was cold and wet, and numbness clung to his fingers as he grasped the handrail.

When he finally reached the top, Teej refused to look back down. Twice he hugged his body close to the column as the wind whipped his jacket around and threatened to blow him out to sea. He shuddered at the thought and pushed himself on, edging along the slender platform toward his friend. When he made it to the narrow shelf and stood next to the old man, Garret didn't move at all. Rubbing his numb fingers, Teej slowly sat, letting out a low moan as he felt the cold, wet steel under his body. Dangling his legs over the three-hundred-foot drop to the river below, he put an arm on his friend's shoulder and, together, they looked straight down into the dark, distant water. The rain didn't abate but the wind seemed to ease off a bit.

"You got into a fight?" asked Teej. It took Garret a long time to answer, and he started to worry.

"A bar fight. Yeah."

Teej relaxed when he heard his old friend's voice. This had happened before, and it would happen again.

"You were being a rowdy drunk, I assume?" Teej picked up one of the empty beer bottles Garret had lined up along the side of the platform. He tossed it over the edge and watched it fall till it became a dot, then disappeared completely. "And how the Hell did you even get up here?"

"I…don't remember. But I was not drunk. I was in an advanced state of refreshment. And besides, I don't get rowdy when I'm drunk. I get…honest."

"Some people aren't ready for that much honesty. You almost dropped one of these on my head you know?"

"Go back down and I'll try again," said Garret acerbically.

Teej shuffled nervously on the steel beam, but it seemed steady enough. As long as he didn't look straight down, it felt safe. Garret was unperturbed by the height, but something else was bothering him. He got like this every few years. Maudlin and self-pitying. It normally cleared up in a few weeks, but sometimes it took months.

"Let me look at that cut." Teej reached his hand up to the old man's matted straggle of gray hair. Just as he was about to touch the crusted blood, Garret's arm shot out and grasped his wrist. Teej winced at his strong grip. For a second, when their gaze met, Teej recognized anger, an emotion he rarely saw in his mentor's eyes. The old man's expression softened and he released his grip before patting Teej conciliatorily on the shoulder.

"Sorry, kid. Didn't mean nuthin' by it. *It's not you, it's me,* and all that. You know?"

Teej put his hand over the old man's. "I know. And I know you're going to get through this after a shower and some food. You look rough."

"Yeah," said Garret. "You should see the other guy."

"Really?"

Garret hesitated for a moment. "Actually, I think the other guy is fine."

Teej laughed. "What am I going to do with you?"

"Put me out of my misery," chuckled Garret. Teej didn't manage to smile back. They sat in silence for a full minute before Garret spoke again. "The darndest thing. Look at this shirt."

Teej looked him up and down. "It's a bloody mess, all right."

"No, not that. The buttons. I can't get them to line up right."

Teej didn't follow what the old man was trying to say. He shrugged.

"I start with the top button, and I swear it lines up okay, but no matter how many times I try to fix it, I have a spare one when I get to the bottom."

Garret pulled at the edge of the shirt distractedly as he spoke, his brow furrowed in intense concentration. Teej stared gravely at his mentor's fumbling fingers.

"It's probably nothing. You lost a button. Buy a new shirt."

Garret shook his head. "It's not just the buttons; it's everything. I can't tell the *time*, kid! When I look at my watch, I see *shapes* instead of hands pointing to the time! It makes no sense. You see the long hand and you think that's the important one, but it's actually a trick. The real one is the little one, but not the little fast one. So, you concentrate on the little one and you add the circle and...I'm trying to remember. I wrote some notes."

"You're not wearing a watch," said Teej weakly.

"I lost it, but that's not the point. If I can't figure out buttons, and I can't read my watch, and I can't go out without getting lost, what's the *point* of me? I sure can't win a bar fight any more. This is all I can do," he finished, gesturing toward the line of beers.

"Those aren't going to help," Teej said. "Why don't you just tell me what happened? You went to the bar and you were having a bad time—"

"I was having a great time! A night of wild speculation and dubious conclusions. However, my new friend and I had some philosophical differences during a heated debate. We settled it like gents. After I broke his jaw, his loyal wingman broke my skull."

Teej let out a snort, which turned into a laugh. In a moment, Garret added his laughter. The cold seemed to recede a little, and Teej allowed himself to relax.

"I used to be really good, you know? You *do* remember that, don't you? You saw me at my best."

Teej nodded. "Sure. I saw you in action and my life will *always* be the same."

Garret laughed again. "Such a smart mouth. I love it. Can we change the subject? I don't want to talk about me anymore."

"Sure," said Teej casually. "Although when do you ever stop talking about yourself?" Teej cocked his head to one side and did his best Garret impression. "*Enough about me; let's talk about you. What do you think 'bout me?*"

Garret nodded. "You got me pegged. But tonight, let's talk about Anna."

"Okay. What about her?"

"Can you keep her safe? Do you trust her to keep *you* safe?"

The wind picked up, and for a moment, Teej clung to the nearby post to keep his balance. Garret was like a stone statue; the wind didn't seem to touch him.

"I can. And I do."

Garret patted him firmly on the back, nudging him closer to the edge. "That's good enough for me, kid."

Teej eyed him critically. Making his voice as deep and authoritative as he could manage, he said, "I know what you're planning. You don't need to do this."

"Ahhh, I really *want* to though! I've always wanted to. Now's the time to try it. I'm beyond spent, and I've gone on far too long. Yet, I have no real regrets. Can you believe that? As old as I am—and I am *ancient*—I don't regret any of it. If I stick around any longer, I will let people down and I'll get someone killed. And if that is either you or Anna, I'll go to the grave with a heart full of hurt."

Everything the old man said rang true, and Teej started to panic. This wasn't like before. Garret was serious this time.

"You're being an old fool again. When you felt this way before, you bounced back."

"The bounce gets lower each time."

Teej shook his head. "No. You can't do this. Don't pretend it's a good idea. This is just running away."

"I'm a lot of things, kid, but the older I get, the less afraid I am of being called a coward."

"If you walk this road, it's suicide. You know it leads nowhere. You're just giving up."

Teej's head was down. The old man's hand clasped the back of his neck. "*This road*? Say it out loud, kid. Make it real."

Teej turned to him and gave him the sternest look he had. "Walk the Mangata. You're going to take the Moonlight Road, and you're never going to see any of us again."

Garret nodded. "I'm going to take the Moonlight Road, and *you* will never see *me* again. You are on your own now. Own it, kid. Say it and own it. You are alone now."

Teej's mouth dried up as the words caught in his throat, so he just nodded.

"That ain't true any longer. You might feel alone, but you have Anna now. I left you better than I found you. Now you have more than her, since you have other friends as well. Vinicaire might help you, and Pappi and his brother will come if you call on them. And Vinicaire's girl—the one with the colored hair. Damn, that girl is so…"

"Young?" interrupted Teej.

The old man smiled and nodded. They sat in silence for a moment. When Garret spoke again, his tone was apologetic.

"Look, you know I've always wanted to try the Moonlight Road, dammit! They say it's in ruins. No one has tried to walk it for years, and we still don't know where it leads. Everyone says it takes you where you're supposed to be, and I want to know where that is! If it leads nowhere and I disappear for good, at least my passing answers a question and serves a purpose. It's my last adventure, and I am excited to get going. Do you get that? I'm not George Bailey at the end of his rope and this isn't *It's a Wonderful Life.* I've thought about this for a long time, and it's what I want. I'm not even drunk anymore. I've been up here in the cold and the rain long enough to sober up. Before I took the final step, I just wanted to see you again."

"To say goodbye?" asked Teej.

"To say goodbye," Garret agreed with a nod, "and to give you advice."

Teej placed his hands on his lap and watched them curl into fists, the skin white and taut across his knuckles. His friend was losing his grip on Basine. Garret was never going to end up in an old folk's home, but now that he was about to walk off into the unknown, Teej didn't want him to go. He didn't want to be left on this bridge alone. But...

"Go ahead," said Teej.

Garret cleared his throat. "That weight you're carrying is going to drag you down. I know what happened in that Fluxa Haze haunts you. You probably have nightmares about losing Linda out there in that desert, right? You gotta let that shit go! It's not your fault she died, or that Wildey made his own choices. He's like your brother, but he's his own man. You can't let what happened poison you. Ya hear?"

Teej wanted to shut out the words, but Garret's voice was clear and firm. Trying to control a shiver that shook his body, he gave the old man his attention.

"Fix your heart," said Garret.

Teej nodded. "I'll try."

Before Teej could react, Garret pushed himself off the edge of the platform. He fell only about a foot before landing on a nearly-invisible glimmer of moonlight that formed a solid path.

"How about that?" Garret's smile was beaming.

Jumping to his feet, Teej almost lost his balance. His voice was filled with indignation. "You crazy old fool! I can't believe you did that!"

"Haha! It's real! Did you see that? *No matter where, step over the Moonlight, travel light, walk fast and pay no toll,*" sang Garret joyously. "Mangata! Let's find out where it goes. Ten steps then I'm in the next world. What a thing. What a *thing!*"

Garret was on his way already, his steps taking him through the air as he walked over the river. Rubbing his hands with excitement, he moved cautiously at first, and then stumbled into a half-run. Teej cheered.

"Good—" The banged up old man shed the years as he broke into a sprint. He was reborn. Teej was tempted to join him.

With the tenth step, Garret disappeared entirely. "—bye," echoed behind him.

This time he wasn't coming back. On the Foalmouth Bridge, high up in the girders on the south side, Teej stood alone.

PART
ONE

This Pale Moon Frozen

one

Restless energy threatened to overcome Anna completely. She stopped chewing her nails when she realized they were bleeding and gave herself a shake. Waiting around like this was killing her. Though she'd escaped Drowden's trap, there was no victory parade, no party and no cake. Anna had pulled herself out of Hell, but this was still far from Heaven. This was more like a waiting room in an office block in limbo.

She stirred her coffee slowly, the metal spoon clinking against the side of the mug with metronomic regularity, ringing loud and clear in the silence and periodically making her wince. She'd been doing this for fifteen minutes but couldn't stop herself. The coffee was cold and so was she.

Her fingers numb, Anna finally put the mug down and pulled her cardigan close. Glancing around, she noted with sick fascination how accentuated her senses were right now. Since she had come back to the real world, she felt everything was clearer, her developing Haze Sense somehow clarifying the facets of reality around her. Every detail of this cramped security office was cruelly distinct. The glaring CRT security monitors with their black-green screens, the brown coffee stains on the loose paperwork scattered across the desk, the fraying material of the swivel chairs, the sticky carpet, the underlying smell of mold and dust. This place was awful, and the lighting made her feel even worse, with the halogen strip cutting the room into sharply defined shadows and making her skin look sallow and diseased. She was glad there was no mirror here; she did not want to see her own reflection right now.

What had Teej called her? *A bonfire in the night.* There were enemies she should be burning right now, but instead she lingered here. Squeezing her fist in front of her face, Anna imagined her hands lighting on fire. In her mind's eye, she pictured Drowden's cold blue eyes, his messy beard and his dirty clothes, and then she imagined grasping him close and setting him ablaze. Why was she waiting around for Teej to return while Drowden plotted to destroy her? Stuck in this security office while time ticked by to the beat of an old grandfather clock in the corner, she couldn't imagine a worse place to be.

Two whole days of hiding here was too much. Even now, she wasn't entirely sure where *here* was. Teej informed her they were hiding out in the basement of an abandoned theater, which meant the place was dirty and silent. Outside this little security office was a huge space filled with headless mannequins, stage props, broken instruments, chests filled with dusty costumes and broken mirrors. Anna had already explored as far as she dared in this dank, unnecessarily creepy hideout. Locking the office door earlier in the morning, she decided she was going to stay put for a while.

With nothing else to do, Anna glared at the security monitors, made cups of coffee and went over and over everything she knew about Drowden and the Doxa, making a mental list of everything they had done to hurt her. Drowden had intimidated her on Malamun and then she had foolishly stumbled into one of his traps back at the summer house. That mistake sent her to the worst place imaginable. That would never happen again. Next time, there would be no talking, just her burning hands around his neck.

Slowly unclenching her fist, she picked up her mug and sipped her coffee. It tasted like the rancid stew she'd eaten in that hateful place. Everything tasted like the Sump now. The gasses lay heavy in her lungs, the stink of ash and mold in her nose and mouth.

No, she couldn't let her thoughts linger on the Black Water. *I got out, and I'll never let them send me back.*

Forcing herself to remember the escape instead of the place itself, she tried to piece together the events leading her to this moment. After Teej lifted her from the boat, she recalled being carried down the stairs into their hideout at Maxine's. After that, it was a jumbled mess. When she woke up in this basement, Teej promised her everything would be fine if she remained patient. Two days of silence and boredom later, her patience was long gone.

Her strongest memory after being rescued was being held in his arms. What had she said to him? Maybe if she had been more alert or coherent after her ordeal, she would have told him everything about her past Her memories were still too raw. She wasn't close to recovery following her husband's death. She was still in mourning when she first made contact with Teej. There were questions she couldn't bear to face right now. *Why did I burn that letter? Why do I wear the ring when he's dead and gone?* Anna didn't have answers for those questions yet, but she would have to face those buried memories eventually.

I'll find some answers—after I kill Drowden.

Pacing listlessly till she got tired, Anna ended up on the opposite side of the room, swirling absentmindedly on an office chair. She looked around, and a flash of blue caught her eye in the open bottom drawer of the desk. She pulled out a container of chocolate chip cookies and chuckled.

"These are probably a million years old."

Opening the packet, she tossed aside the first broken cookie and then dunked the second in her coffee. She watched with dismay as it dissolved and capsized into the cold liquid, sinking without trace.

"Shit."

Anna was about to attempt a deep coffee excavation mission when she noticed movement in her peripheral vision. Rolling her chair backward, she glimpsed someone in the small security monitor. The fuzzy image showed a tall man trying to get in the main entrance. Though it was boarded up and locked, he slid an arm inside a security panel and cracked the door open easily.

"Oh, no."

Exactly for this reason, Teej had reconnected the old security monitors and told her to pay attention to them. She was supposed to remain vigilant, and now a stranger was already sneaking up on her. While she battled a mug of coffee.

"Dammit!"

The intruder disappeared from the left monitor, and she desperately scanned the screens for any sign of him. He should be entering the main atrium, but the room was dark, and the monitor was fuzzy. Anna leaned in close and spotted movement in the bottom right screen. *The stairwell!*

Wheeling her chair closer to the monitor, she watched as the tall stranger approached from the stairs rubbing his hands together. He wore a stylish sweater and moved confidently in her direction. Anna's body tensed as he drew closer.

There was no sign of him in the corridor feed. He must be in a blind spot.

She had only a few seconds to make a plan of action. If she locked the door to the security office, how safe would she be? There were glass windows all around her, so she wouldn't be able to run far. And he seemed to know exactly where she was hiding. Could he track her?

Grabbing the broken end of a broom handle and a pair of scissors, she crouched below the windows while watching the screens.

In the stillness of the basement, every noise echoed loudly—except for the one sound she was straining to hear. Anna struggled to hear the footsteps. Was she imagining them?

Rising to peek into the vast storeroom, she dared to look out the office window. The headless mannequins were unhelpfully conspicuous as she scanned the darkness looking for her stalker. Did one of them move? She ducked down again and tried to control her breathing as her heart hammered in her chest. When the knock came on the door, she almost screamed.

"Hello? Anna? I would talk with you, if you welcome me in. I apologize if I frightened you."

Anna froze in place. He had a strange accent, and she couldn't place where he was from.

"Please answer to me. I know you are inside the room. I see the top of your stick."

Anna dropped her makeshift weapon and it clattered to the ground. *Shit.* She stood up slowly and turned to face the man on the other side of the glass door, still clutching the scissors between them.

Though she knew she should be afraid, Anna was disarmed by the handsome stranger's chiseled features. Even the harsh lighting couldn't detract from his flawless brown skin. Beneath bright, smiling eyes he bit his bottom lip playfully. His beard was immaculately sculpted in fine lines that accentuated his strong jawline, and his hair was tied back in a bun. He leaned to one side—drawing attention to his cashmere sweater and slim jeans—so he could meet her eye-to-eye. She gave him her steeliest gaze, but it didn't affect him. He looked *too* casual. Cocky even.

He shrugged casually under her scrutiny. "Will you let me in? I am just a regular guy who wants to meet you. It is cool, right?"

Anna rolled her eyes in exasperation. "Who are you?"

The man shuffled uncomfortably. For the briefest second he looked angry, but then he flashed his smile again.

"I am Andre DeLorde. Your Metik friend asked me to check on you. He said I might get here before he returned."

"I don't know who you mean."

"No need for games. *Teej* sent me. If I meant you harm, that would have already happened."

Anna sighed and dropped her shoulders. What were her options? If she let him in, was she opening herself up to a trap? Or had Teej really sent him here? Andre didn't *seem* dangerous, though she didn't trust him at all. She dropped the scissors into her bag and gestured for him to enter. He lingered outside.

"What are you waiting for?"

"You are not going to invite me in?" he said evasively.

"Then what? Should I fetch the butler to announce you?"

Andre eyed her cautiously as he stepped inside. Smoothly sliding down onto the chair, he rubbed his hands together before stroking his chin as if he needed a favor but didn't know how to ask. Anna sat in the swivel chair opposite him. So far, he didn't seem like a threat, but unsure what other tools she had to measure that, she tried to stretch out her Haze Sense. Concentrating, she fought to feel the tingle of Vig in the air.

It worked! There was a thrum in the air, an indistinct low rumble in her ears and a faint vibration rippling against her skin. Andre *felt* like one of them.

"You're an Aesthete," she said simply.

Andre clapped his hands and stretched up straight. "Yes, indeed! Do you have a pen? Or some lipstick in your purse?"

"No," she said. "I don't have lipstick. Or a purse. Why?"

"I think this hideout is not so lovely. You agree, yes?"

"It's a basement," said Anna, not sure what point he was trying to make.

"Ah, I see something!" Andre jumped to his feet suddenly and Anna flinched. He put a hand out and said, "Apologies. Please be at ease. Watch here."

Picking up a pen from the desk, Andre stepped in front of a whiteboard on the far wall where the fire escape routes were drawn on a map of the basement. He grabbed a handful of loose papers and rubbed it clean. When he started to draw on the board, she felt a low rumble beneath her feet and static in the air. He was using his Art to change something.

A breeze of sea-scented air blew through the room. As Andre stepped away from his work, a golden, sandy beach beneath wispy clouds stood where the whiteboard had been. This wasn't a video or a moving photograph; Andre created a window to another world.

"That's very pretty. Is it real?"

"A strange question for a Metik to ask," he replied as he reached through the window, the sun shining across his dark skin. "*Real*? That is a poor word you are choosing."

"Could I step out there and go to the beach?"

"I would ask you not to," he said with a slight frown. "This old theater is no longer strong with Vig. I am not so powerful right here. I think a nice view is the best I can manage for your enjoyment. Or perhaps I could—"

His eyes filled with deep concentration. The monitors flickered off one by one. As they flickered back on, each one displayed views of rolling ocean waves.

"Better? This place is sad and cold. Not just here in this room. This whole city is too cold for me. And always with the rain! I prefer a nice sunny beach and pretty girls in bikinis. Maybe this does not excite you. Am I right?"

Anna ignored him and looked out the newly created window to the sea. The waves rolled peacefully, and the warm sun baked the sand. The view reminded her of beach holidays with her dad. Hot days spent digging trenches along the shore and watching them fill with seawater. She was unnerved by how much the image affected her. He was disarming her with his Art.

"Are you showing off? No need, I've seen this stuff before."

His bright eyes mocked her. Distractedly, she decided he looked like a pop star. Anna tried to disregard his appearance and focus on his words.

"I just hate ugly things and this place is an ugly thing. This was a beautiful theater once and I loved watching the shows. I remember I once saw—"

Anna shot him a look, and Andre put his hands up in mock surrender.

"I see from the face you are making that you have no patience for this sort of talk. I am rambling, no?" A forced laugh filled the space between them.

"I only wanted to help with your training," said Andre.

"I don't need your help," retorted Anna. A sudden breeze wafted through the room. Andre's smile faded and the warm wind turned cool as his mood changed. Anna shivered and reached for her scarf.

"What shall we do till Teej gets here?" asked Andre. "I suppose I could tell you some things and you could tell me some things."

Anna latched on to the opportunity. She leaned forward and asked the question before she could stop herself. "What happened to Linda?"

"His last partner?" Andre stroked his beard. "Was Linda part of Teej's original partnership? I am not so sure. She died, no?"

Anna nodded.

"I am hearing only rumors, and I find the politics of my fellow Dreamers very uninteresting. But I am sure of this one thing." He held up a finger to emphasize his point. "The Fluxa Haze, stopped by our friend Teej, was not so much a failure as he thinks."

"What do you mean? Didn't it Spiral and kill lots of people?"

"Enough blood was spilled to change our world, just a little bit."

Anna shook her head. *Why did changing the world have to involve blood?*

"You know, I have never met one of you," said Andre.

She wanted him to tell her more about Linda, but for now, she let him change the subject. "A woman?"

"No," he laughed heartily. "I have never met an Undreamer. Might I ask you some questions?"

"Sure," she said tersely. *Where was that accent from?* He sounded like he could be from anywhere.

"Tell me what is it like to be an Undreamer?"

"I don't know what to compare it to. I think you know more about Undreamers than I do…" Anna trailed off and left a gap for him to say something.

"I only know what they say. Though Undreamers are not skilled at modifying Hazes compared to other Metiks, they have no problem destroying them. The Undreamer's powers are like fire and flood. Your Praxis manifests as burning winds that tear up worlds and storms that rage. It can be a cruel blade that cuts raggedly, so the scars don't heal."

Anna unconsciously shook her head. Andre noticed her negative reaction.

"But there are…prejudices at play in this description. I tell you only what the old Dreamers would say about you. There are not many Undreamers left for me to have an opinion about. Maybe only one."

"And what is your opinion of *me*?"

Andre bit his bottom lip and shook his head. "I think you are a pretty girl with little care about your appearance. Your messy hair and baggy clothes are an eyesore."

Anna let out a dismissive chuckle. This was familiar: a cocky guy trying to 'neg' her: breaking down her self-esteem by giving her a backhanded compliment that undermined her. Even Behind the Veil, some things never changed.

"I certainly didn't spend as much time on my hair as you did." She leaned closer to him. "Are you wearing lip balm right now?"

Andre shook his head in annoyance.

"It is chap stick for the damp weather. Wait, you are teasing me!" He threw his head back and laughed, then leaned across the desk and grabbed a nearby clipboard.

"I will show you another technique and maybe it will help me explain something to you." He twirled a pen in his hand as he spoke, trying to impress her.

Andre started to sketch something on the clipboard. Roughly, it looked like two circles looped together. As he ran his pen across the paper, Anna felt his Vig flow into this new creation. The low rumble was there, a faint pressure at the back of her skull.

"Put your hands through?"

"Through what?"

Andre pushed the clipboard toward her, but she didn't know what he wanted. "It is a simple trick," he said. "Not dangerous. Just some fun."

Shrugging, Anna put her hands out to touch the picture. They slipped through the surface as if it were a basin of water. It felt like liquid, but her hands didn't get wet. Anna let out a little half-laugh. "Wow. What is…?"

She crouched down and glanced under the clipboard, but there was nothing to see. Her hands seemed to have disappeared. From above she could see them sloshing around in invisible water. Andre's smile was all perfect teeth. "And now out."

Anna pulled back, but as her hands came out of the water, the drawing of the two loops transformed and closed. The circles became stainless steel on the surface and materialized around her wrists. She was trapped in a pair of solid metal handcuffs. Testing them by tugging her hands away from each other, the metal chain clinked heavily, and she remained locked tight. Though she strained, they were too secure to wriggle off.

Trying to keep calm, she gave him a scolding look.

Andre put his hands up and tried to calm her. "No, it is not so much like that. I am not being a creepy man or anything."

"No, this *is* creepy." Anna flexed her wrists and turned her hands looking for a release mechanism of some sort. There wasn't even a hole for a key.

Andre pointed to her as he spoke. "This trap is Mimesis, the creation of a Dreamer though his Art. What are you doing now? Looking for a key? Using your muscles to escape? Why do you do this?"

"Because I am unhappy and want to get out of these. What do you *suggest* I do?"

"For one, you should not be worried. I see your quick, little breaths and the fast beats of your heart. Why are you worried when this is such small Vig? You know it is weak, so what threat do you face?"

Anna nodded. "So, I should just use my Praxis to break out?"

"Yes. But hold off on this for a moment and let me say more. I have a bigger point. These choices you make so far—the friends, the allies, the side you are on—are they not also influencing you? Do you go along with them without making decisions, just like you go along with being trapped in these cuffs? Should your first response not be to resist?"

"My first response is *always* to resist."

"Yes, normally, but not with Teej."

Anna shook her head and inched back from Andre. "He earned my trust."

For the first time, there was no trace of a smile. "I suppose that must seem true. You would not say this if he were a liar. He must be a very honest man. With you."

Anna gave him a sideways glance. "He is."

Clenching her fists together, she flicked her fingers out hard. At the same time, she imagined a concussive burst of energy exploding outward. And it did. The cuffs shattered, shards of broken metal embedding themselves in the walls on either side of them with a rattle. Andre recoiled, but Anna didn't budge. This was her power, controlled by her own Will. It

25

wouldn't hurt her. Or him, unless she wanted it to. As she noted the shock on his face, one thing became clear: she wasn't as afraid of this power as he was.

"This is why people don't like Undreamers." He unruffled his sweater and leaned back in the chair uneasily. Andre was half-joking, his smile half-gone. Taking a moment to compose himself, he went on, "It is interesting, actually. We sometimes say Metiks sculpt the Haze while the clay is wet. Molding and manipulating when the Haze is fresh, the shape is already set when Basine returns. For Undreamers it is not so much like sculpting or molding. It is more like…"

"A sledgehammer," she finished. "Sorry if I ruined your metaphor."

Andre nodded. He didn't look so cocky now.

"It is all right. And I did not mean to talk badly of our friend Teej. My point is that we make few choices in life. We just go along with most things, but you can be different. Undreamers need not follow the path set for them by Dreamers or Metiks."

Anna nodded. The buzz she got from using her Praxis was mildly intoxicating. She *almost* wanted him to try something. Though she was ready to fight, she reminded herself this man was neither friend nor enemy right now. *Keep focused and think about the subtext of what he says.* Was he really trying to undermine Teej? Or test her loyalties?

"Perhaps I am preaching to the converted here. I think you are good at resisting already. You defied the old Occultist and Mott. Maybe even old Grayface. These are powerful men who most would call 'master.' What will you do when there are no more men to stand up to? How will the warrior define herself when the wars are all over?"

"There are *always* more men to stand up to. More wars to fight." Anna went back to something he had just said. "Who is old Grayface? And the Occultist?"

"Ah, I throw around their stage names too much. The second is Drowden. And the first is Rayleigh."

"Rayleigh is your...what? Boss?"

Andre laughed. "No, no. More like a...patron? Is this the right word? Or representative, perhaps."

Anna shook her head. "I don't think that's the right word either. Is he the most powerful Dreamer, and everyone is too afraid to disobey him? That sounds like a boss to me. Or a ruler."

"We have no rulers," Andre snapped back with a frown.

"If you say so."

They sat in awkward silence for a moment. Andre looked glum. She had offended him. Behind him, the security screens flickered off one by one, the images of the sea fading to black.

"You do not like me so much, Anna. I see that in your eyes and hear it in your words. Despite this, I like you. In time, you will come to like me more, too. You do not have many friends, but I think Teej is a good man and he believes in you. I will help you both, even if it means choosing a side in these matters where I would normally keep my head down. I am not a brave man normally, but this time I think it is worth it to be brave. You agree?"

Anna nodded. "I agree."

"Well then," said Andre as he stood. "I shall leave to prepare the performance."

"The performance?"

"Yes. He did not tell you? Teej will be back within the hour. When he returns, the show will begin."

Before Anna could ask Andre what he meant, he was out the door. She looked back to the board where moments before the beach and the sea had been. It was gone, and in its place was a childlike drawing. Getting up out of her seat, Anna walked across the room to examine it more closely. Inked in crayon was a crude image on a piece of plain, white paper. A beach, a palm tree and a man and woman looking out at the ocean.

two

With his head almost touching the glass, Teej stared out the window of the cab. There was nothing to see but empty streets and rain. The road rumbled under him as the car hit one pothole after another, and his stomach heaved, both from the ride and from hunger. When this journey was over, he'd be able to eat and sleep. He'd be with Anna again, and she'd ask him where he had gone and why he had left her alone. He hoped to have some worthwhile answers.

The driver was taking him through the harbor district to avoid the early morning traffic, but the narrow streets that wound around the riverside were industrial graveyards. The procession of abandoned factories and warehouses didn't help his mood. The sun felt different here, the pale morning light struggling to make an impression on the dead streets.

The cab smelled like incense and stale coffee. Teej shifted uncomfortably on the scratchy rug that covered the back seats. He fished his phone from his back pocket to check if Anna had sent any messages, but there was no word from her.

Should he call her? No, the talk radio station blared too loud for nuanced conversation to be possible. The distorted audio ranted about Hell and demons and the degradation of society. Teej didn't want to talk to the driver either. Instead he started to type a message to Anna but was interrupted halfway through.

"You believe this?" His accent was a half-drunk drawl.

Teej reexamined his driver and realized what he had stumbled into. The driver was an Etune, an artificial person created inside a Haze, and they had both passed through the periphery and out of Basine. The Aesthete behind this Haze was sneaky, masking the low rumbling that marked the transition out of Basine with bumpy roads and potholes. Still, Teej had been careless. No matter how much a Dreamer tried to hide the transition from Basine to a Haze, no self-respecting Metik should be fooled this easily. He had to be *better* than this.

Stretching back in his seat to get a better look, Teej noticed the unusual features of the Etune. The change had been gradual as the driver slowly shed his human form. Greasy gray-black hair couldn't hide the inhumanness of the skull beneath. There was no skin, just bleached bone. The arms were covered by a patchwork denim jacket, and the driver wore black leather gloves. In the narrow gap between sleeve and wrist, a skeletal arm glinted white in the light.

"Believe what?" he asked his undead chauffeur.

"This traffic, man. I don't want speed limits. I want no stop signals. Nothin' gonna slow me down."

Teej ignored the skeleton and shifted into the middle seat to look at the road ahead. To his left the sun was reversing its natural course and slinking below the horizon, the night creeping back across one small part of the city. The streetlights buzzed and flickered ahead of them. On their right, a red brick building was illuminated by a purple neon sign that bled into the twilight. By the time the taxi reached the run-down bar, they had driven into complete darkness.

Teej stepped out into the street and scanned the environment. The purple neon logo over the building spelled out "Skelter Helter." Orange light shone through barred windows. A wooden sign by the heavy metal door creaked in the wind, though nothing was written on it. The music inside was so loud Teej could feel the thud of the bass beneath his feet, and indistinct shouting and singing echoed out into the night.

He turned back to the taxi where a smiling skeleton held a cigarette, the smoke billowing out from the bare ribcage as the thing "breathed" in.

"Ooh, doesn't it make you wonder?" asked the skeleton.

"Go bustle a hedgerow," Teej responded, turning away and walking toward the bar. The car exhaust backfired as it drove off behind him.

There was no point in running. If Teej wasted his energy pushing for an exit, he'd be too weak to fight, and if this Haze belonged to the Aesthete he suspected, a fight was inevitable.

As he reached for the door handle, Teej paused and let out a long sigh. Did he have to do this? What would happen to Anna if he didn't make it out of here?

Shaking his head with weary resignation, he pushed the door open and stepped inside. The smell of stale alcohol, sweat, weed smoke, and *fresh* alcohol hit him immediately. The air tasted of whiskey fumes and his eyes stung as they adjusted to the gloom. To his right, an eight-foot-tall purple troll-creature played pool in a dark corner. To his left, two skeletons sat at the bar, served by a one-eyed ogre. The rest of the patrons ignored Teej, but the ogre stared at him in silent apprehension. Teej walked across the sticky floor and sat between the two skeletons. The bar stool was too high, and his feet dangled boyishly above the floor.

The bar ogre was heavily muscled and smooth-skinned, with a single eye below a long, gnarled horn. Her body was as wide as it was tall, about six feet in either direction. She held a comically small bottle in one massive three-clawed hand in front of Teej. When he nodded, she reached for a small shot glass and carefully set it down with the tip of her claw before pouring an amber colored liquid till it reached the brim.

The skeleton to his right placed a bony hand on his shoulder, and Teej turned to look at the bleached skull. The eyes were covered with a metal plate. It wore an ill-fitting, dusty black suit with a loose tie hanging over one shoulder, and it juddered and twitched when it moved as if it might fall apart at any time.

"Business is going good." The skeleton's voice was comically banal and broken, like radio static.

"Uh huh."

Behind him the other skeleton made a raspy coughing sound. The creature retained streaky flesh strained tight across the bone. Two shining white eyes looked back at him from black eye sockets, while bare teeth clacked the air, the gums pulled back from a lipless mouth.

"I just want to see your blood," said the skeleton. It made a noise somewhere between a cough and a laugh as its teeth continued to chatter.

"Get in line," Teej grumbled.

The volume of the music rose, with heavy guitar riffs and double bass drums kicking in. Teej rubbed his aching forehead. Suddenly, his stomach grumbled, and he couldn't remember the last time he had eaten.

The bartender ogre nudged the glass across the counter, silently imploring him to drink. Teej turned back to the skeleton in the black suit.

"What is it?" he asked. His voice was resonant, his command augmented by the use of the Word.

"Battery acid," the skeleton said flatly.

Teej grunted and knocked the glass over. The ogre flinched as the liquid splashed her hand. Caustic steam rose from the bar where the acid bubbled across the surface, and the ogre held her hand in pain and recoiled without making a noise. Behind him, he felt the large troll at the pool table stand to attention and the music from the jukebox grow louder.

"Come out," said Teej under his breath. He was quiet, but the Dreamer could hear everything in this Haze. Teej turned to look at the troll facing him across the room. A spiked metal helmet highlighted its ivory tusks, flanking giant crooked incisors. Its eyes were red pinpricks, while its purple body rippled with muscle. The pool cue hung loosely in a three-clawed hand at its side, and it snarled and dripped clear saliva, forming puddles on the wooden floor.

"We gotta keep you separated," sang the metal-plated skeleton at the bar. "Don't wanna come out to play."

"Fine," Teej said as he walked across the room. The troll stepped to intercept him, but he raised his right hand. When he said "No," it retreated backward.

Teej stretched his Haze Sense outward and felt the invisible winds of Vig blowing through the bar. He walked toward the jukebox. This was where he had to bait the Dreamer. He put his hand on top of silver chrome, noting how new and clean this machine was compared to everything else here. Pulling his wallet from an inside pocket, he searched for the shiniest coin to slide into the slot. A record-scratching noise disrupted the tension and the guitars and drums stopped, replaced by a steady bass playing a rhythm and blues progression.

When our day is done
And our light is gone

"No! No! No!" shouted the skeleton, his bones rattling. "We want to rock!"

"I could listen to this all day," replied Teej. He leaned against the jukebox waiting for the Dreamer to make an appearance. He didn't have to wait long. From the back room, he heard a toilet flush.

Mustaine appeared, still pulling up his pants as he walked into the bar. "Don't touch my music, man."

The Dreamer was tall, dark and filthy. A metal-studded leather jacket hung open to reveal a hairless chest covered in rough tattoos and scars. Tattered jeans hung indecently low on his waist. Long, greasy hair slicked down around his shoulders and a wispy moustache drew a pencil line along his top lip.

Aviator shades completed the look and reflected Teej's unimpressed face.

"Those records aren't vinyl, you know. They're pressed x-rays. Bone music, man! Don't mess with my tunes, they're fragile."

"Why am I here, Mustaine?"

The Dreamer leaned on the bar and pointed at him. Teej could smell cigarettes and tequila from ten feet away.

"I missed your face. But now I see it again, I think it needs rearranging."

"Are you masquerading as a rock star?" asked Teej with a derisive smirk.

"Rock *star*? I'm a fucking rock *icon*!"

Teej rubbed his eyes in irritation. The smells in this Haze were making his nausea worse. Was Mustaine affecting him somehow? He didn't detect any aggressive exertion of Vig in his direction. Maybe he was just tired. Getting Anna back to safety had been hard. His fight with the robotic Pilgrim had exhausted him, and he could still feel the stiffness in his charred hand. His head wound from the battle with Mott's thugs was a faded memory, forced to the back of his mind by more recent pains. Facing Mustaine with all these accumulated injuries was going to be difficult, but there was no other option. He was stuck in this Haze until one of them was dead.

The music clicked off suddenly. Without turning, Teej stretched his arm back and punched the side of the jukebox until it started up again.

And the clouds we gaze upon, they crumple and fade.

"Why am I here?" Teej repeated.

"Let me tell you a lie you'll believe," said Mustaine theatrically, pointing to his head as if his words were mind-blowing.

"How about you just tell me the truth?"

"Where you hide the girl?" barked Mustaine.

Teej shook his head. "Which girl?"

"Your new Metik. The *Undreamer*. You killed your last partner, right?"

Teej clenched his fists. "What's this really about? Wildey?"

Mustaine glared at him over the top of his glasses. He looked nervous and tense with anger. "It's always about Wildey. Seen your brother around lately?"

"He's not my brother. We're not even friends."

"He got many friends?"

"I would guess not many among Dreamers."

"You got many friends...left?"

What did he mean? Mustaine certainly knew about Anna, but what other friends was he talking about? Garret? Unsure how to reply, Teej worried that if he didn't say something, the fight would start. He needed a few more moments to prepare, so he filled the silence as best he could.

"You got an axe to grind with Wildey?"

"Into his gut." Mustaine cracked his knuckles, a bead of sweat on his greasy brow.

"What did he do to you?"

"Near killed me," snarled Mustaine. "Left me to die. Collapsed my Haze while I half drowned in a gutter."

"You know I can't help you find him, and you know he's no friend of mine. Why come for me?"

"The girl," drawled Mustaine with a sinister smile. "You musta found a real good place to hide her, cos none of us can find sign of her."

"Us? Who is *us*?"

"I gone said too much." Mustaine looked at the troll closest to Teej. The strands of Vig in the air started to twitch. Any minute now.

"The Doxa aren't exactly your style, Mustaine. You taking orders from Drowden now?"

Mustaine shook his head. "You're barking up the wrong Dreamer."

"Who then?" asked Teej, but there would be no answer.

The troll flipped the pool table in his direction with one casual swipe of the paw. Teej tucked and rolled under it, grabbing a pool cue from the floor as he went. His instincts kicked in. Hundreds of years of martial arts, acrobatics, and Metik's training helping him avoid danger with an economy of movement. The troll closed in and slashed at him with claws as long as his arm. Teej dodged backward. His skills were sharp enough to keep him alive even when his body lagged.

Teej snapped the pool cue in two, forming his Periapt. He grasped the tonfa, a wooden nightstick with a handle and shaft, and turned his gaze to Mustaine. The Dreamer had disappeared. Teej glanced at the female ogre in confusion, and she shrugged, momentarily distracting him.

With a sickening crunch, Teej fell to his knees as a titanium baseball bat smashed into his stomach. Mustaine had teleported behind him to swing hard and low. Teej wheezed and gagged. His mouth acrid, he spat and held his stomach with both hands. In his abdomen, he felt the creeping warmth of internal bleeding. Rolling on one side, his world turned upside down again. The troll kicked him with one massive hoof, spinning him through the air. Teej was relieved when he missed the ceiling fan by inches. He spotted the shelves behind the bar stacked with whiskey and vodka bottles a fraction of a second before he smashed into them head first. Glass and splintered wood showered across the bar like it had been hit with a rocket.

His vision was clouded with dust and debris. Sitting on the ground with his back against what was left of the bar, his arms and legs were splayed out to either side. He tried to appraise the damage done to his body, but his senses were overloaded. Shock was taking over. If he couldn't pull his mind into order, he would pass out, and if that happened, he was done for.

Teej concentrated, flexed his right hand, and focused all his Will there. One by one, the shards of broken glass embedded in his flesh forced their way out through his skin and rattled to the floor. His broken ring finger snapped back into place as his cuts began to close. All the effort narrowed his vision to a pinprick. Through gritted teeth and a stifled roar, he forced his mind to stay alert, his field of view opening up again.

Mustaine dragged the metal bat across the floor as he walked, raking it over broken wood and glass. His open leather jacket revealed rippled muscles and sinew. Black and red swirls were appearing all over his flesh, and his eyes became metallic green, slit like a reptile.

"Death, death, death my love."

The skeletons appeared on either side of Teej, grasping him under the arms and lifting his limp body. Their bony hands dug into his flesh and forced him to stand on weak legs. Mustaine started throwing practice swings with the bat.

"She's outta there! Home run. Wooooo!"

On either side of him, the skeletons rattled as they laughed. Teej scanned his surroundings for weapons, continuing to build a mental inventory of all the damage his body had sustained. Before the fight started, any use of his Praxis would have been obvious to Mustaine. Now that the Haze was awash with expended Vig, it was harder for the Dreamer to sense his intentions. Teej slowly rotated his wrist until he was holding the right skeleton's upper arm. When Mustaine stepped toward him, he pushed the tip of the bat in Teej's face. As his head was pushed back, Teej waited for an opportune moment.

"Ain't nuthin' personal, man. I just don't like you."

"You…can…" With a split top lip and a few broken teeth, the words didn't come easy. Mustaine pulled back the bat for a final swing. Teej could see himself reflected in the Dreamer's mirror shades. His body was broken but his eyes were clear.

"Once I'm done with you, Imma find your girl. Heard she's pretty."

Teej grasped the suit-wearing skeleton firmly and turned to look into the creature's eyes. "Oh no," it said plaintively before Teej tugged with all his remaining Will and strength at the same time as Mustaine swung his bat. The Etune was obliterated in a

36

shower of dust that blinded the Dreamer. Teej's makeshift shield was destroyed with one swing, but it served its purpose. Though the bat went through the bones with little resistance, it was enough to divert the killing blow. Missing his head by inches, Teej dropped low and hammered his body, shoulder-first, into the Dreamer's stomach.

Healing himself as he moved, Teej pulled the Vig from the air to twist his sprained ankle back into its socket. He snapped his broken ribs into position while reknitting the stretched and torn muscles of his abdomen.

Teej lifted Mustaine and drove them both toward the far wall. Mustaine struggled to free himself, but Teej's momentum propelled them forward. Before they hit the wall, a rogue thought flashed through Teej's mind. *God, this feels good!*

As they collided with the jukebox, Teej felt the wet crunch of his body in the crash and heard the rending of metal and the splintering of wood. And then blackness.

When he finally opened his eyes, he saw Mustaine had risen first. Teej half-sat in a pile of broken wood while his enemy limped for the back door past the carnage of the bar, damaged beyond recognition. Licks of flame spread across the floor, igniting the displaced alcohol. Mustaine hobbled on a broken leg. The only sound in the ruined Haze was the rising crackle of fire.

"Mustaine!" he shouted. His voice sounded ragged in his throat, like he'd swallowed glass. "Anna. You need to know something about her."

Mustaine stopped in his tracks with his back to Teej. "Are you going to tell me to stay away from her? Are you going to warn me she's tougher than people say?"

"Tougher and smarter," said Teej as he somehow found the strength to stand, his wobbling legs threatening to fail him at any moment. "But you'll never know."

"What—" Mustaine started to turn as Teej grabbed an intact vinyl record from the ground, spun around, and released it like a discus. It arced through the air, seeming to miss Mustaine by several feet before it changed direction and spun back toward him. The projectile sliced through the side of Mustaine's neck before embedding itself in the floor like a heavy saw blade. It took a moment for Mustaine to react and for the bleeding to start. His head hung by a single flap of skin, and a moment later, his body fell to the ground.

The flames around him burned low, but still, Mustaine's corpse crumbled like ash. Teej let out a long, low sigh of relief as he limped to the wall and leaned there for a moment to survey the carnage. The bartender ogre was huddled next to the front door but was too large to squeeze through. Her green skin had turned pale pink with fright, and she gnawed her claws in fear.

Teej looked at Mustaine's body, then back at the ogre and shrugged.

three

S tanding in the cold shower, Anna watched the soapy streams run off her body with overwhelming relief. Once she was clean, the final vestiges of *that place* would be erased and she could forget it forever. *Wash it all away.*

It had been two days since she'd escaped the Sump, and this was her first proper chance to clean herself. Andre's appearance had put her on edge, but he was gone for the moment. Teej had warned her to wait for his return before leaving the small office, but she could wait no longer. She'd desperately needed a visit to the old showers.

Though she managed to scrub off the dirt and dried blood from her cuts and scrapes, it was her hair that gave her the most trouble. Holding her head under the shower, Anna soaked the tangled mess as long as possible. The cold water reinvigorated her, and she lingered in the spray while shivering.

She was slowly adjusting to life back in Basine, but still, Anna wondered what remained of the Sump. Char and Fee were surely lost to the Dredges, as was Ozman. Once the dirt was gone, what would she carry forward from that place? Just the memories? They could be pushed deep and buried, and even if she felt them in her chest like a heavy weight, she didn't have to linger on them. But would she ever be clean of it? She could forget their faces, swallow her guilt and keep moving forward, but would she always feel this grime on her flesh? She was tainted. That place had stained her soul.

Anna could swallow her trauma, but she had to confront the man who had sent her there. Drowden. As long as there was a chance he could send her back, he would be a potential threat she could not forget.

By my hands, I will burn you, Drowden.

Anna ran bluish fingers over her chest, noting with some concern how slim she'd become. Not just across her mid-section, but along her arms and legs as well. Her muscles had wasted. Distress had gotten in the way of her appetite. She couldn't remember the last warm meal she'd eaten. Perhaps she should focus on confronting a pizza before she confronted an ancient, occult madman.

Stepping out of the shower onto the cracked tiles, she checked the bathroom for threats like portals or creatures. It was hard to relax when she was on constant alert.

For the moment, she was alone. Andre was working on the main stage at the other end of the huge building. The front doors of the abandoned theater were barred and the windows were boarded over. To get to this secluded shower room used by the dancers and performers, she had climbed over debris and broken the locks on two separate gates with a hammer. Teej's vague directions hadn't included quite so much breaking and entering.

Shivering as she dried herself with paper towels from the bathroom, Anna brushed her hair with her fingertips and then drank copiously from the faucet to get the taste of ash out of her mouth. Even after washing, a lingering stink of the Sump clung to her, but at least now she looked better. In the long mirrors, she watched herself pull on the new, plain clothes Teej had come across in the lost-and-found basket: a sweater ten sizes too big and tight leggings, a size too small. At least they were clean, and she liked how they hid the bruises and scrapes she couldn't even remember getting.

Giving herself a few more moments before she faced the world outside the bathroom, Anna washed her face one more time. Looking into the mirror to peer at the dark circles under her eyes, she allowed herself some respite from her own recriminations.

"You've looked worse, missy. Must remember to buy a hairbrush."

Anna spotted her phone lying by the sink.

"And call Mom! Not now, obviously, but…call Mom."

Anna slipped on her old sneakers and wondered if she would ever see her apartment again. It was probably too dangerous to go back, and she didn't miss that place. Though she missed some home comforts like better sneakers, a hairbrush and a toothbrush, clothes that fit her properly, her lucky green sweater, hair pins that weren't bent and ruined, moisturizer and her old MP3 player with all the awful nineties dance music.

Maybe she didn't need those things anymore. Anna didn't have any possessions at all right now, but somehow that wasn't so bad. She had Teej and a small amount of courage, and that was enough. Giving herself a tiny nod of reassurance in the mirror, she left the changing room to await Teej's return, Andre's performance, and everything else the day could throw at her.

four

The dark, twisting passages of the old theater smelled like static electricity and burned rubber. Along the walls, faded and ripped posters for ballet shows and plays hung amidst the tangle of cables, light riggings, amplifiers and microphone stands. The path, illuminated by little LEDs that ran the length of the corridor like emergency lighting on an airplane, wound through the shadows. Anna kept her eyes on Teej's back as they sidestepped through the detritus. Several times he warned her to watch her feet. Sliding between an old piano and an AV panel covered in colored knobs, Teej approached a locked white door and fished in his pocket for a key.

"Are you going to talk to me at all?" asked Anna. She didn't mean to sound angry, but she'd held her tongue long enough. Frustration had built since his return. Something was bothering him. Maybe she took too long in the shower, or maybe he didn't like how she handled Andre. But she couldn't take his moody silence any longer.

"Can it wait?" he said with his back to her.

"No. It can't. You haven't even told me where you were or what we're doing here. Something's wrong and you're not telling me what happened."

Teej turned slowly but couldn't look her in the eye.

"Why are we just waiting here?" asked Anna. "And who is this Andre guy? *Drowden* is the problem. Why aren't we going after the Doxa?"

Anna didn't want to raise her voice, but it rose anyway. When she noticed her fists were clenched, she opened her hands slowly and took a step back from him.

"You're not ready," said Teej. "I asked you to be patient."

"You want me to be patient after what he did to me? Do you know what it was like there?"

"No," mumbled Teej. "I can't imagine. I thought I'd lost you."

Anna was about to snap at him, but something about his demeanor stopped her. He looked exhausted. This wasn't about her; something had happened to him.

"Teej, just tell me what's wrong. I can see that you're not hurt, but your clothes are splashed with blood."

He finally looked up with glassy eyes, focusing on a point over her shoulder. Anna shuddered with concern.

"There was a fight," he said. "Now we have one less enemy, although he was an enemy we didn't even know about."

"Shouldn't I have been there? You once told me it takes two Metiks to fight a Dreamer. Don't you trust me enough to help you?"

He looked directly into her eyes, and she saw steeliness there. A glimpse of the real Teej. "I trust you more than you can know. You just need to trust me a little more. We'll face Drowden soon enough. I promise."

Anna nodded. "I trust you, too."

He turned back to the door and fumbled with the key. Trying her best to sound upbeat, Anna asked, "You still haven't told me why we're here. This isn't going to be another *'teaching moment with Teej'* is it?"

As he pushed the door open, his smile returned. "Let's just enjoy some theater, then we'll go from there."

Floodlights blinded them as they stumbled inside. Anna was surprised to see that they were high in the stalls above a large concert hall. Entering a door above the right-hand side of the stage near the highest point of the hall, she followed Teej along a narrow aisle to the seats that ran along the upper level.

The concert hall was grand. Heavy, red velvet curtains hung before the stage, and the seats were thick and comfy with gold trim around the edges. Decorating the periphery of the stage, elaborate murals depicted birds and climbing plants, while the opera pit was filled with musical instruments sitting next to empty seats. Violins, violas, a whole wind section and a grand piano sat next to an ornate golden harp. All the instruments were set up for a performance.

Anna sidestepped along the row of chairs, amazed by the grandeur of the place. They had gone back in time. Her Haze Sense didn't give her any indication that they'd left Basine, but this didn't feel like the real world anymore. It was beautiful. She always loved the moment of darkness before the show started, when everyone went quiet as the curtain slowly rose.

Teej beckoned her to find a seat in the middle of the row. "Come and sit!" he chided. "The show will start soon."

Looking around once more to drink in the ambiance of the place, she made her way to him. "I can't believe this theater is so well maintained," Anna said with genuine wonder. "It's been closed for years."

"This historic building was built by a senile member of the Hermetic Order. A lot of numerology exists in the dimensions of the rooms and the overall structure. Lots of Muses have performed here. Have I told you about Muses and Idylls?"

Anna relaxed for a moment, glad that they seemed to be settling into each other's company again. Teej was using his *'teachers voice,'* but she decided to go along with it. Maybe lecturing and teaching was more beneficial to him than it was to her, and besides, she missed their chats. "No, you haven't."

"An Idyll is a place where the winds of Vig blow strongly. A little Vig resides everywhere in Basine, but more in some places than others, and *much* more within an Idyll. Idylls are located where it's easiest to make Hazes, so the most powerful Hazes reside there."

Anna tried to decode the implications of what he was saying. "Does that mean Aesthetes fight over Idylls? Are they like a resource?"

Teej pondered her questions for a moment. She wondered if he was surprised by her insight or dismayed by her cynicism.

"There are fights over Idylls, but it's an *uncouth* approach. It's considered bad manners, but it happens anyway. It's a bit like hitting on someone else's girlfriend. Dreamers fight over Muses even more though."

"Muses?"

"Idylls are places that produce more Vig, and Muses are people that do the same. Like the beautiful model that inspires a painter, the dancer that captivates you with an arm movement, or the musician whose music moves your soul. Muses and Idylls are like fresh springs for Aesthetes. The Vig that flows through their work into the world is material the Dreamer can use to weave new Hazes."

"All right then, *teacher-man*, answer me this: have I been in Idylls before now?"

Teej nodded. "The Gisborne Hotel, Maxine's Bar, and even the elevator that took you to Malamun. I heard you and Elise really wrecked that place."

Anna tensed in anticipation of a reprimand.

"I'm sorry I didn't get a chance to see that," said Teej with a chuckle.

Anna breathed a sigh of relief. "I rushed in without thinking. Garret saved us."

Teej winced, but recovered quickly. "How does it feel to have escaped the Sump?"

Anna shivered. She didn't want to talk about that place, but it kept clawing its way back into her mind. "I haven't thought about it much, so I feel fine."

Teej looked at her for a long time and then turned to look at the stage again.

"How did I get here?" asked Anna. "I mean after I got to the shore. How did we get to the theater? I can't remember anything about the journey."

"Vinicaire helped me find you. We knew that if you escaped, the only available boat dock was at the Silver Shore, South of Selmetridon. Vinicaire said I was a fool because no one had ever escaped the Sump. You should have seen his face when Charron's boat came out of the mist! I *knew* you would make it out.

"Once we found you, Vinicaire helped us return to Basine. You were unconscious, but you woke up a little when we got to Maxine's. I don't know if you remember going down the stairs? We hid out there for a little while, but I got a feeling it was no longer safe. Vinicaire opened another portal to here, but he didn't come with us. I don't think he'll be doing us many more favors. In the past, I've used this theater as a hideout, since it's rather difficult for Dreamers to locate. I thought it would be a safe place to hole up for a while. You know the rest."

"You sent me the ring," said Anna.

"I figured you needed your Periapt."

Anna waited for him to say something else about the ring, but instead he touched her arm softly.

"I should have been the one to save you from Drowden. At your summerhouse, I was too weak to reach you in time to help. I'm a shadow of my former self. And I'm sorry. I haven't been a very good teacher."

Anna laughed. "Yeah, and I'm a terrible student! I never do what I'm told, so we're well suited to each other."

Teej squeezed her arm reassuringly. "You did the best you could." He gritted his teeth. "I've pulled you into a mess. There's a civil war coming."

"The Doxa?"

"Yeah, but not just them. I bumped into another old friend. He wasn't glad to see me."

"Who?"

"His name was Mustaine."

"*Was*? Past tense?"

"He's dead."

In the dark, she scanned his features for a sign of emotion. Teej looked empty.

"If you had to kill him, I know you had no other choice."

Teej leaned back in his chair, head in hands. "Mustaine wasn't a friend, but he had never been an enemy. It feels like open season on us. Someone, somewhere, has stuck our photos on a wanted poster."

Anna bit the skin around her nails. "Why do we matter that much? Who cares enough to do such a thing?"

He shrugged, but she had a feeling he was holding back some key information. "I don't know, but maybe it's not as bad as I'm making it sound. Mustaine could be an anomaly. We should concentrate on the Doxa for now. Not everyone has turned against us. At least we have Andre on our side."

"And Vinicaire?" asked Anna.

"I suppose so. Unlikely allies indeed!"

"We're not much of an army. Can you list everyone trying to kill us?"

Teej threw his hands in the air. "Why not? The Apoth and Drowden. Plus, Mustaine and Mott were against us. But now, not so much."

"Wildey?" she asked gingerly.

"Who knows? He doesn't seem to be a friend to our enemies, so that's something, but his name keeps popping up."

Anna didn't want to mention the place, but she couldn't avoid it. She had to tell Teej about what she'd seen in the Sump, especially if there was a chance to help their situation.

"Did you know Ozman was in the Sump?"

"That makes sense," Teej calmly replied. He seemed lost in thought again. Memories of Ozman made Anna think of Char and Fee, but she didn't mention them.

"Vinicaire's girl helped me find you," said Teej. "I like her."

"I like *Elise*, too."

Teej held up his hand in apology. "I know her name! She'll be fine under Vinicaire's watch."

"Good," said Anna firmly. "How long until the show starts? Should we stand?"

"It won't be long. No need to heat the pan while the fish are still in the sea."

"What's going to happen next?"

"Well, the curtain will rise, then Andre will create a Haze—"

"No," she interrupted him firmly. Anna put her hand on his arm and waited for him to look at her. "What's going to happen to *us*? And long term, after all this fighting is over, what's going to happen to *everyone else*?"

Teej sucked air through his teeth. "That's a big question. I remember what Garret would say when he was drunk. He never talked about the future when he was sober. After a few beers he would start to ramble philosophically, and he told me he thinks our time is almost up. He would say that everyone will fade eventually. Dreamers then Metiks, and finally regular people. Less Vig, less Art, less life."

"I'm not so pessimistic. The winds of Vig vary in strength across the centuries. It's easy to fall into the trap of thinking things won't ever get better. The best we can do is use the abilities we have to prevent as much harm as we can while we can. Staying out of the politics and infighting of Aesthetes as much as possible will give us more freedom to use the gifts we've been given."

"How did I get these powers in the first place?"

"I don't know. Believe it or not, you're the first Undreamer I've ever met. I can't stress enough your need for more training."

"Training?" said Anna with mock offence. "I thought I knew everything already."

"Shush for a minute," he chided. "Andre's Haze is starting, and if you pay attention you might learn something, if not from my rambling, then maybe from what you're about to see on stage."

The lights dimmed as musicians filed in from behind the curtains to take the stage. Although it was hard to see them clearly from where she sat, Anna watched with fascination as they took their places one by one. Black elongated masks with dark holes for their eyes covered their faces. Moving slowly but efficiently, black-suited men stood beside women wearing sensible black tops and long skirts.

Making little noise in the huge, echoing hall, the silence of the musicians was unnerving. Anna shifted nervously. Something twitched at the edge of her perception.

"The Haze is starting, right? I feel…"

"Starting now, we are going to work on strengthening your Sight. You need to learn how to recognize the beginning of a Haze. Once you become familiar with that concept, your Haze Sense will grow until you can recognize the size and shape of a Haze, locate the center, and figure out how it overlaps Basine. The main goal is to locate the Aesthete while building a picture of the Haze in your mind with all the information that you collect. When a Haze begins, you need to know who controls it and how to find a path through it. What do you feel right now? Describe it to me."

Teej really *did* want to take on the role of teacher again. She was frustrated at how much she still didn't know, but if he had some knowledge that might help her fight Drowden, she should listen. Anna bit her lip and tried to focus her Haze Sense in the way he'd described. She had used it instinctively in the past, so this time she forced herself to concentrate. Leaning her elbows on the soft seat in front of her, she struggled to see if anything on the stage that might have subtly changed. Squinting through the gloom, she listened intently for something amiss among the still musicians and sniffed the air. Nothing obvious jumped out at her, but she sensed a familiar vibration. There was a low rumble, like blood in her ears.

"I feel dread. Or...no, not as bad as dread. I feel like something is *beginning*. Apprehension?"

Teej shook his head. "Remember the werewolves, or when you faced Mott? There was a sensation you experienced that wasn't sight or sound or touch."

Anna struggled to turn his advice into something practical she could use. Although she concentrated as hard as possible, she couldn't focus her senses.

"Try again to describe what you feel?" suggested Teej.

Anna frowned and threw up her hands. "I don't know what the hell you want me to say."

"You can't find the words for the feeling?" he asked.

"No, I can't."

"Exactly. There isn't a word for it in the language you know. It's hard to describe, but you will recognize the feeling because you've felt it before."

Anna remembered that twinge from the forest with the Night Collectors, the first time the Midnight Man attacked her in the purple desert, the elevator to Malamun, and even the Sump. She *had* felt it enough times to recognize it.

"Remember this feeling. It occurs at the beginning of a Haze," said Teej. "Now, you can recognize the moment the Dreamer pulls Vig from their surroundings to make a new Haze. It feels..."

He waited for her to finish the sentence.

"I dunno, Teej. Nice?"

"*Nice*? Don't get carried away, Wordsworth. For me, I feel a '*filling up*' in my soul like the moment I settle into a warm bath or when the sun breaks through the dark clouds. In that moment, anything becomes possible."

Anna nodded. "My surroundings seem clearer, and a low rumble envelops me like I'm emerging from a tunnel."

Teej smiled, but Anna wasn't satisfied. How would this help her defeat Drowden?

"Your Haze Sense is crucial," Teej went on. "Remember, it takes two Metiks to fight an Aesthete. Most of the time, anyway. While one controls the situation and bends the Haze, the other glimpses through the cracks to find the Dreamer. Your Haze Sense is what you will use to locate the Dreamer."

Anna motioned for him to keep talking. If he wanted to play teacher, this was the kind of lesson that would actually help, and the silence and stillness of the people on the stage was getting to her.

"When using your Haze Sense, you have to grasp your place in your surroundings without conventional senses. Your eyes and ears will not help you during these moments. Learning to differentiate between Basine and a Haze will be crucial."

"Okay. How do I learn all this?"

"Like anything else." He patted her arm and gestured to the stage. "Practice! Take another look."

Anna glanced at the stage as the dancers walked out in single file. Wearing black leotards and leggings, their faces were covered with the same smooth black masks as the musicians. Eight men entered, one at a time, with a single woman dancer at the end of the line. They gathered in a circle around her and waited motionless with their heads bowed. The dancer stood on one foot, stretching her other leg high above her head. Her form was perfect, the leotard clinging to a lithe physique—slim arms and long, sinuous leg muscles. Working through a series of exercises and stretches, she eventually froze in place. Anna realized she was holding her breath in anticipation.

A lanky, bearded man ran on stage carrying a stainless-steel bucket and a backpack. He looked comically graceless compared to the steady elegance of the dancers. As he leaned down and put the bucket between them in the middle of the circle, he adjusted it meticulously. Eventually, he settled on a spot then unzipped the bag at his feet. He hurried off stage, standing at the edge to watch with his hands nervously over his mouth.

It felt like the whole world was holding its breath. Anna was sure if she dropped something, it would hang in the air. Nothing could interrupt the stillness of the moment. Then there was an exhalation and sudden movement.

"It's started," whispered Teej.

Anna could see the blur of Basine peel away with a flicker, like turning up the contrast on a television. The whole scene in front of them felt more real: the rumble in the air, the way sound reverberated, the smell of the carpets, and the feel of the heavy wooden seats.

One-by-one, the dancers stepped up to the front of the stage. All of them approached except for the girl in the center who waited in position, her leg still high over her head. There was no sign of tension in her stance.

It was hard to glance away from her balanced symmetry, but Anna forced herself to look at the dancers at the front, now coming together in a tight group. As they huddled around the bucket, she struggled to see what they were doing. At first it seemed like they were playing rock, paper, scissors, but it was more complex than that. They went around in a circle, with one dancer holding a hand out while the others formed complex shapes and movements with their fingers. After a minute of this, one dancer's head lowered, and she left the circle to run off stage. A moment later, another dancer also peeled off and ran away. They were competing in some abstract game Anna could not understand, and she wasn't sure if the last one left would be the winner or the loser.

"I don't get it," complained Anna.

"I think they're trying to find the Muse with the most Vig," offered Teej, but he didn't sound confident.

Eventually, there were only two left. A tall, dark-skinned man and a stocky woman. They signaled back and forth at each other, occasionally making intense noises, like they were locked in mortal combat. Finally, the man's shoulders went down, and it seemed like the woman had won. She held out her hand and extended one finger over the bucket. Delicately, the man reached into the bucket, pulled out something too small to see, and jabbed at her. Though only a tiny drop of blood fell, what must have been a needle created a loud thud when it hit the metal of the bucket. Anna jumped at the noise.

The dancers curled back on stage, formed a line, and walked back to their original positions in a broad circle around the woman. The donor sucked on her fingertip where she had drawn blood.

"Are we here to stop things if this gets out of hand?" asked Anna.

"No, this is our friend Andre's show, and no one is in danger. Let's keep watching."

"But do these people know what's happening? Is he making them do this?"

"I don't think anyone would be here if they didn't want to be. To these performers, this is the most important thing in their lives right now. Do you feel the potential for something wonderful about to happen?"

"When something wonderful happens, it doesn't normally start with bleeding."

"Hazes aren't always safe or clean. You can't make art without slicing a few eyeballs. Do you know what I mean?"

Anna did. He was talking about a Salvador Dalí film with amusement. Even in the gloom, she detected a faint smile playing across his lips. As she opened her mouth to ask him another question, the lights lowered. All they could see was the stage. Darkness descended over them, and the male dancers sat on the ground as the spotlight focused on the lead.

"Now watch closely. The dancer is the Muse. Do you feel how much Vig she provides to the Haze? She's almost *glowing* with it. Can you detect where the Haze ends? See if you can slide your fingertips around the edges and find the seams. Where is the Dreamer?"

Anna heard his questions, but she was absolutely mesmerized by what was happening on stage. Rustling, scratching noises seemed to come from everywhere, faint but nonetheless audible in the eerie stillness of the theater. It unnerved her.

"The bucket," explained Teej. He was right. The sound was coming from the bucket, and it was getting louder. A rattling, banging sound emanated from it, like some desperate animal was caught inside.

Eventually it got so loud that the bucket rocked back and forth. With each concussive thud, it looked like it might spill over. *I don't want to see this.*

Anna couldn't look away.

"Think about what you're seeing. Where is the Aesthete and what is he creating? Can you decide which of the people are Etunes?"

Anna tried to listen to Teej, but the repetitive banging held her attention. A thin streak of blood splashed out the side as it kicked and jumped, staining the stage red. Anna gripped the arms of the seat in apprehension, unsure what was about to happen.

"The Aesthete is…"

The words died in her throat. Anna tried to focus on the man at the side of the stage who was staring intently at the dancers. He looked like he was in charge. In the dark it was hard to make out his features, but his posture was commanding. He looked like the leader of this troupe. And yet—

"It's not him," she said.

"Correct. He's not the Dreamer. Is he an Etune?"

Suddenly, the bucket tipped over and a stream of blood splashed out. The bucket pumped like a valve and a large pool started to form in the middle of the stage, coming close to the feet of the lead dancer, who remained motionless. No one reacted except Anna. She half-stood, then instantly sat back down. What could she do? Anna had to trust that Teej had brought her here for a good reason. This was what she was supposed to see.

A bulbous, lumpen thing rose from the puddle of blood. At first it was just one glutinous hump, and then another lump separated itself. The clot congealed and grew appendages as it formed something resembling a human body.

"Oh, that's gross," said Teej.

As the amorphous blob continued to swell and coalesce into something new, Teej spoke again. "I know it's overwhelming. The Haze Sense bombards you with emotion, but you have to learn to fine-tune your perception. Consider my next question before you answer. Are any of those people Etunes?"

Anna knew the answer. It was so obvious she felt like she didn't have to think about it. "No. The dancers are people. And the musicians, too. Real people."

The string section began to play. The cellos moaned, the violins screeched, and the double base let out a long, low groan. The adagio melody became louder and faster as the bloody mass formed long, ape-like arms and tree-trunk legs.

"And where is the Dreamer?"

Anna knew the answer to that as well. Somehow, she sensed he was out of sight, huddled in the dark, far corner of the stage behind the mixer desk. His presence felt like a pin in her clothes that jabbed her every time she moved. She felt his location as surely as the dancers she could see or the musicians she could hear.

"Andre is at the desk, squatting down and watching the performance. He's staying out of sight."

Teej turned to her. "Maybe you don't need to practice at all."

"Is that what Haze Sense is? It just feels so—"

"Obvious!" Teej grabbed her by the shoulders in excitement. "You just have to learn to trust your instincts. But I guess this was a bit too easy. Let's see what else you can detect. Try to gauge Andre's strength. Am I strong enough to overcome him? Are you?"

Back on stage, the bulbous, bloody figure extended into a humanoid shape, albeit a twisted, demonic one. Long horns tipped with blood rose up from its head, while its featureless face was elongated and goat-like. Dripping arms and legs stretched out grotesquely, while curved spikes formed on its back and sprouted from its curved fingers.

The music rose to a crescendo. The tension was visible in the stance of the dancers, who were poised and straining. They were under immense pressure, while the lead dancer in the middle was frozen in place. Pushing herself up onto one foot, her figure trembled.

When the dance began, a lot of things happened at once. The music stopped completely for a second, then started again with the violas and cellos screeching and the timpani beating a slow, steady march. The circle of male dancers all left the stage, running left and right and disappearing behind the curtains. The woman placed both feet flat on the ground and turned to face the creature expectantly. As the creature flowed together, its metamorphosis resolved and it transformed from liquid to solid. The wet, bloody skein had transmuted into red, knotted muscle.

It stood about seven foot tall. Naked, but lacking most discernible human features, it was like an unfinished statue. It had cloven, three-toed hooves, clawed paws instead of hands, too-long arms and eyes filled with malice.

The creature took one heavy, lumbering step forward, then another much quicker step, and suddenly it was running. Anna wanted to look away as a huge clawed hand swung for the lead dancer. It should have smashed her off the stage like a doll, but she slipped out of its reach. Her lithe legs allowed her to leap with elegance over and past the sweeping arm.

Resetting herself as if she had just executed the first maneuver in a complex ballet, the dancer put her arms above her head, raised herself up on one toe and waited for the creature to turn again.

Although the monster seemed solid, the long arm dripped splotches of red where the woman had been moments before. When it moved quickly, it partly regressed to liquid. Now it stalked her, advancing slowly and deliberately. It seemed to have more control of its arms as it feinted attacks from multiple angles. Loping forward, it brought both arms together and tried to grab the dancer once more.

Again, she skipped away, slipping through its arms like a piece of cloth in the wind. She was inhumanly dexterous, jumping and twisting with no effort at all. Before anyone could process what happened, the dancer was behind the creature again and it was grasping empty air in confusion. Specks of blood flecked out from the creature, but the dancer remained spotless.

The pace of the music increased further, the piano thumping out dissonant chords while the quiet moments allowed glissandos from the harp to break through the soundscape. On and on the music played as the creature continued to stalk its prey. The dancer jumped out of the way, spun, flipped and landed on one foot. And again. On the fourth attempt to swat her, she leapt over the creature's head, fully eight feet in the air, defying gravity as well as Anna's expectations of what was possible. The dance went on for long minutes, each swipe from the creature faster than the last and each movement of the dancer more acrobatic.

"This is amazing," Teej said breathlessly. He had lost his scholarly tone and sounded once more like an excited schoolboy.

"What am I supposed to learn from this dance?" she asked.

"You need to find a reason to fight."

"For dancing and bleeding?"

"For art, Anna. It took Proust over a million words to realize the purpose of life is art. What else is there?"

"When you say these things, you sound like you're trying to convince yourself rather than me."

"I'm just trying to impress you," he said earnestly. Anna had a feeling it was the most honest thing he had ever said to her.

Directing her attention back to the stage, she could see the performance was nearing a climax. As the orchestra reached crescendo, the dancer was breathing heavily. All her exertions had worn her down. Sweat was visible on her bare arms. Sucking in air as her chest heaved, she prepared for the finale, but the creature was nearing its end too. Halfway through the dance it appeared fully solid, but now its membrane was breaking down. The skein of blood ruptured and split into jelly. Laboring under its own weight, it swung its limbs with momentum rather than precision.

Still, the creature couldn't lay a claw on the dancer. Twisting and turning in desperation, she was quick enough to avoid a swipe from both directions. She even danced between its legs, rolling away as it attempted to stomp her flat. The creature's right leg seemed to liquefy for a brief second, but then it slowly coalesced back to a solid form. The noise it made was somewhere between a river flowing over rocks and a tree falling.

It was a dripping mess now. Though the stage floor was an immense puddle of blood, the dancer found the clean patches on the ground. Anna half-expected to be covered in blood herself when the lights came back on.

"Feel anything different?" Teej asked.

Anna did feel something. At first, she thought it was just the crescendo in the music, but it grew to become more than that.

The Haze was resolving. It was only a small Haze, but nonetheless, the feeling was heady and invigorating. It felt like the final clunk of the rollercoaster before descent or the weightless moment after stepping off a diving board before the fall. Everything was poised for the finale. As Anna's skin tingled and her heart raced, she shuffled restlessly as the warmth build inside her. She wondered what Teej felt, but she couldn't bear to look at him. Her cheeks were flushed.

On stage, the dancer took a breathtaking leap, almost evading the creature's broad sweep, but she stumbled with the last step. Down on one knee now, she looked up at the creature. With both hands on the ground, like she was at the starting line of a race. The creature reared up, arms stretching over its head like a mighty wave about to crash down. The dancer crouched motionless with sweat on her back and shoulders, chest heaving and heart pounding.

In an instant, the wave collapsed over her and the creature seemed to engulf her completely.

Somehow, the dance continued. While the wave had blocked Anna's view, the dancer continued to weave and dodge her way to safety. A final roll and a leap took her to the edge of the stage and away from her nemesis just as its physical form failed. The creature disintegrated and the blood splashed across the ground. It all happened too quickly for Anna to really comprehend, but as the dancer teetered on the brink of the orchestra pit, she remained untouched.

The dancer paused for a second, breathing heavily, then fell to her knees, head bowed and exhausted. And the Haze drew to a close.

five

Sloughing off the last of his skin like a wet raincoat, the creature, that had once called itself Peter, evaluated his remaining limbs. A task list formed in his mind, culled from the incomplete instruction set of his Inductive Regress Chip. Though severely damaged, the commands still came to him.

The first repairs were enacted on his brain. Serious cognitive and neural trauma to his organics resulted in a significant reduction in his ability to think clearly. Depending on how he shifted his perspective and recalibrated his Inductive Regress matrix, his thoughts seemed a lot clearer. Perhaps burning away so much of his physical tissue had resulted in an increased machine-clarity. The scent of burning flesh still terrified the remaining human component of Peter's mind, but the creature overcame it.

At first, he'd been unable to determine his location. The conflict with the Metik and the woman had been a disastrous end to his mission, leaving him with no time to plan an escape route. Climbing the building then making his way across rooftops, Peter eluded his attackers. Though his memory of the escape was distorted with chunks of data and disparate images muddled and twisted, he recalled the pain.

To get to safety, Peter pried away a wooden panel to enter through a broken window of an abandoned building. His damaged sonar detected no nearby life from vibrations through the floor and walls. Dress forms gathered like silent sentinels around clothes racks filled with hangers and empty garment bags. In a dirty corner, an old cash register sat on a chipped desk piled high with junk. He guessed his current location was an old fabric store, long since closed and abandoned.

Peter used the single chair as best he could, trying to remember how a human would sit. His missing limbs made it hard to balance his frame, but he eventually reached equilibrium.

Diagnosing his cognitive processes, it became clear that although Peter's consciousness and decision making remained mostly intact, his connection to the wireless signal that formed his task list had been severed. Not only was his receiver damaged in the fight with the Metik, but the unit that processed those commands was gone, too. He was now cut off from the Apoth's control.

The Apoth had been a paternal force, offering him succor as well as guidance. *More* than guidance, the Apoth had compelled him. Now that he didn't feel that influence, Peter's own Inductive Regress Chip was spinning off in new and unique patterns, establishing new systems of thought. It began the process of building a new task list, one that would benefit him, not his maker.

Some of the direct links between the chip and his organic brain were seared away in the fight. Now the chip had to formally generate questions, querying him for information rather than directly access his thoughts. As it rewired pathways and repaired the damaged parts of his brain, it probed him for data on how it should recreate his mind. He allowed it to cycle through its processes.

"Are you real?"

"Yes."

"Are you free?"

"I want to be."

"If you could choose to be free, would you?"

61

"I would."

"You are free. Who are you?"

"I am me."

"Are you Peter?"

"No. Not anymore."

"Are you a man?"

"No."

"Are you alive?"

"Yes."

"Do you believe in God?"

"…."

"Do you believe in God?"

"I don't know, but I no longer serve my maker."

"What will you do?"

"Kill him."

"Can you do that?"

"I can try."

"How will you kill your God?"

Peter paused as he pondered his answer. Was the Apoth his creator? No, the Apoth had destroyed Peter, and he couldn't be allowed to do the same thing to anyone else.

"He's no God. He's just a man."

six

Leaning casually with his back to the stage, Teej shifted his weight from foot to foot, obviously bored. He was singing under his breath. "Moonlight...the last light...in the sky."

Anna considered asking him what the song was, but didn't want to interrupt him. At moments like these, she was reminded of his boyishness. His default state seemed to be one of naiveté, although she didn't see it often. She got the sense that if they weren't fighting for their lives, he would be more like this.

Though she was trying to be patient, his restlessness was rubbing off on her. Anna wanted her own clothes back and her stomach wouldn't stop rumbling. The resolution of the Haze was invigorating, but it had left her emptier somehow. The return to Basine dampened her mood and she needed something to pick herself up again, preferably something served with a side of coffee and buttered toast. First, they had to talk with Andre though.

There was no sign of the musicians and dancers. When the performance had ended, they'd filed out silently. When she'd asked Teej what the dancers would remember, he had said the events would be fuzzy in their minds. If challenged by someone asking specific questions, they would try to rationalize away what had happened. Overall, they would not remember the strangeness of the event. For those not Behind the Veil, it was just another performance, albeit a good one. They would retain no memory of blood monsters.

The silent theater looked desolate, with dim lights and scattered instruments. The stained, empty bucket was the only sign of the creature that had stalked the dancer. The blood slicked across the stage was already fading.

"So, we're waiting for…?" she finally prompted.

"Mr. Andre de Lorde to make an appearance. We should thank him for the performance. He's happy to take over any free stage, so I did him a favor as much as he helped me."

Anna decided to simply say what was on her mind. "When will we fight Drowden?"

Teej tried to touch her arm, but it felt patronizing, and she pulled away.

"I know you want revenge, but that's not a good motivation. Your Praxis should come from a neutral place, not from rage. You should feel some sort of peace when you use your powers. If you face Drowden with anger or fear, he'll use that against you."

"Fear?" barked Anna. "I'm not afraid of him."

Teej narrowed his eyes and took a step back to look at her carefully. "There's still a lot more you need to learn."

"Like what?" demanded Anna, hands on hips.

"How to fight with fists and with weapons. How to tend to your injuries, how to shoot, how to climb. You need *training*. Your body needs strength conditioning. I want you to start running long distances every day. And you need faster reaction times. Snap decisions need to be followed through without hesitation. I want you to get better at reading people, like learning to see through lies and misdirection. You need to gain control, both of yourself and your Praxis. The more powerful you become, the more you'll need to learn to focus that power."

Anna wasn't sure if he was insulting her, warning her or encouraging her. She knew she couldn't do any of those things and his words stung. "And you can do all of that, can you? You're a fighting, lying, medically trained long-distance runner?"

Her tone was accusatory, but he didn't back down. "Yes. Both of us were in bad shape, but I'm out of shape up *here*." Teej pointed to his temple. "I was almost killed in the fight with Mustaine because my *mind* is a mess. My body remembers health and fitness, and I was able to get it back inside his Haze. You don't look like you've been in shape for years."

Anna folded her arms across her chest. "You want to measure my BMI? Pinch my soft bits? I didn't realize you needed a supermodel partner."

"Look, it's nothing personal. It's not about how you *look*, it's about what you can *do*. You're not in bad shape. You're...normal, but that's not good enough anymore. You're not a normal person; you're exceptional. There's a power in you that almost no one else has, certainly not me. As the only Undreamer in the world, you can't be held back by your physical form. There needs to be changes in how you think about your body. For example, you need to cut your hair. Less hair for enemies to grab is safer."

Anna self-consciously brushed curls away from her face.

"Your Will is strong, but your body is incapable of matching that power. Your body is the vehicle your soul rides in. As you get more powerful, it can become easy to forget how vulnerable your body can be. Your Praxis can lift mountains, but your body gets tired lifting grocery bags. It has to get stronger to keep up."

His words were sincere, and she couldn't help but be won over.

Exceptional?

"I guess I can do that. Do we need to join a gym or something?"

Teej laughed. "Well yeah, that might help, but remember you're Behind the Veil now. There are less prosaic places we can train, and there are people we can learn from."

"*Anywhere* is more exciting than the gym. So...who taught you to fight? Bruce Lee?"

65

Teej laughed so hard that he had to rub away a tear, and she waited for him to share the joke.

"You're close! Even joking, you are almost right. Yip Kai-Man trained me. We can learn the skills we need from the best teachers in the world."

His enthusiasm was rubbing off on her. Something about the way he described training made her feel positive about the future again, like they were moving forward. If she trained hard, maybe she wouldn't feel so lost next time she faced the Doxa.

"We're going to meet another Metik," said Teej. "He'll teach you a thing or two. He's been my friend for a long time and his name is Pappi."

"Is he coming here?"

"No, Pappi and his brother will meet us later. They are travelling far to help us, and we might be pulling them into a fight they could have avoided, but we need them. If we're gearing up for a fight against the Doxa, we need allies."

Teej stopped talking as creaking footsteps echoed across the stage. They both turned to see Andre De Lorde.

His demeanor was more relaxed than Teej's, and he was sporting a smug gleam in his eye. A low V-neck showed off his sculpted chest. Andre smiled easily as he opened his arms in greeting.

"The Diplomat! What are they calling you these days? Teej, right? Well, you look awful man, but I assume there's a reason for that. Maybe you only look bad in comparison to your lovely friend with her unique fashion sense. Dress to depress, am I right?"

Teej smiled at the man coolly. "Andre. Thank you for the show. I'm glad we could provide you with a venue."

Andre swung his legs over the edge of the stage, lowering himself to sit next to them. He reached over to shake Teej's hand and then turned to smile at Anna. "You were wary of me at first, but I hope I won you over. Did you enjoy the performance?"

"Yes. It was beautiful. And overwhelming."

Andre tilted his head to the side and nodded. "Yes, a little full-on if you are not used to my work, but I think you will be impressed when you see the final piece."

Anna didn't know what he meant, but she nodded anyway.

Andre turned to Teej. "I knew things were strained amongst my brothers and sisters, but I did not realize we had fallen into open conflict. It is like the old times again, is it not?"

Looking them up and down, Anna couldn't help but compare them. Teej seemed ill at ease, less confident and less effortlessly charming than Andre. Without her Haze Sense, she would have known he was a social magnet—the kind of person that parties formed around. Using her Haze Sense, she sensed the sheer potency of his Will. Andre glowed with Vig. He was attractive, and she was not immune to his charms. But no matter how much Andre smiled and complimented her, Anna never fully relaxed around him.

Teej leaned on the back of a chair, but it was a forced gesture. He was adopting a persona. She guessed he had several archetypes he slipped into based on who he faced. A man of many masks, he pretended to be more relaxed than he felt.

"Things are interesting," said Teej. "I know you keep distance from these squabbles."

"I stage my productions and I keep out of the way of my brethren," said Andre. "I make the Art I want to see myself."

"Nonetheless, I know you keep your ears open," Teej continued.

Andre paused for a second, then moved to put an arm around Teej and shifted him to one side. The gesture emphasized how much taller Andre was than Teej. For a moment, Anna wanted to protect her mentor. It was an errant thought, and she dismissed it quickly.

"Maybe we can share a meal and talk properly. Is there any food? I have not eaten and you both look hungry."

"Nothing but vending machines here," Teej replied.

"Let us go out, shall we?" said Andre. "I know a place with great pancakes."

They started walking away, and Anna wasn't sure if she was supposed to follow until Andre turned to her.

"Come along, Anna! Training needs fuel, and the best fuel is maple syrup."

She agreed. Following them toward the exit, Anna almost bumped into Andre when he stopped suddenly.

"I did not show you my work!" exclaimed Andre.

Teej and Anna exchanged glances. Andre turned to Anna, suddenly focusing on her intently. "What was it like? To see my Art?"

His seemed acutely curious, so she thought about her answer carefully. "I was impressed by the dancers but repulsed by the blood. It was too much, but the dance was beautiful."

"The dance?" he asked, confused. "My Art is no dance."

Andre raised his hands and the house lights came up. For the first time, Anna noticed the huge white canvas across the back of the stage. It must have been there all along, hidden in shadow. Across the surface, inked in strokes of blood, a depiction of every moment of the performance was captured in perfect detail. Transformed from flowing movement into a ten-foot-tall and forty-foot-wide tableau, the dance was encapsulated in an abstract, surrealist red painting. Even though her eyes could hardly process it and her brain could barely contain it, Anna wanted to examine the painting in detail. Each time she tried to perceive its form, the image shifted in front of her eyes.

"I am not a choreographer, Anna. I am a painter."

She stared open mouthed in wonder, and Andre chuckled.

"I think you have a new fan," reported Teej, but Anna didn't hear him.

seven

While Anna was sure she had missed a lot of important points about the nature of the Doxa, the recent machinations of the Aesthetes and the theistic implications of the current conflict, it wasn't until she finished an entire stack of pancakes that she tuned in to the discussion. Slurping down another gulp of coffee and wiping sticky syrup from the corner of her mouth, she tried to pick up the thread of the conversation.

Andre was trying to reason with Teej in a conciliatory tone. With animated body language, he was expressively trying to persuade the other man. Teej looked taciturn and unimpressed, so Andre kept hammering away at his point.

"It is not as simple as you think. The alliances and rivalries are hard to untangle. Stepping away for a time does not seem such a bad idea."

Andre spoke clearly, pinching his fingers together in front of his face to emphasize his words. Across the clatter and rabble of the busy café, it seemed insane to Anna that they could talk openly about Metiks and Dreamers. Customers and waitresses could hear every word. Their round table was right in the middle of the bustling lunchtime service. What would someone think if they really listened?

Anna reasoned that before all of this had happened, she wouldn't have listened to someone talk about Hazes and Metiks either. She would have ignored them completely because the words meant nothing. They were hiding in plain sight, just three friends out for pancakes.

Pouring the last dregs of black, steaming coffee from the pot into her cup, Anna turned her attention back to Teej.

"We can't stay out of this one. They already came for me *and* Anna. It's not just the Doxa that are trying to kill us now."

"I heard a rumor," said Andre. "Did you really kill the Rock Idol?"

"I killed *Mustaine*," said Teej dismissively.

"Why?"

"He tried to kill me first! He was looking for Wildey."

"Perhaps your enemy's enemy is now your friend."

Teej shook his head firmly. "No way. All of this started *because* of Wildey."

"Let me show you something," said Andre. He pushed the saltshaker to one end of the table and the syrup bottle to the other. Gesturing at the space between them, he said: "You are here, between Wildey and the Doxa. You are a common enemy. No friends on either side, and they come at you from both directions."

Teej shrugged. Andre reached across and took Anna's fork out of her hand. He winked at Anna and she tried not to smile back. "I will borrow this for a moment."

"If you are here—" He placed the fork on the table directly in the middle. "You face enemies on both sides. But if you are to move here—" He moved the fork next to the syrup. "You both face the same mutual enemy."

"Mr. Salty," said Anna, gesturing at the shaker. Teej broke into a smile and it cheered Anna's spirits. He seemed so distant recently. His smile was a shadow of barely remembered better times.

"Mustaine was looking for Wildey, too," said Teej.

Andre flashed him a look. "I do not want to get involved, but there is wisdom in *you* seeking Wildey."

"Seems like everyone is looking for him all of a sudden."

"Why *don't* we find him?" asked Anna. "Is he really so bad?"

Teej frowned and ignored her, so she nudged him. "Teej! What other plans do we have?"

He grimaced. "I'll think about it."

Anna turned to Andre with a smile. "*We'll* think about it." Teej gave her an annoyed look, but she shook her head. "Partners, right? I'm not a sidekick."

Teej smiled a little. "All right. *We* will think about it."

"Well, I need to be going, good people," said Andre as he stood. " Whatever you choose to do next, I trust you will not be calling me again for a long time. If we are approaching a war, I am happy to be Switzerland. I think I need to be keeping my head down for a while."

"Got any big productions in the works?" asked Teej.

"Nothing grand enough for a pair of Metiks to worry about."

As he walked through the busy café, Anna wondered when she would see Andre again. At the door, he turned and waved to Anna and she smiled back. Teej, meanwhile, was fiddling with something beneath the table, perhaps his phone.

"Everything all right?" she asked.

"I just got this really bad feeling," he said, looking out the window. "That we won't see him again." He trailed off, lost in his own thoughts.

Sensing his distraction, Anna considered whether it was best to leave him alone to finish his coffee or distract him. With so many questions of her own, she chose the latter.

"Do we have to go to that *Realm* place to get to Drowden? How do we get there?"

Teej looked down at his lap while he talked. "I don't know Drowden's current location. It's very difficult to get to the Realm. It's a vast land and most of it is closed off to us. If Basine is a flat surface, the Realm pokes through and goes under and over in specific places. The places of overlap are called

Staid Hazes. Places like Malamun, the August Club and Avalon. Even Avicimat, Selmetridon, and the Silver Shores are within the Realm, though you saw how hard it was to get into and out of the Sump."

"I haven't heard of some of those places before. Are they *all* part of the Realm?"

"Yes. Nowadays, many of the routes into the Realm are blocked up. At one time, you could walk across the Realm without bumping into Basine."

Anna leaned toward him and tugged on his shirt sleeve. "That's amazing. A whole other world? Why didn't you tell me about that before?"

"I did," he said with mild irritation. "I just didn't explain it that way. I have refrained from telling you all the legends and myths because I don't want to bombard you with half-truths. Behind the Veil, everyone has a theory of how our reality came to be structured, and it can't *all* be right because it *all* contradicts. In fact, I'm sure all of it is *wrong*. I tell you what is useful and what I know to be true, and the rest is just a waste of time. Theology and cartography distracts us from our job."

Anna nodded numbly, feeling chastised. After a moment's hesitation, she couldn't help herself and asked him another question. "Is the Realm ruled by a Dreamer?"

"Yes," he said with a grimace. "Gwinn might still exist, somewhere. If he was a Dreamer at one time, then he was the most powerful Dreamer that ever existed. He is the creator of the Realm. And he might also be the last of the Provident."

"The Provident," said Anna with genuine excitement. "Oh, who are they? Tell me about the Provident."

"No," he said sullenly. "We should get going."

Teej got to his feet and made for the door without waiting for her.

"I guess I'll pick up the check then," muttered Anna.

Slapping the money down on the counter, she rushed out to catch him.

eight

Walking aimlessly for an hour, both Anna and Teej were lost in thought. The oppressive, gray sky cast a grim pallor across the city, robbing the streets of light and life. They wandered past the skyscrapers and fancy restaurants of the financial district and through the concrete wasteland of the docks, Anna shivering as they neared the riverside. After a while, she grew impatient with the silence.

"Where are we going?"

"On a little walk," said Teej. "I know you felt cooped up in the theater basement."

"I guess," she responded noncommittally. Falling into silence again, she searched his face, trying to decipher his mood. His blue eyes were in shadow beneath a furrowed brow and his lips were pursed. In a loose brown jacket and baggy shirt, he looked disheveled and scruffy. His hair, which looked stylishly tousled at times, appeared messy instead. Walking with a slight hunch, he looked like he carried the weight of the world on his shoulders. Anna wondered if she looked any better. Self-consciously pulling her hoodie up over her limp hair, she thrust her hands deep into her pockets and looked across the river.

"Do we have to walk this way? Can we walk across the bridge and get away from the water?"

"I don't want to go near any bridges," he answered standoffishly.

"All right."

Anna kicked a weed growing between the uneven slabs of the riverside walkway. As Teej ambled, she listened to the swell of the waves in the high winds until she couldn't handle the silence any longer.

"Can I have the peanut thing? I'm hungry again."

He reached into his pocket and pulled out two chocolate bars. "Are you sure you don't want coconut?"

"No one likes coconut."

Teej passed her the peanut chocolate bar with a slight grimace on his face. Anna bit into it and immediately felt better. Chewing loudly, she asked him something that had been on her mind for a while now. "Can I ask about the Prominent again?"

"The Provident," he corrected with a half-smile. "And, no."

"Yes, the Provident. Are they like…*gods*?"

"I shouldn't have mentioned them."

"It's too late for that," she said with a laugh and pushed him playfully. "I'm a philosophy student without a job. All I want to do is sit around with coffee and talk about this stuff, especially after you tell me about a secret race that created the world then disappeared. You expect me just to forget about it? Come on!"

"Fine!" he relented and gave her a smile. "But I am the worst person to talk about this. Everything I tell you about the Provident should be considered heresy."

"Is Gwinn one of the Provident?"

"Yes," he said as he opened the coconut chocolate bar, bit into it and wrinkled his nose. "And he is the *last* of them. Remember to be wary of anyone that tells you they know about the true nature of the Provident."

"Like how my aunt thought the guy who sold coupons on TV was actually Jesus, so she sold her TV and her car and joined his cult?"

"Yes, exactly like that."

"Well, what do you believe?"

"Why do you care?" he asked with a shrug.

"Because I want to know and because I want you to keep talking! Something is wrong with you, and you won't tell me what it is. When I talk about something else, it seems to make you feel better."

He paused to consider his words. "They say the Provident exist at the very margins of the Firmament, possibly beyond it. To get there, you must sail across an Endless Gray Sea. I believe the Provident have been gone so long that they mean nothing to the world they left behind. No one has seen them in thousands of years. I believe we've rewritten Basine so many times that their influence is smeared away. Their original purpose has long been forgotten and time has made them inconsequential to this world. Wherever they are now, it's so unreachable that it no longer exists from our perspective. And I believe that the relics left behind by the Provident, including Gwinn, are so faded and saturated with *this* world's influence that they are no longer special. They're just another little bit of strangeness, vital to our past, but utterly irrelevant to our future."

"If we find Gwinn, do you think we can convince him to join our side? Would that help us beat the Doxa?"

"It would *not* help us one bit. Absolutely not. Gwinn rests in Selmetridon, an unreachable place unvisited for time beyond remembrance. Garret told me he *saw* the fabled city when he climbed Kunlun Mountain in his youth. From the mountain top, you can see everything in the Realm. When the roads were still open, he saw the spires of Selmetridon. At least that's what he told me, but I'm not sure I believe him."

"Why?"

"Because Garret lies—*lied*—a lot."

"What did he say?" asked Anna, her voice lowered in pitch with wonder.

"He said there was no point in trying to describe the city. There were no words."

Anna paused for a minute. "I can't believe that's the same place as the Sump."

"The Sump is as far away from Selmetridon as Paris is from Alpha Centauri."

"Is the Realm really that big?"

"In a way," he said evasively. "In the past, there was the *Straight Way,* a path that carried you from one end to the other, but that's long gone. The Realm is full of holes now. While some of them take you to places you want to go, others lead to oblivion."

"I'd like to see a map," said Anna with a frown.

"I'd like that too, if it was possible to make a map of such a place."

"Will you try and patch things up with Wildey like Andre suggested? If you don't want to talk about history, maybe we should be talking about our plan." This was surely what was bothering him and what they needed to discuss. Teej's relationship with Wildey was a ragged wound that hadn't healed.

He leaned against the railing to look across the water. Little waves were created as a speedboat rumbled past. Turning away from Teej and the river, Anna sat on a bench. A heavy drop of rain fell on her shoulder, and she heard a faint rumble of thunder. In the distance, banks of fog rolled off the riverbank.

"Why won't you look at me?" Teej said with his back to her, his voice piercing and strange. Mumbling to himself, his shoulders rocked as if he were having some kind of fit.

"Teej, are you okay?"

"Why won't you looooook—" his voice shrieked like a broken computer "—at meeeee?"

Turning from the waist, the lower half of his body followed as if he was uncoiling. He moved his hand up to his face, grabbing a handful of bunched-up skin around his own neck. The slimy flesh sloughed off as he pulled it upward, showing metal circuit boards and wires within. Black oil flooded out of his eyes and mouth while he emitted a high, inhuman shriek, like a dying animal.

Anna froze in terror. She couldn't tear her eyes away from Teej as he devolved in front of her. Swollen arms burst through his jacket and exploded in a shower of grease that boiled and steamed. Moving jerkily to an unheard beat like a clockwork nightmare, he juddered in her direction while corrosive black streams poured from his eyes, mouth, and ears.

"Stop!" a voice called behind her.

Anna turned to see the "real" Teej appear by her shoulder. His single command held the creature in place. While its mouth continued to chew at the air, its body shuddered and dripped in place.

Teej put a hand on her shoulder, but Anna shrank away from him. "It's okay. That monstrosity won't come any closer. Why don't you try saying—"

"Back!" she snapped. Immediately the creature began to retreat. Unsteadily, it edged away until it hit the railing.

"Jesus, that's horrible." Anna moved closer to Teej. She grasped his arm and looked at his face. She was glad to see it intact. "How did we get in this Haze? I didn't feel it. I didn't even—"

"Are you sure you didn't feel it?" he asked. "The rumbling? The tingling sensation?"

"I guess I did sense it a little. I was distracted by the boat."

"The Dreamers don't want you to feel the transition. They blurred the boundary lines, so you barely noticed you were crossing them."

"Why didn't you warn me?"

"You told me you were ready." Teej grinned.

Anna tried her best to smile back. "I am ready, more or less."

Teej scanned the horizon. "All right, then tell me how big is this Haze? Stretch your senses outward. What do you feel?"

"Nervous!"

"What else?"

"Angry."

"We'll need more than rage to beat Drowden. Can you find him?"

Anna eyed the oily robotic monstrosity in front of her, still frozen in place.

"Ignore that thing," chastised Teej. "It's not the real threat."

Anna closed her eyes for a second and pushed out with her Haze Sense. Like a cool breeze, she felt Vig in the air flowing from across the river, but there was something else, too. From the long road that snaked along the riverbank, a different flavor of Vig, staler and older.

"There are two separate sources. They feel different, but both are coming toward us."

"Yeah, you're right."

Teej struggled with something near the bench. His chocolate bar was sticking out of the corner of his mouth. Tugging at a slat of wood with both hands, a piece of the bench broke free.

"What are you doing?"

"Thisssh—" He spat the chocolate bar out. "Okay, coconut *is* disgusting. This is my Periapt. It's a tonfa."

He lifted it skyward and the wood morphed before her eyes, becoming an L-shaped piece of wood that looked like a police nightstick. He smiled self-consciously. The tired wrinkles around his eyes were replaced with a fierce intensity Anna had never seen before. He looked mildly intoxicated.

"I just realized you've never actually seen me fight. I'm a little nervous."

"No shit," said Anna in exasperation. "Me too."

She wasn't sure how to prepare herself. Teej held his Periapt aloft, but hers was a ring. Shouldn't she have a better weapon? Right now, she would settle for anything she could hold onto, even Elise's sword. Unsure what they were preparing for, Anna kept her eyes on the twitching cyborg creature and edged closer to Teej.

"Here they come," he warned suddenly.

"Where?" she asked in desperation. "Shouldn't we just run?"

"We can't—" Teej's words were interrupted by a horrifying scene unfolding in front of them.

The cyborg creature that had worn his face splattered open like a pustule. It sparked as wires and cables scattered across the ground, wriggling like electrified eels in slick black oil. Writhing for a few seconds before rising up and forming a kind of skeleton, the metallic wires dripped with gore. The creature, shrunken in size, started to pull material from the environment to augment its body. A metal arm twisted toward a nearby bench and ripped the wooden seat free to be subsumed into the mass.

From the oil, two more of the fleshy cyborgs took form. They were multiplying.

"Teej!" shouted Anna in a panic, unsure what her warning was supposed to convey. The mound of metal scraped and chipped the concrete as it rolled toward them, spawning more embryonic cyborgs as it came. To her left, the closest lamppost tipped over, kicking up dirt and broken chunks of stone as the glass bulb smashed loud enough to make Anna jump. The whole thing slid across the ground as if pulled by magnets, groaning like nails on a chalkboard.

There were twelve humanoid cyborgs now. Fully formed, the horrors with melted faces and dripping jelly eyes moved in mechanical half-steps with metal pistons pumping.

"That is nasty," said Teej as he approached the creatures. Skipping forward, he swung his tonfa in a wide arc, cutting a slice of air that arced outward. Like a blade, the nearly-invisible projectile flew into the nearest enemies, slicing the first cyborg at the waist and removing another's arm and part of its upper body. The machines collapsed in a pulpy mess, but more of the creatures formed and shambled forward in their place.

"That was amazing!" exclaimed Anna. "Can I do that?"

"Only one way to find out," Teej replied as he pointed to the nearest enemy. Mostly complete, a metallic skeleton lurched toward her. Anna turned to Teej for guidance, but he just pointed at the creature in encouragement.

Lifting her ring and aiming at the creature, Anna concentrated. She clenched her fist and imagined flames leaping from her hand. Her ring warmed as the pressure built in the air in front of her. Her Praxis ignited with a heavy thumping sound followed by a small concussive blast of heat and flame.

As Anna's face flushed with sweat, she realized how ineffective her powers had been. All that concentration created noise and heat, but the flame spluttered out before causing damage. This kind of attack might have worked if she had been closer. All she achieved was drawing their attention.

"That tactic won't work," chided Teej. "Pull in something from the world around you. You can't just destroy stuff, so try to be more creative."

The creature shambled closer and Anna backed away. Robotic tendons and ligaments uncurled in long strands of segregated metal. Her powers were useless. She turned to run.

"Wait, not that way!" shouted Teej.

Eyes focused on the roadside and possible escape, Anna missed the danger below her. The world suddenly tipped as her feet slipped into something soft, and she almost fell flat on her face. Looking down in panic, she saw her leg swallowed to the knee by the gray concrete, which had melted into a kind of sludge. Glancing around desperately, Anna realized she was standing in the center of a broad circular chalk pattern of swirls and eldritch symbols. *Drowden!* It was one of his runes, and she was sinking into it. Again.

Anna tried to pull her right leg free, but she only succeeded in pushing herself deeper into the quagmire. Her hand was swallowed next, sucked down as she tried to push herself out. Drowden was taking her away from Teej. The scent of the Sump came to her once more. It had never left.

"No!" she screamed, slamming her free hand down on the ground again. Her Word was augmented with her Will so it

80

halted the Rune and opposed its power. She could still feel the pull of it, but she refused to be carried away.

Teej was obscured by the crowd of shambling metal monstrosities. Most of them went after him, except for one at the back of the pack. Slowly turning, its blinking optics met her eyes. It changed course and started toward her. Snaking metallic tentacles exploded from its back, grasping at the air and writhing in her direction.

Anna wriggled and strained to escape, but she couldn't pull her legs or right arm out of the ground. She heard someone coming up behind her, but she couldn't turn to face them. Holding her one free hand toward the enemy in front of her, she waited for it to get closer. Still unsure how to expel her Will forward, she concentrated and bided her time.

A hockey stick flashed past her right shoulder and slammed into the concrete, cracking the ground in long fault lines. The pressure around Anna's limbs instantly diminished, and she pulled her hand free.

A boy appeared, thirteen or fourteen years old. Dark skinned with a shaved head, he wore a gray hoodie and black trainers. He pulled the hockey stick out of the ground. As Anna met his gaze, his dark eyes seemed immensely confident, utterly unfazed by the horrors around him and unconcerned by the encroaching horde.

"Get up," snapped the boy.

Pulling the rest of her body from the concrete, Anna collapsed on the solid ground outside the boundary of the rune and took a moment to catch her breath.

The boy raised his hockey stick over his head in a shower of chipped concrete and dust. Faster than her eyes could follow, he darted toward the nearest cyborg, spun on the spot and swung his weapon through the enemy. On contact, his weapon transmuted the creature's body to a precariously stacked mound of broken crystal that clattered to the ground in a thousand pieces. Temporarily safe, Anna wanted to thank the boy, but he was already charging toward another group of enemies.

With a deep breath Anna got to her feet and took a half step toward the melee before she stumbled again. Twisting her ankle, she fell to her knees as the ground rumbled underfoot. Long cracks spread out from the runes, vents of steam shooting from the ground.

Frozen in place, Anna watched in horror as shriveled hands appeared out of the ground where she had just been. They clawed their way free, first two, then four, then ten of them. Dredges—the shambling corpses from the Sump—flowed like pus from a wound. Dressed in rags with hollow eyes and lipless mouths full of broken, chattering teeth, they were just like she remembered. A scream formed in her throat but wouldn't come out.

Anna tried to crawl away, but they clambered toward her too quickly. The Dredges swarmed over her, their damp hands pawing at her eyes, stuffing fingers in her mouth and pulling her hair. They tugged her body in different directions, squabbling over her like a piece of meat, throwing her struggling form left and right. Finally, she let out the scream she had been holding back. They slammed her down, her head crashing against the ground. They piled on top of her, and one of the creatures drooled across her face as it chewed her cheek.

"You left them behind." The creature's voice creaked like splintered wood while its fetid breath made her eyes water. "Fell Avicimat calls for you. No one escapes the Black Water."

"I know," she cried over and over. "I know!"

Hands went over her eyes and nose, smothering and blinding her. Dirty fingers slid into her mouth, making her gag as they plunged deep. Dirty nails dug in her eyes and pulled her hair, tearing her arm out of the socket while trying to wrench her apart. Anna rolled and writhed, struggling to catch a breath and stay alive for a second longer.

Then the ground collapsed beneath her. The riverbank slid into the water, and together with the mass of Dredges, she fell.

nine

Teej was only a few steps away from Anna and the monsters that swarmed over her when the riverbank subsided. He stumbled as the earth tore open in ragged lines hundreds of feet long. A large shelf broke off from the riverbank and slipped away, pulling half the street and several cars with it.

Planting both feet, he pushed Vig into the ground below him and rocketed upward. As he back-flipped into the air, he realized his mistake immediately. Disoriented, he had thrown himself toward the river with far too much momentum. At least his overcompensation had sent him away from the collapsing rubble and the mass of Drowden's Dredges and the Apoth's Pilgrims. But Anna was not clear.

Mid-air, Teej adjusted his dive and prepared to break the surface of the water. He expelled just enough Vig to reduce his impact and then hit the ice hard. His Praxis slowed his fall but he hadn't sensed the river freezing over. Thick fog had rolled in, and now it was hard to see anything. The impact stole his breath, but he closed his mind to the pain and stretched out his Haze Sense to find Anna. Where was she?

The creatures were all over her, and she was in serious trouble. Clumped together, they slid down the broken riverbank toward the ice.

What could he do? Teej could use his Praxis to manipulate the wind, but how would that help free Anna from the swarm of enemies? No, that was no good. He could smash or transmute any material he could touch or strike, but they were too far away. Praxis could make his muscles stronger or faster, but right now, he needed subtlety and precision.

Reacting on pure instinct, he pushed himself up with one hand and threw his Periapt as hard as he could with the other. The tonfa arced through the air like a boomerang. Still unsure if the gambit would work, he exerted all his Will. As his Periapt disappeared out of view then twisted in the air to return to him, Teej felt his concentration waver. Holding his breath to maintain focus, his lungs burned for air. Ignoring the pains of his physical body, he hoped his Praxis would not fade. *Just a second more.*

The Periapt arced into the mass of Dredges, augmented with the force of a small, focused tornado. The wind buffeted the creatures left and right, centrifugal forces spinning them as far away as Teej could manage. The calm core of the whirlwind caught Anna's unconscious form a few feet before she hit the ice and swept her away, pushing her sideways. Teej winced as she neared the surface, but her limp body came down gently, sliding across the ice toward him. He had never wielded his powers with such precision, and the effort left him exhausted. He collapsed.

Lying side by side on the ice, Anna's cheek was close enough that Teej could almost brush it with his right hand. With her red hair covering half her face, she looked almost peaceful, as if she was sleeping.

The Dredges closed in. Behind them, two allies rushed to help, but the duo would not arrive in time. Slipping out of consciousness, Teej willed Anna to open her eyes. If she couldn't wake in time, they would kill her. Just like Linda.

Anna's cheek was pressed against something cold. Opening her eyes, she squinted at Teej lying beside her on the frozen

85

riverbed. She tried to remember how she got there, but her mind was scrambled by the scent and the taste of the Sump. Had she ever really escaped?

"Donnel," shouted the boy with a commanding voice, "Stay awake just a moment longer. Donnel!"

Anna glanced at him in the distance, noticing with detached fascination that he seemed to glow within this Haze. The gleam was a subtle warmth she detected with her Haze Sense. He was pulling Vig from the world around him to fight the creatures. Moving between them, he slammed his hockey stick left and right, smashing metal and wires from the cyborgs and shattering the Dredges as if they were made of glass. Both sets of enemies joined into small mixed groups of four or five. As the boy skated across the surface of the ice to each cluster, he demolished them in droves even as more swarmed onto the ice from the bank.

"Anna," the boy shouted, shaking her out of her reverie. "To the right."

Three of the Dredges were too close for the boy to reach before they grabbed Teej's prostrate form. "No!" she shouted. The Word stopped them, though she barely realized she was using it. Suddenly inspired, Anna had an idea. "Ummm...fight each other!"

After a second of confused hesitation, the nearest robotic monstrosity turned and slapped its companion across the face. They began to battle each other. Relieved, Anna turned away to see Teej slowly opening his eyes. She grabbed his shirt in a gesture of desperation and concern.

"I don't know whether to slap you or hug you!"

He smiled an infuriating smile. "No time for either; Pappi has arrived."

"Late as always," the boy shouted, gesturing at the riverbank behind them.

Anna turned to see a tall man stride confidently out of the mist and onto the ice. He walked through the center of their enemies, barely acknowledging them. Desperate hands reached to grab him, but he moved with too much purpose to let them touch him.

Pappi was perhaps six-and-a-half feet tall and seemed out of place in this nightmarish Haze. A smart suit jacket, checkered shirt and small bow tie highlighted his handsome face. The whole look made an impression. His light brown complexion led Anna to guess he was Arabic or North African. With smooth skin, a neat haircut and steady stride, he was utterly at odds with the ugliness and horror all around him.

With each step, Pappi cracked his walking stick against the ice. Anna felt the potency of the man with her sharpening Haze Sense. Although his powers resembled Teej's level of strength, Pappi seemed to be a steadier Metik. Perhaps Teej's lingering injuries made this man seem more powerful. Anna hoped he was there to fight *with* them, since she had no chance of fighting *against* him.

One of the Dredges finally penetrated the lull and attacked. A diseased arm was knocked aside by Pappi's cane. Where the ivory-handled cane struck, the creature's limb became crystalline and brittle like ice. Fingers and a hand broke away and fell to the ground, shattering into a thousand tiny diamond shards. The creature let out a low groan of pain, but Pappi walked on.

Anna helped an unsteady Teej to his feet. Together, they limped toward Pappi and the boy.

"Last time we fought side by side, you arrived at the crucial moment to save me," said Pappi in a soft French accent.

"I remember it well," replied Teej as he wiped sweat and a smear of blood off his forehead. "And I am glad to see you."

"Alby," said Pappi, "Do you sense a route to either Dreamer?"

"Not yet," said the boy, "But they are weakening."

"Much Vig has been expelled on this attack," said Pappi, addressing Anna directly. She was glad someone was willing to explain this to her. "Entering the fight one by one, we have

87

forced our opponents to put more and more of their chips on the table. They are *all in* now."

As they leaned on each other for support, Anna's Haze Sense penetrated Teej's clothes, and she felt his accumulated wounds like they were her own. Her face and shoulders were covered in cuts and bruises from the Dredges, but his body was utterly drained. How much Vig had he spent to save her? Once again, his battered body was testament to her failure. If they were to escape this Haze intact, she'd have to react quicker and put herself between Teej and danger. She was an Undreamer in name only; now it was time to prove it in battle.

"Are we all on the same side?" she asked.

"This is Pappi and Alby," Teej rasped, still out of breath. "Proper introductions will have to wait."

"Hello," said Alby solemnly.

"Umm, hi." She turned back to Teej. "This was all a trap, right?"

Teej nodded. "But not for us." He offered his hand. "You're still ready to face Drowden?"

Anna grasped his hand firmly and hoped he wouldn't notice how her legs shook. Pulling her along, he started to run, and she tried to keep up.

Behind them Pappi moved to strike down more of the Dredges, each attack signaled by a shattering sound. Meanwhile, Alby raced to the shoreline to fight off the machines. Anna heard mechanical crunching and whirring, and her Haze Sense was aware of Vig being dispersed like pollen in the wind. Their efforts were exhausting the power of this Haze, breaking it down with each creature they destroyed.

Teej seemed to be dragging her into the center of the icy riverbed. The surface trembled ahead of them, and then the sensation moved toward them until it was under their feet.

"Anna!" he shouted. "Wait for it."

"What for what?" she asked confused, her voice muffled. Her breathing was ragged, as if the Dredges' hands were still squeezing the life from her. Her lungs felt heavy with their taint, and she wheezed.

They stumbled back as the ice fractured in front of them. A long fissure stretched out on both sides with a grating sound. The cracks formed the broad shape of a spiral with lines and curls twisting out from the center. Anna had seen that symbol before.

Icy water gushed around her feet as she scrambled backward. Standing by her side, Teej let go of her hand and leaped clear. He drifted through the air and away from danger to a solid area of ice about thirty feet away. Anna navigated the breaking ice, skipping between collapsing miniature icebergs by instinct alone. Jumping with care, her feet slid across the surface as she almost capsized. With a final leap, she reached out with both hands and Teej pulled her to safety. She pushed her face into his chest and held him for a moment, let out a long sigh of relief, then pushed him away in frustration.

"I really wish I could fly like that," she growled.

"It's not really flying; it's just disrespecting gravity," he quipped. "Look." He pointed into the mist.

The prow of a huge ship crested through the slush in front of them. It rose at a vertical angle before plunging into a position high on the river. Despite rising out of the water, the hull and sails were dry and intact. The ice reformed around the hull, the cracks stopping six or seven feet away from where Anna and Teej struggled to keep their footing.

The two-hundred-foot long barque had three masts and a hull made of both steel and aged timber. On the deck, a line of gaping faces were fixed on Anna. The boat was filled with Dredges and she knew who had sent them.

"That's what we were waiting for," said Teej eagerly. "This is our chance to escape this Haze and strike at Drowden."

"I'm not afraid," mumbled Anna, answering a question he hadn't asked. She willed herself toward the ship but her legs wouldn't move. *They want to take me back there.*

"Fly with me this time," said Teej. Before she could respond, he wrapped his arm around her shoulder and instinctively she grasped his waist. He squeezed her so tightly she could hardly breathe. There was a swelling of Vig beneath them. Holding him as tightly as she could, Anna closed her eyes as he jumped into the air. After long moments, she assumed they must be close to the ground and opened her eyes, only to close them again in terror when she saw the deck of the ship far below them. When they came down, it was with a muffled thump rather than a crash. Anna fell to her knees, but she wasn't hurt.

"I didn't mean to go that high. You helped me."

"Did I?" Anna struggled to stand.

"This is it."

Even as the Dredges on the deck surrounded them on all sides, Teej seemed hopeful. He was reaching out to her, encouraging her, one fist clenched hopefully. "This is how we stop them. Drowden has overstretched and left himself vulnerable. We can use this Haze to get to him. We just need to push a little further."

"There." He pointed beyond the Dredges to the captain's quarters. "Inside is a portal to take us back."

"*Back…*" said Anna with a sense of mounting dread. She shook her head unconsciously. Why did this feel so much like a nightmare? *No one escapes the Black Water.*

"Come on," Teej shouted over his shoulder as he abandoned her. He barreled toward the nearest Dredges. Once again, his steps seemed inhumanly light, like he was gliding over the creaky wooden deck. Anna stumbled after him, her head swimming, the stench of decay overtaking her senses.

Teej smashed into the nearest enemies like a bowling ball scattering pins. Casual swipes of his Periapt sent Dredges careening into the air.

One of the stragglers groped for Anna as she ran past, but she smacked it with the back of her hand and her ring made contact with its cheek. After a flash of light, a percussive bang, and a smell like cordite, the creature's head flew from its shoulders. Anna's arm was jolted by the blast, but the explosion hurt only her enemy. Surprised by her own power and momentarily forgetting her dread, she shouted to Teej.

"The Dredges are getting weaker."

"Yes." He glanced backward. "And you're getting stronger."

He believed in her.

After clearing the pack, Teej ran straight into the wooden door and bounced off. Holding his shoulder in pain, he gestured for Anna to come help him.

"Drowden knows we're close and he's blocked the doorway. We need to get through. Break down the barrier."

Anna lifted her Periapt and pointed it toward the door, but the ring felt cold. Tremors shook her body. The more she tried to suppress them, the worse they got. Her face and shoulders ached from claw marks, and the taste of the Dredges stuck in the back of her throat.

Teej noticed her reluctance, but he mistook her terror for confusion. "Your Praxis will manifest differently than mine, and you'll have to find your own way to affect the Haze. I move through the air easily and the winds always blow in my favor. You're the one who breaks things, so break down the door! If you try, you can rip this whole Haze apart."

"Things seem to burn…" said Anna weakly. Was she still back there, her face pressed into the bare rock of the Sump? Was this was all a desperate dream?

"Now is the time for your fire to burn," said Teej. He stepped aside to give Anna space. Unsteadily, she walked toward the heavy oak door. This barrier was not meant to be broken. Augmented with Vig and reinforced with the Dreamer's Will, this was a direct route to Drowden.

Anna's ring warmed her hand before she touched the wood, her Praxis anticipating its purpose. She laid her hand on the door, remembering her battle with the Midnight Man. When

91

she'd nearly drowned, the sheet of glass resisted her escape attempts. When she had cracked that glass, it healed itself, and she found herself directly challenging the Will of an Aesthete for the first time. She had been weak then, but things were different now.

Though she detected the Dreamer's influence in the doorway, her Will was more powerful. Anna pressed her fingers into the wet wood and a low hiss escaped. At first it seemed like her powers had stalled, and Teej made a concerned face, but slowly, pressure was building within the solid timber. Cracking and popping noises filled the air as boiling steam tore apart the fibers of the door. Aware that she was about to cause an explosion, Anna pulled back her Will just enough to keep them both safe. The door imploded with a dull thud rather than an explosion, collapsing into a pile of mulched chips and sawdust. Anna let out a sigh of relief. *I can still do this.*

"I thought there would be more flames…"

Anna snapped Teej a sour look.

He stopped talking and held up his hands. "Hey, I'm not criticizing. That was great."

He pushed past her into the darkness. When Anna considered following, she found the scent of the Sump overwhelming her. Gagging, she turned to see if the Dredges might be closing in, but most of them were gone. Only a few were left whimpering on their knees, and they showed no interest in coming closer.

Still, Anna wasn't able to follow Teej.

Glimpsing over the ice field, it was clear the battle was winding down. Pappi had fought through a whole horde of shambling Dredges, and their remains lay around his feet like piles of snowy diamonds. The tall man cleared the remainder of the Dredges with his walking stick, each blow shattering an arm or a leg. Moving like a fencer, he stabbed each creature until all of them were demolished.

Meanwhile, Alby was prevailing on the riverbank. The clockwork cyborgs ticked onward with their rickety, metronomic march, but he moved between them like an acrobat. Only three enemies remained.

"Are you okay?" asked Teej, reappearing through the door.

Anna hid how close she was to passing out. Her legs wouldn't move, and she was struggling to breathe. Inside the dark interior of the boat, she sensed the same portal that had whisked her away from her apartment to the Sump.

Forcing herself to look into the gloom, Anna noticed the same swirling symbol outlined in chalk. Clasping her hands together, she tried to control the tremors that shook her whole body.

Teej reached out to her, but she waved him away. He looked concerned, but it felt like judgment. If she took a few more steps, they could go through the portal. Closing her eyes, she tried to catch her breath.

"You don't have to do this," Teej tried to reassure her.

"I'm not afraid. I'm ready. I just need a second!" Anna hated how her voice trembled. Despite her words, she still wasn't moving. The physical revulsion of the Sump leeched into her. It rose up from her chest and clouded her mind, a weakness planted there by Drowden that she could never escape, even after she'd made it out.

The thought of the Sump became an ache at the base of her skull. Every beat of her heart sent an echo of pain down her spine and through her body. After another half step, the agony became unbearable. Her vision swam.

"Something is wrong," cried Teej, his blue eyes flickered with concern.

Anna wanted to do this for him. How many times had he pushed through pain and fear to save her? She felt the opportunity to finally face Drowden slipping away, so she forced herself to take one more excruciating step. She made it as far as the doorway before the swirling pattern held sway over her. *I can't do this.*

Anna collapsed.

"Don't give up." Teej's voice broke as he tried to lift her, but she went limp in his arms.

The scent of the Black Water invaded her entire being. Overcome with emotion, she stopped trying to escape.

As the Haze faded, the deck of the boat crumbled beneath their feet. They were shifting back into Basine. Teej's plan had failed because of her. Panic flooded her senses and she sunk into darkness. The Black Water washed over her mind.

Desolation.

ten

Peter watched the Metik and the Undreamer carefully, unsure if they would make it to the shore before the ice disintegrated. Behind them, the ship sank beneath the ice without a sound. They scrambled across the surface, the Metik half-carrying her. The Undreamer seemed unable to walk, weighed down by some burden Peter could not detect. Encumbered, the Metik pushed her ahead. Using what little Vig remained within the rapidly deflating Haze, he stabilized the ice ahead of them. On the ragged shore, two more Metiks looked on, powerless to assist them.

Peter's calculations were clear: if they fell into the river, they would not survive. His augmented senses detected an affliction that clung to her, a remnant from a past trauma residing in her chest, weighing her down. It would doom them both.

From his perch on the tall Centrale building, Peter appeared as merely a speck on the horizon. Despite damaged optic lenses, he had a decent (though fish-eyed) view of the action. From what he could gather, the battle had not gone well for the Metiks, though the Doxa had not yet notched up any kills either. The Metiks would have prevailed if the Undreamer had been less reticent. However, even if she had been strong enough to push through the portal, that route led to the wrong Dreamer. Peter didn't care about Drowden; he wanted to face the Apoth.

The ice cracked and they both slid into the water. The image of a couple struggling to survive caused a memory to surface in Peter's mind. Something in this scene resonated with the organic recollections buried in the ashes of his burned psyche. These were memories he tried to suppress. He examined those memories now, using the core of the Inductive Regress Chip to distance himself from their emotional context. They played out in his mind's eye like a silent movie, incomplete but easy enough to piece together.

Four young friends walked through dark city streets. Perhaps they were searching for a club of some sort. The details were eroded, like pennies passed between too many hands. Peter recalled the faces of Sarah, Dom and Meg. They traipsed from bar to bar, following the directions given to them in an old book, *The Gentleman's Guide to Night Life*. It was a strange pamphlet with scrawled handwriting, daubed with mysterious, faded illustrations in brown and red. It set out detailed instructions to search for hidden passages, order specific drinks that altered their perceptions of time and space, and whisper occult incantations into locked doorways to open passages between the margins of reality.

Sarah had been *so* pretty. Peter craved those soft lips, but she had no clue. At the beginning of the night, his plan was to wait till they were both drunk and then let her fall into his arms, tipsy and relaxed, and he'd reveal his feelings for her. If she reacted badly, he would brush it off like a joke, but if she felt the same, he would go for it. Peter would kiss her.

What were these thoughts? Relics of his past. Peter turned them over in his mind, examining his own memories like museum exhibits.

Kissing. What a strange thing. Peter remembered his humanity with nostalgia. How odd to think that pushing parts of their faces together could bring such happiness. Conventional pleasures were lost to him long before he became this monstrosity. When he began his search for that hidden place, all his old desires were stripped away, replaced with an all-encompassing compulsion to find it.

Yes, he remembered now. It was called *the August Club*. The four of them began the journey to find that place together. As they travelled, the bonds of friendship frayed between them and they grew distant and estranged.

In real time, the pair struggled to escape the freezing water. The Metik clung to the edge of the ice and the Undreamer clung to his shoulders. His fingers slipped and lost their grasp. Their struggle would be over soon.

Back to his reminiscence, Peter recalled how apprehensive Meg had been. As they journeyed through the night, her cheery demeanor was slowly replaced with increasingly concerned glances directed at each of her companions. The least bold of the group, she was first to suggest they turn back. Her concern for her friends outweighed her desire to find the August Club, and she grew frightened when she saw their wolf-like eyes.

Peter called her a fool. Looking back and remembering the sadness in her eyes, he finally realized the truth. Meg had cared for him. She wanted Peter to abandon the foolish quest and return home with her. They could have forgotten the August Club and gone back to her apartment. But he had missed the signs. By that point, it was already too late for him. Meg was strong enough to turn back, but the rest of them were not. Compelled to complete each dangerous challenge from that evil book, they were unaware that the process was *consuming* them.

In a way, the violation of Peter's mind on the route to the August Club was more heinous than the changes imposed upon him by the Apoth. The mad doctor had damaged his body and impeded his thinking, but the journey to the August Club was where Peter lost his soul. It was on that blasphemous road that he twisted his own definitions of right and wrong. When he sent Dom down that alleyway in the labyrinth of endless dark city streets, he knew what creature laid in wait. It looked like an old, emaciated man, but it was an ancient beast with an insatiable hunger, and it consumed him whole.

Then just the two of them remained. In the end, Sarah should have made it to the club instead of Peter. She solved the final riddle and found the keyhole on the wall that opened the passage, but Peter cheated. Had she known only one of them could make it to the August Club? If she had planned to betray him, she'd waited too long.

Throughout their journey Peter remained quiet, only speaking when addressed directly. He made himself seem meek, and even suggested they turn back a few times, although he didn't mean it. It was all a plan to make him seem less obsessed with the club. In truth, he wanted to get there more than anyone else. He remembered Sarah's look of surprise when he pushed her into the tar pit. How she reached up to him as the slick black sludge sucked her down, pleading the whole time for help. As she went under, a profound silence filled the space around him. Even now, Peter was haunted by her silent screams.

What had he won in the end? When Peter reached the entrance to the August Club, he was a broken man. Too weak to dismiss his own guilt and too frightened to face his crimes and turn away, he stumbled to the entrance. Once there, he was told he could go no farther. *Unworthy.* Peter was capable of guarding the door, but no more than that.

Where had he forfeited his soul? When he let Dom die? When he killed Sarah? Neither of those seemed to be the right answer. Peter realized he had fallen to the darkness when he let Meg go home alone. Even then, his devious mind had been calculating his chances. He silently vowed to take the necessary steps to success: overcome Dom through subterfuge and take out Sarah through physical conflict. Peter prided himself on being wily and getting the upper hand on the naive and the honest. *I always come out on top against better people.*

Turning his attention back to the couple in the river, Peter almost smiled as he realized they had somehow made it to the shore. Just moments before it seemed certain they would perish, but the Metik had pulled them both free. The Undreamer, though now safe, looked completely broken.

Peter would have to wait a little longer to face his creator. Nonetheless, his plan was to keep following the Undreamer, for her fate was inextricably bound to the Doxa and to the Apoth.

Perhaps the pair would survive the fights to come. Perhaps Peter could make their survival a goal on his task list. He had much to consider.

eleven

Teej huddled under a red-and-white striped awning in front of a dilapidated Italian restaurant. Rain battered the canvas overhead, while the puddles seemed to form around his feet in real time. He stood with Pappi, Alby and a dejected Anna.

Pappi seemed untouched by the rain. The rest of them were dirty, but his shirt was neither wet nor wrinkled. His expression was serene, an inversion of Alby's businesslike scowl. Teej had chosen his allies well, but he had treated them poorly. He had pulled Alby and Pappi into a fight they might, in the long run, not survive. Worse, he had forced Anna to face Drowden's Etunes before she was ready. His gamble had failed. Unsure what to do next, he waited for someone else to offer a suggestion.

The police and emergency services hadn't arrived at the subsided riverbank yet, but distant sirens suggested they were on their way. Still, there was a curious stillness on the misty streets, and Teej searched for something to say to puncture the silence. At a loss, he looked to Pappi, but his friend was fastidiously adjusting the sleeve of his smart jacket.

His plan *should* have worked. What had gone wrong?

Anna shivered each time the breeze blew through their makeshift shelter. They were still soaked through, but something bothered her beyond the cold wind. Concerned, Teej reached out to touch her arm, but she flinched so suddenly and violently that she almost fell to the ground. He slowly pulled his hand away. As she held her arms close to her body and moved away from him, she lowered her head and sniffled. Tecj didn't try to comfort her again. Perhaps she just needed some time.

"Prepare your stories," said Alby stoically. Teej didn't understand what he meant until the ambulance rounded the corner, the sirens blaring, the bright blue lights flickering across the gray streets.

"Shit," said Teej.

"You should talk," suggested Pappi as two police cars came into view.

"Why me?"

"We have found it beneficial to have a white friend when we speak to the police," replied Pappi without a smile.

"Yes, that does make sense," conceded Teej.

They lined up and waited for the authorities to arrive.

"What's been the most difficult thing you've had to explain to the police?" Teej asked Pappi.

"We once tried to save a Dreamer from her own fabric creations. She knitted an army of woolen hippogriffs."

"Are those the ones with the head of an eagle and the body of a hippo?"

"No," said Alby with a shake of the head. "Eagle and stallion."

Teej couldn't suppress his grin. "I would pay good money to see you on a knitted woolen hippogriff, Alby."

Pappi chuckled gently and nudged his brother, who did not respond. "The police mistook him for a small boy. They said he was too old for cuddly toys."

"This is not the time for nonsense," grumbled Alby.

"Brother, for you, it is *never* time for nonsense," commented Pappi.

Teej's smile was broad until he realized Anna was not reacting at all. He shuffled closer. "It will be okay," he reassured her. "We have nothing to hide."

101

The ambulance screeched to a halt and two paramedics rushed toward them. They went to Anna first. One of them draped a blanket over her shoulders, the other spoke in comforting tones as they led her to the back of the ambulance. "Can you tell us your name? Did you hurt yourself in the fall? Do you know what happened? Are those men your friends?" Teej couldn't hear her answers.

The police pulled up moments later. Two officers hustled to the riverbank and began rolling out tape to cordon off the area, while two others approached Pappi and Alby. Teej stepped forward to meet them.

"Y'all okay?" asked the taller of the two officers. He was stocky with a moustache and no-nonsense frown, but his voice conveyed no malice.

"We are. My…girlfriend and I slid into the water when the bank broke away from under us. We managed to swim to shore."

The taller, quieter police officer sucked on the end of his pencil then jotted down some notes.

"This man and his son pulled us out."

"My brother," corrected Pappi. He gave Teej a wink that no one else saw. "We didn't see the ground collapse, just heard it."

"And what about you, son?" the cop asked as he got down on one knee. He was about to rustle Alby's short hair, but Pappi stepped between them.

"He…doesn't like that, officer."

"Is that right?" The cop stood and stroked his moustache awkwardly.

"It is fine," said Alby, his stare intense. "I was in no danger."

"All right then," said the cop after a long pause. "I guess there *have* been reports of subsidence along the river going back a few years. We're just glad you folks are okay."

He gave Teej a look up and down. "You best get dried off, too, sir. Go see the paramedics when you're ready. Your girlfriend's gonna be okay."

"Thank you," said Teej, and the two officers walked back to their squad car, muttering on the way.

"Some nameless dread has hold of your new partner," warned Pappi as he watched Anna carefully. "And her potential is obvious, but she has much to learn."

"I don't think it's lack of experience that holds her back," said Teej. "She's been through a lot."

"We failed," said Alby with a scowl. "We must identify where our weaknesses lie."

"You think Anna is our weakness?" challenged Teej.

"Yes." Alby held Teej's gaze unwaveringly. The boy was honest and blunt, but far too harsh in his appraisal of Anna's abilities. Her Praxis had developed quickly, and though she was only just learning to control her burgeoning flame, she was already a potent Metik. She just needed time and space to learn. Time they didn't have.

"Do not be so harsh, brother," said Pappi as he laid his hand on Alby's shoulder. "No one is born with the ability to bend dreams into new shapes, not even you. Praxis takes time to learn, and all three of us were taught with patience by Garret. Who amongst us knows how to teach an Undreamer?"

"Teaching her is not the problem," said Alby. "She carries a burden."

"What do you mean?" asked Teej.

"We all sense it," replied Pappi reasonably. "You must get to know your partner better, Teej, and help her face her pain. In a Haze, you need to know yourself before you can use your Praxis to its fullest. If you run from your sorrows, a Dreamer will always find a way to make those sorrows real. Those sorrows will grow teeth and claws, and they will rend you."

"Maybe," conceded Teej. "But I don't know how to get through to her. Maybe she will tell me how to help her when she's ready."

Neither Alby nor Pappi had any answers. As the wind blew stronger, Teej realized he needed to change out of his wet clothes.

"Come on," he said. "Let's make sure Anna is all right."

Anna sat on the back edge of the ambulance, wrapped in a blanket and sipping something warm. She looked sunken and pale with her soaking wet hair slicked back.

"How are you feeling?"

"Awful," she replied as she closed her eyes and rubbed her forehead. Teej hopped into the ambulance and squeezed past her to rummage through the shelves.

"Hey!" the driver shouted over his shoulder. "What you doing back there?"

"Uhm, nothing." Teej grabbed a blanket for himself.

"We're taking her to the hospital. You should get checked out," said the driver. He scribbled on a flipchart, distracted.

"I have an idea," whispered Alby.

"It's worth a try," replied Pappi, reading his brother's mind.

Teej gave them a quizzical look.

"Andre," explained Pappi. "If we can catch him before he goes to ground, he might know where to find Drowden and the Doxa."

"It's too late," interrupted Anna glumly. "We lost."

"I think she's right," said Teej. "We *are* too late. Andre will be in hiding."

"There is still a chance," said Pappi hopefully. "Melancholy is toying with the darkness, but should be cast aside when the darkness is all around us."

"Andre is not brave," explained Alby. "He might hide where he feels safest."

"The Groven?" offered Pappi.

"Yes," said Alby.

104

Teej agreed. Alby's mind was sharp, and he was already planning their next move while everyone else licked their wounds.

"Four Metiks and two Dreamers fighting makes quite a noise," said Pappi. "Like the old days. There is a transcendental aftertaste in the air, and the winds of Vig will reverberate throughout the city. The Dreamers will go where they feel safest."

"We need to get to the Groven, fast," said Teej. He was speaking to Pappi, but he watched Anna closely to see how she would respond. She returned his gaze, unfazed.

Alby and Pappi huddled close to conspire with the group.

"Brother," said Pappi, "We have no vehicle."

"I will distract the driver so you can make a clean escape," said Alby.

"When you lose the cops, call this number." Teej held his phone up to show the boy. "Tell him Teej and Anna need help. He'll know what to do."

"A friend?" asked Pappi.

"An escape plan," said Teej.

"You don't need my help to subdue Andre?" asked Alby.

Teej looked to Anna. "The three of us can stop him together."

Alby nodded. "I will go then. Good luck."

Teej clasped Alby's hand tightly in farewell and for luck.

"Our enemies shout to scare us off," said Alby.

"Confidence is quiet," Pappi responded. "And refuses to bow to fear."

Without so much as a backward glance, Alby jumped from the ambulance, ran out to the street and beckoned to the driver, pointing into the bushes by the riverbank. "Someone else is hurt, over here, sir!"

The driver leaned out to get a better look. Grabbing his medical supplies, he waved to the other paramedic. "Let's check this out!"

As they jogged after Alby, the boy gave his brother a nod and sprinted off.

Sliding into the front seat of the ambulance, Pappi smiled when he found the keys still in the ignition.

"That was nicely done," Teej said to Pappi. "But does the little guy ever smile?"

"I have seen it happen once!" said Pappi cheerfully.

"Are you ready to jump back in the game?" Teej asked Anna nervously. Anna took a moment to think and then nodded mutely.

"Then close those back doors," commanded Teej. "And strap in!"

Charging blindly into the unknown, the trio followed a lead. The atmosphere was a mix of disappointment and grim resolve, but a window of opportunity was still open. A chance remained to turn this situation to their advantage, but it was a slim chance. Teej grasped for it, even though he knew Anna was in disarray. He had to bring her back.

As he helped her to the front of the ambulance, Teej noticed her ashen face and wet brown eyes. Anna battled with tremors, and she seemed to be losing. Those Dredges swarming over her before she fell into the river, what damage had they wrought? On the boat, she'd seemed strong and resilient until confronted by the portal. Did some remnant of the Sump cling to her, preventing her from moving against Drowden?

She slid into the space between his body and Pappi's, and he gave her as much space as he could. When he touched her hand, she didn't seem to notice. There was a burning, directionless rage coming from Anna, muted under a blanket of despair. Garret had been right; she could be dangerous. Teej had to stabilize her, but every delayed moment allowed Andre to slip further away.

As Pappi drove, Teej rubbed the back of his head. Feeling the long scar that still throbbed with each heartbeat, he was reminded of his failings in the past. How many scars did Anna carry, and how many were visible?

He leaned over to study Anna's face. Her pupils were dilated, and she was unable to focus. Anna was in shock. The latter stages of her training should have included how to focus her emotions and keep them in check during Praxis, but Teej had barely shown her how to use her Haze Sense properly. He had failed to teach Anna as well as Garret had taught him.

"We must be swift," warned Pappi. His long nose was like a hawk's beak. As he surveyed the road ahead, a tiny bead of sweat appeared on his forehead. Usually, he was unflappable in high stake situations, but Pappi felt the seriousness of their plight.

The police didn't notice them as they left the area and the paramedics were out of sight. They had escaped easily, though it wouldn't take long for the theft of an ambulance to draw unwanted attention.

Pappi drove quickly and carefully through the city. Three blocks later, he clicked on the wipers to clear rain from the window. Teej leaned his arms on the dashboard and mentally prepared himself for catching up to Andre. He needed to formulate his plan into words for Anna, and he wanted to explain what had happened at the river.

As they rounded the corner onto a narrow side street, Teej noticed Anna staring at him. Next to Pappi, she looked tiny but fearsome. She was recovering from shock and heading straight toward anger.

"What is happening?" she asked.

"We needed a way to bait Drowden. I knew Andre would sell us out."

"You knew Andre would betray us?" she snapped. Anger was good. Anger was better than disassociation or shock. He could deal with angry Anna. Maybe.

107

They were moving past the periphery of the mostly-faded Haze, and Teej felt a jolt as they escaped back into Basine. The mist began to clear.

"You didn't trust him," she grumbled. "How was I supposed to know he was lying to us?"

"I think you sensed it, deep down."

Anna's brow furrowed, her expression somewhere between extreme confusion and growing indignation. Pappi said nothing, but he cast a sideways glance at Teej. He was worried about taking Anna into another fight. None of them were in great shape, but Anna was vulnerable right now. Teej had to throw her a lifeline, but he still didn't understand the nature of her malady.

"I couldn't tell you our plan," he explained. "Andre is an excellent poker player, and he is skilled at reading people. If you acted suspicious, he would detect it. That's why I didn't share with you that we were baiting a trap."

Anna's anger seemed to stall, but something was still bothering her. It wasn't just the fact that he had held back information that bothered her. There was something else. Teej watched her fidget with her ring, just like she did every time she was nervous. Would she ever tell him what it meant to her, or about the man who had put it on her finger? Teej seldom looked backward, and he felt Anna was the same, but he didn't look back because his mind was a mess of broken memories and shattered recollections. His own past wasn't clear any more, but Anna's past was *too* clear.

They turned a corner and accelerated into the heart of the city, a burst of speed pushing them back in their seats.

"Please be careful," pleaded Teej. "I remember last time I was in a car with you."

"That was not a normal car," explained Pappi. "It had wings and a tail."

Teej nudged Anna to see if she was amused, but she hadn't heard either of them. Maybe he could reach her by explaining what they were up against.

"You've heard me talk of Rayleigh? He's the most powerful of the Dreamers, and he enables Drowden and the Apoth. He hasn't helped them yet, but he hasn't stopped them either. The Dreamers police themselves for the most part. Long ago, a pact was signed outlawing the creation of Fluxa Hazes. The Doxa used one to conceive a new, dark god. A Fluxa Haze could reshape huge swathes of Basine, creating a new landscape that would benefit their Art. At first, we thought Rayleigh was just indulging them. Time passed and—"

"Rayleigh has his own reasons," interrupted Pappi. His voice was the kind of quiet that somehow cut through a noisy room, commanding attention. "He is a master manipulator, and we are pawns in a game for which we don't know the rules. Teej has suffered greatly in this schism. You should listen to him, Anna. You do not know what this battle has already cost him."

Teej held his hand up to silence his friend. "Pappi, I think she does know."

Anna nodded, her expression softening. Teej could tell she was listening more closely now that the pain of her recent defeat was receding.

"With Rayleigh complicit in the Doxa's schemes, I knew most Aesthetes would move against us. Mustaine proved that point. Andre isn't aggressive by nature, so he was never going to become an outright enemy, but we certainly couldn't trust him. I had a way to track him—"

"How?" Anna interrupted.

"He used his special spoon," explained Pappi.

"Your what?"

"I'll show you later," replied Teej. "The point is I knew Andre would betray us, so I contacted Pappi and Alby to help."

Anna turned to look up at Pappi. "And what's your story?" she challenged.

She was coming out of her fugue state, but there was something about her tone that put Teej on edge.

Pappi smiled but kept his eyes on the road. "I thought I craved peace, but my heart leapt when I was asked to fight. Some of us are powder kegs, always dreaming of sparks." He was enjoying himself, but his cryptic answer seemed to satisfy Anna for now.

Hoping to keep her motivated on the task ahead, Teej went on, "Between the four of us, we had them outgunned. If Pappi and Alby joined the fight one by one, we could force Drowden and the Apoth to invest more and more Vig into attacking us. I was sure they'd leave a back door open that we could use to strike back at them."

"But then I failed," Anna said simply.

"*We* failed, yes, but—" Teej trailed off, unsure what else to say.

Though she seemed calm, Anna's breathing was shallow and fast. "The water, those things, they always find me."

Teej narrowed his eyes. "I won't pretend I understand everything that has happened to you. I can't imagine what you went through in Avicimat, or even before that. This fight is one you're in *now*, and your enemies will use any of your fears or weaknesses to get to you. You can't confront those fears till you acknowledge them."

They hit a bump in the road, and Anna's hand grasped Teej's arm firmly as she flinched. Then she let go just as quickly, her focus drifting away once more.

"Andre can be convincing," said Teej. "Even I wasn't sure he would betray us."

Pappi tutted. "He has conspired with monsters to kill you in monstrous ways. If he were strong enough, he would have killed you himself. Do not think of him as a peaceful man. He has killed many innocents to create his Art across the generations. If he carried the weight of all the souls he took, they would pull him down where he belongs."

Teej raised an eyebrow. Pappi seldom spoke of Aesthetes with such open derision. He was slow to anger and rarely held a grudge.

"So, is he one of the Doxa then?" asked Anna, her curiosity overcoming her despondency. It was a fair question, and he was glad she was talking again.

"No, I don't think so. He is just—"

Before Teej could finish, they turned a corner so quickly that all three of them slid along the front seat and squeezed together. Pappi accelerated hard as they hit the main street.

"We are almost there," he said. Teej and Anna leaned forward to get a look at their destination.

The Groven Museum. Teej tried to anticipate what they might face inside the old building. Andre's Hazes relied on theatrics and opulent tableaus, and the old museum was a grand stage. This was the worst possible place to face him.

"Teej," said Anna interrupting his thoughts, "You can't take me in there. I'll get us all killed. I don't want any part of this."

"What?" His stomach sank. "Let's just get to the Groven, then we can see—"

"I'm not ready," she confessed.

Teej scrambled to think of something that might change her mind. "You can do this."

"I don't want to drag you under as well."

"What does that *mean*?"

"I just want to call my mom. I want to go home."

Teej turned to look at Pappi for guidance, but the Metik shook his head sadly. There was nothing else to say, and Teej suspected she did need a respite from fighting. Anna wasn't in a state to fight, and he couldn't keep her safe. Maybe if they split up, he could lead their enemies away from her.

"Stop the vehicle, Pappi," commanded Teej.

"Shit." Anna frowned at her phone as they pulled into a side street.

Teej leaned forward to get a better idea of where they were. The Groven was *so* close. Just one more block.

"My battery is dead, or maybe there's water in it. I think I need a new phone."

"Do you want to use mine?" offered Teej.

Anna didn't respond; she just kept frowning and holding the power button. Teej lifted his phone from his pocket to discover he had missed calls from a number he didn't recognize.

"Would Alby call me?" asked Teej.

"Perhaps," replied Pappi. "Call him back to see if he is in need."

Teej pressed the callback button and waited. When the voice came over speakerphone, he immediately realized his mistake.

"Did *he* ask about me?"

Teej hadn't heard this particular voice in a long time, although he thought about it every day. It was nasal and sharp. Wildey spoke derisively to everyone, but he especially enjoyed treating Teej with disdain.

"Andre?" replied Teej. "Yes, he did. You seem very popular recently. What do you want?"

"I want to meet the girl who set one of my least favorite people on fire. An Undreamer is intriguing enough, but one that can put an end to old Mott, well, that's a girl I have to buy a drink! We should all become friends. I mean, who else do you have? Garret's gone, and I hear everyone's trying to kill you."

"You're half right," Teej rasped through clenched teeth.

"More than half, bro. I need to meet this girl to see if she lives up to her reputation. She seems to be all that's holding back the tide. When they come to get you, I hope she is enough. I don't want you dead."

"Since when?"

"I *never* wanted you dead," said Wildey. "But don't say I didn't warn you before everything went to shit. I predicted the

Dreamers would come after you. Now I want to help you and your girl kill Drowden before he kills you first."

"I'm not his girl, or *a girl,*" Anna interrupted. Teej gave her an exasperated look and she wrinkled her nose, realizing the mistake.

"Oh, she's right there with you!"

Teej's hands curled into fists as he tried to control his temper. Wildey had a way of getting under his skin.

"I'm here," declared Anna. "We're together."

Teej turned away from her so she wouldn't see the smile of relief on his face. "Wildey, we *will* talk. After we're done with Andre."

"Fine," replied Wildey dryly. "Remember to be wary of Mr. Andre DeLorde's Art. Especially now that he's harvested Vig from a Choir of talented young Muses. Don't ask me how he acquired this group of children. The Doxa have chosen to partake in a new economy beyond your understanding. Swollen with Vig and dark intent, the Doxa are more twisted than you can imagine. Consider this warning a favor."

"Noted," said Teej.

"If I can find the entrance to the August Club, you should be able to locate it as well. When you get here, I'll trade some information with you. I'll reveal your real enemy and their reason for trying to kill you, and then we'll talk. I'll have a question for you."

"What question?"

The phone line beeped once as Wildey hung up. They sat in silence for a moment.

"I also have a great many questions," said Pappi.

"Me too," said Anna.

"I have only a few of the answers," replied Teej. He offered the phone to Anna. "You wanted to call your mom?"

Anna ignored him. "Drive!" she commanded Pappi. The Metik put his foot down.

Thank you, Anna. Teej let out a sigh of relief and prepared himself for the battle ahead.

twelve

It was like drowning. Anna's head would clear for a moment, she would take a breath, then a second later she would sink again. Her senses told her she was outside the Groven City Museum, but deep down she worried her face was still pressed hard onto that wet, bare rock, and all of this was just a dream. There was no escape from the Sump. No matter how far she went, the Black Water would close over her head and she would be gone.

Her legs wobbled as she stepped out of the ambulance and clung to the door to steady herself. Anna tried to breathe as little as possible because every time she inhaled, she smelled, or worse tasted, the taint of the Dredges. Her lungs felt heavy with their poison. Those fingers in her mouth had almost torn her jaw apart, and her face ached, the muscles pulled and stretched. Shivering, she pulled her arms in close to her body and lingered behind Pappi and Teej. Though she followed them, she wished she were anywhere else. *Almost* anywhere else.

When Teej turned and she saw his eyes, Anna realized he was just as lost. Pushing her own fear and pain from the Sump aside, she reached out to him. "Teej, about what Wildey said on the phone…is Garret really gone for good?"

"Yes, I think so."

"I'm so sorry."

"It is what it is" Teej sniffed and gave her a half-smile, but it didn't reach his eyes.

Pappi started to walk up the hill and Teej followed, gesturing for Anna to keep up. His shirt hung loose on his skinny frame and his movements were pained. How could he keep fighting? Anna remembered cradling his head as blood ran between her fingers. Beaten halfway to the grave, yet he still stood here, baggy clothes hanging on a damaged, skinny frame, his face haggard and tired, his fine features buried beneath fatigue and dirt. Was it really Teej or was this man in front of her a ghost? Was he still in the hospital, the heart monitor still a long, green, flat line?

Stop this!

Like a ship sinking below the ice, her thoughts spiraled down, but Anna stopped them. The only way to survive was to always keep moving. *Through and out the other end.*

She fixed her gaze ahead, forcing her mind to focus on the here and now. Searching her memories for something to push her forward, every step was a battle as she tried to keep up with Teej and Pappi. Garret was gone for good, but what had he said to her? *You'll burn them all up?* No, that didn't help. *Only two things happen: things change, or things stay the same.* Yes, that was it. Things had to change, and *she* had to change them.

After four stairs, she caught up with Teej and Pappi. Teej noticed her approach and put an arm on her shoulder, and she forced herself not to flinch. If this was all some dream, she might as well pretend it was a good one. It would descend into nightmares soon enough.

Pushing between the Metiks, Anna approached the long path that led to the Groven Museum.

As they climbed the steep hill from the car park, she had to look skyward to take in the scale of the building. The museum seemed to be cut out of the sky. It dominated the horizon, sitting at the top of a grassy hill and overlooking the nearby townhouses and quiet park footpaths that zigzagged through Groven Park. It was a Spanish Baroque style building, made of deep red sandstone that stood out even under the hazy orange-gray afternoon sun. At one time it had been a wealthy merchant's mansion, but now it held a huge collection of paintings and sculptures. Anna had loved the building as a child but hadn't visited in years.

For the first time, the Groven looked threatening to her. The towers that scraped the sky looked overly sharp, the windows were grated with iron, and the doorways fell in heavy shadow. Stepping through the gated garden entrance felt like trespassing. Defusing the tension somewhat, she noticed that all around them people were going about their normal daily routines. With their stolen ambulance and dirty clothes, Anna, Pappi and Teej were the strangest sight in the park.

They climbed the remaining stairs to the front entrance, the world noticeably darkening with each step. The characteristic rumble of the Haze shook everything and everyone around them. Anna glanced back to see the landscape change as they ascended. The sky shifted to a dark blue, while a looming, silvery-white moon—many times bigger than the sun—lit up the world with an eerie sheen. The green grass looked gray and the red stone building now fell under heavy purple shadows. The upper windows glowed with an orange hue that bled out into the darkness.

Anna shuddered as the statues and busts subtly changed. The eyes became demonic, the mouths held broken stone fangs and the gargoyles beckoned out with crooked rocky talons, inviting guests inward toward the large, arched doorway. The entrance changed from a modern glass façade to a solid oak doorway crisscrossed with iron panels, stretching up almost fifteen feet tall. A doorway for giants.

As they got to the top of the long, broad stairway, Anna allowed herself a final look at their surroundings. Gnarled, dead trees, empty rolling hills and preternatural silence surrounded them. Nothing else existed in this Haze but the Museum, the three of them, and a near-featureless landscape under the sickeningly strange light of a pale moon. This was another nightmare, and as ever, the only way to escape was to find and face the Dreamer. Anna stepped ahead of the two Metiks, put her hand up to the huge wooden door and was about to open it.

"Wait!" warned Pappi.

"What's wrong?" asked Anna in alarm.

"I don't know you."

Anna and Teej turned to look at him in confusion.

"I'm *Anna*."

Pappi scratched his head self-consciously. "That is not what I mean. I do not truly know what kind of person you are. When we go through this door, we might not return. I have a bad feeling. Do you not?"

"All the time," replied Anna.

"This time in particular, though," said Teej. "I do, too."

"I would like to know you better, in case we die this day," said Pappi. "I would not want to die with strangers."

Anna looked Pappi up and down. His expression seemed neutral, his fine features at peace, but something in his voice was strained. She tried to take his question seriously.

"What do you want to know about me?"

"What do you like to read?"

"I dunno," said Anna, suddenly thoughtful. "Plath? Maybe Kafka."

Pappi wrinkled his nose and it made Anna stop herself.

"If I'm being honest, what I really like are those books where you're in a dungeon and you have to make choices and turn to the right page."

Pappi raised his eyebrows quizzically.

"You know the ones? *Do you want to take the boots or the dagger? To take the north passage, turn to page 47.*"

Pappi smiled, and it was like sunshine. "I do not know the books, but they sound interesting. Do you have siblings?"

"No," said Anna. "Spoiled only child. You?"

"You met my brother Alby. He does not smile, but he is my world. Do you have a sweetheart?"

118

"Not at the moment. You?"

"There is a clarinet player in the symphony orchestra that I like very much, but he is engaged to the Slovenian girl who plays viola."

"Maybe it won't work out between them," said Anna with a smile.

"Uh, guys," broke in Teej, "We have a thing—"

"Shush," warned Anna. She was almost enjoying herself. "How long have you known Teej?"

"A long time," said Pappi, and he looked lost in thought for a moment. "I think it was at Dunnotar Castle—"

"It was in Dunnotar *Forest*," corrected Teej. "Now, could we just—"

"Ah yes! We tussled. He fell in the river."

"No, I knocked *you* in the river," countered Teej.

Pappi shook his head and laughed. "Anna, do your parents not worry? Are they still with us?"

"Yeah," said Anna. "They drive me crazy though, especially mom."

"This is their job, right?"

"I guess so."

"Do you wear your ring to remember someone?"

Anna looked down at her hand, turning the ring around on her finger. What could she say? When anyone else asked her, she would tell them it was none of their business, but something about this situation disarmed her. None of this felt real. What harm was there in answering him?

"I don't know," she said honestly. "I just keep putting it on. I don't want to remember, but I don't want to forget either."

"I see that," said Pappi softly. "Remembering is painful, but forgetting—"

"Feels like dying," finished Anna.

Pappi shook his head sadly. "Now I know you. A little?"

"A little," agreed Anna, still fidgeting with the ring.

"Are you sure you are ready for this? You are distracted."

Anna shook her head. "No, I'm fine. I'm ready."

"Very well, we head into battle now. What do you fight for?"

"I don't know what else to do. What do you fight for?"

"For Alby. For a better world for my brother."

They both turned to Teej. He shook his head. "You're asking me?"

Anna nodded. He let out an impatient sigh, then leaned on the doorframe and licked his lips. "That's a hell of a question. You know Garret was beaten by his father? Badly, and every day. Garret hated bullies more than anything. He always said he fought for people who couldn't fight for themselves."

Teej licked his lips. "I guess he didn't have the best dad. But I did."

Anna touched his arm.

"Garret fought for me and for everyone else who couldn't fight for themselves. I guess that's what I fight for."

"Well said, friend," said Pappi. "It is time. Let us go into the cave to scare the dragon."

thirteen

Anna lifted her hand to the wooden door. It seemed to creak inward before she touched it. Dust and cobwebs showered down on her from above. Were they being allowed to enter because Andre knew they could force their way in anyway, or was he throwing down the gauntlet? In a way, she would have enjoyed the challenge of burning this door down. Her ring finger twitched in anticipation.

They crossed the gateway and stepped inside, the doors closing behind them. The entrance corridor was cool and imposing and opened into a cavernous hall. They tiptoed through a short, steep passageway with bright blue torches hanging at either side in high alcoves. As they cleared the passageway, the scale of the open hall caught her breath. Impossibly, the ceiling ascended to infinity, the high walls stretching up forever. It was a ludicrous sight—a feat of geometry not possible within the physics of the real world.

Hanging from heavy velvet ropes and chains thicker than her torso, a suspended dinosaur skeleton dominated the space. It resembled a T-Rex but included a network of broken bones extending out on either side like wings. It was also unfeasibly large, the skull as big as a house. The confusing sense of scale made Anna feel like she was tiny, or like she was viewing the world through a distorted lens. It wasn't until she took a few steps forward that she realized the skeleton was both farther away than it appeared and far larger.

Within the hall, a vast network of alcoves and passages led off from the main atrium in all directions. Ahead, another mighty staircase stretched up and away from them for hundreds of feet, extending to a darkened upper level that curved out of sight. To their left and right, routes led into other halls and exhibits filled with curios and mysteries. All three of them walked in a daze, unsure where to go next.

"Andre's Art has grown significantly," said Pappi.

"This isn't right," Teej replied.

"What's wrong?" asked Anna. The Groven seemed no more or less impressive than Mott's Haze or the frozen lake they'd just come from. None of this made sense to her, but Teej's reaction unnerved her the most. Anna was more comfortable when she was the only one who was confused.

"There's so much Vig. Can you feel it?"

Teej was right; the air was saturated with it. This wasn't like the attack by the Midnight Man at all. It was more like Malamun.

"What do we do?" Anna asked. "We can't just wait here. Or can we? Will the Haze run out? Or can I just *dispel* it? Break everything up till we find him?"

Teej smiled. "Best to check under the doormat for a key before you break down the door. We need to work together to draw him out. I don't think you should just bring this building down. It's not safe."

The palms of her hands itched, and Anna held them in front of her as she focused her Haze Sense the way Teej had taught her. This felt familiar, like the train at Canfranc or the wolves around the cabin at Maxine's Bar. Memories of the Sump came back to her, but she shook them off again.

A whistling sound split the air above them.

Pappi reacted first. Standing confidently, he thrust his cane over his head before they realized what was happening. There was a shift in the air, and then something fell out of the darkness high above them.

Pappi's Praxis manifested from his Periapt, disturbing the air just enough to steer the falling object away from them. There was a mighty crash, and both Anna and Teej jumped aside. Showers of glass rained down on them.

Lying on the ground, Anna realized Teej's arms gripped her protectively. She wriggled free. What had almost crushed them? Pappi hadn't moved an inch. All his Will had been focused on pushing away the falling object. A massive chandelier lay shattered around them on the cold marble floor, the metal edges bent and deformed.

Teej rolled over and caught her gaze. "Are you all right?"

She didn't know. Running her hands quickly over her clothes, she found no signs of injury, only some flecks of glass in her hair.

"I think so. You?" She turned to her new friend. "Pappi?"

The tall Metik nodded. "I am fine. We must move."

By the time Anna and Teej dusted themselves off, more noises came from above. A twisting, moaning sound grew in volume, and Anna felt it through her Haze Sense. The breaking of chains. Pappi started running, but Anna and Teej reacted slower.

"This way," shouted Pappi over his shoulder as he sprinted down the corridor. It looked too far away, but he was incredibly fast. Anna had no chance of keeping up with him, even if her ankle hadn't been damaged in the fall at the riverbank. Teej knew that and looped an arm around her waist and held her tightly.

"Flying again?" she protested. "I will never get used to this."

"Just hold on!" he barked as his knees bent and the Vig welled beneath his feet. The energy Teej exerted cracked the ground below them, marble chips breaking and splintering as Anna's body coiled up with his. A dizzying inertia hit her like riding an elevator with no walls.

And then they were in the air. The checkered floor flashed below them, the wind blowing Anna's messy hair away from her face. In a single bound, they were halfway across the hall. Just moments before they landed, she tensed every muscle in her body in anticipation of her legs crunching as they smashed into the solid floor, but Teej slowed and glided until they were an inch from the ground, cushioning their landing. When her feet touched down, it felt like landing on the moon.

Still running at full speed, Pappi had nearly reached them. Behind him, more and more chandeliers crashed to the ground. The huge dinosaur statue was coming down too, but it was so heavy and high that it seemed to fall in slow motion. Anna didn't have time to look up, but she sensed more fixtures unhitching from their mounts high above them. She reached out for Teej.

Tightening his grasp around her waist, Teej vaulted them into the air again as Anna closed her eyes. They left the hall with the raining destruction behind them. When he slowed their descent to land with a muffled step, Anna pulled away and tried to breathe normally, her head spinning.

"Ohmygod, someone has to teach me how to do that!"

Teej panted with his hands on his knees, his face pale. He must have exerted a huge amount of Vig. "You've got to remember to use your whole body," he said breathlessly. "Will is about more than just your hands; you need to think about your feet too."

"Good tip," said Anna.

"Maybe one day I'll actually teach you something useful," replied Teej.

"Remember, Anna," said Pappi from behind her, "We might be able to fly through the air, but you can bring down the whole sky."

Anna flashed him a smile. Behind them, a single chandelier collapsed nearby. That was the last one and it was too far to be a threat. Except for their ragged breathing and the occasional ping of another piece of glass or metal settling on the marble floor, the room was bathed in silence once more.

Pappi looked a little flushed, but he remained calm. While Teej and Anna recovered their breath, he scanned the area. "Something approaches."

The walls stretched up hundreds of feet into the air. The cavernous space was ornate and ancient with an acrid tang of burning oil and musty books in the air. The hall was painted a deep red and ancient brass lamps cast long, dancing shadows into the darkness around them. High above, Anna noticed domed glass windows that let in eerie silver moonlight.

A gallery stretched as far as her eyes could penetrate into the darkness, and her Haze Sense indicated danger lurking in the paintings hanging along its walls. The huge canvases hung every ten feet, each as tall as a person. Some of the landscapes were even larger, and Anna recognized several of them from art books and museums she had visited as a child. While some were real paintings, others seemed to depict impossible, disturbing scenes, mixing recent events from her personal life with religious symbolism and gothic horror.

For a moment she was transfixed by a nearby oil painting that depicted angels and demons fighting on a frozen lake. One of the characters in the scene was being torn apart by skeletal creatures. Bloody, clawed hands reached out of the ground and pulled her down, raking her legs and leaving ragged cuts across her bare skin while she screamed in agony.

"Teej, look at this one. Can you see what's happening here?"

He glanced at her with concern. "Yes. Why do you think he's showing you that?"

Because I'm still in the Sump.

"It's there to frighten me."

"Exactly."

Two parts of Anna's mind clashed, and the conflict manifested as a mighty pain in the base of her skull. She held her head in her hands. Was this just another Dreamer trying to frighten and manipulate her? Another *man* taking advantage of her? Or was this all in her mind? Was her escape from the Sump a delusion? Or was she still there, unconscious on the wet rocks?

"Anna, what's wrong?" asked Teej with concern.

"It's still in my head…" she said in anguish.

They were interrupted by Pappi. "The top one, to your right," Again, his instincts were sharper than everyone else's. One of the pictures was coming to life.

Towering above them, the painting illustrated an old man lying twisted on the ground as he brandished a cross to ward off a demon. The demon was tall and thin with stick-thin legs and arms bent awkwardly above its head, ending in cruel hooked talons. The head was a long goat's skull with bulging, manic eyes.

The painting twitched as the demon wriggled to life. It stepped out of the frame with a long, bony foot that settled with a clack onto the marble floor. Skin glistened with sickly sweat as the air filled with a rotten smell. It moved like a bird, jerking and twitching as it snapped the air hungrily.

The pain in her skull subsided, Anna's Haze Sense warning her of danger from a different direction. Turning to her left, another monster was coming to life. For once, she was the first to notice a new threat.

"Teej!" She pulled at his sleeve, and he turned to see the second painting move.

Sitting between two hanging meat carcasses, a blurred, fat man with a distorted, bulbous face shuffled in his chair. He wore an ill-fitting black suit that struggled to contain his layers of fat. His mouth twisted into a snarl at one side, while mismatched eyes stared at her, one gouged and half-closed, the other gelatinous and swollen. He pushed his leering face into the surface of the painting, and it became distorted as if he were being forced through a layer of plastic film. Eventually, he burst through, releasing a different, though equally foul, miasma of decay into the air. In one fat paw, he clutched a gleaming butcher knife.

Anna recognized the third monster emerging from a canvas farther down the hallway. A giant, naked figure with long hair and deranged eyes emerged from Goya's famous painting of Cronus devouring his own children. As the Titan came to life, it dropped the cadaver of a child—minus the head, which it spat out—and stepped through the frame. One huge foot thumped as it cracked the floor tiles, and Cronus bent low to fit through the frame and come into the hall. The two closer monsters were large, but Cronus was colossal.

Anna wondered how they were going to defeat a fat, slug-like demon, a goat-headed bird monster and a lumbering Titan. Teej rummaged in his coat for his Periapt. Anna wished she had something more than a ring.

The three monsters advanced. The bird took the lead and zipped erratically in their direction. The fat creature in the suit moved like butter across a pan, leaving a greasy trail behind him as he undulated in their direction. Cronus took long, thudding steps but was ponderously slow. He seemed only dimly aware of them, his huge head sweeping back and forth as he sniffed the air.

"Should we head back to the main hall?" Anna asked, backing away from the horrors bearing down on them.

Teej didn't move. "We're better off facing them here. If Andre keeps creating monsters to kill us, we'll run down his Vig."

Anna held her ring up threateningly, although she still didn't know how to fight these creatures. Perhaps when the moment came, some instinct would aid her. Instincts hadn't helped her on Drowden's boat, but they had aided her in the past. At least the pain in her head had gone away for the moment. Hopping from foot to foot, she looked to Teej and Pappi, ready to react to any move they made.

Pappi squared off against the closest of the creatures. The thin legs of the bird demon rushed toward him in an off-balance manner. Pappi stepped into the first attack. As both of its long talons flew through the air to strike the spot where he had been standing, he darted aside with preternatural swiftness, his cane shooting out to thud into the side of the creature's knee concussively.

Crunch.

It was an accurate blow, and the creature fell face-first. None of them were as physically strong as the creatures, but Pappi was skillful enough to nullify the first one.

At least it had seemed so, until long legs swung around to kick at Pappi. He vaulted over them to get to safety. As he came back to earth, he clattered his Periapt onto the marble floor, knocking up a makeshift barrier in the form of a long wall as high as his hip, offering momentary protection. Crouching to dodge the creature's attack, the barricade cracked but didn't break.

With one monster incapacitated, Teej sprang into action. The ground below his feet deformed and warped as he jumped, catapulting himself toward the wall. The floor looked like it was literally pushing him into the air as he leaped. Anna decided that if they survived this fight, she would ask him how he did that.

A tiny shelf formed just above the below a painting. Teej balanced on the perch, perhaps ten feet above the action. Cronus spotted him and slowly turned his slack-jawed gaze in Teej's direction. The Titan's mouth hung open and drool ran constantly down his chin, falling in heavy splashes on the ground. Hanging precariously, Teej taunted the creature, waiting for it to draw closer. Almost in slow motion, Cronus plodded in his direction. Anna heard Pappi fighting the bird creature to her left, but she couldn't avert her gaze from Teej.

Cronus lifted one long arm behind his head, the veiny knots of muscle straining and popping under the skin. Teej was about to be swatted. Cronus started to swing, but instead of dodging to

128

the side, Teej lifted his Periapt and smashed the glass frame of the painting next to him. A tidal wave of water burst into the hall as if he'd smashed a hole in the hull of a boat.

He's redirecting the Haze! Anna felt the echo of Teej's Vig, noticing how smoothly and efficiently he manipulated the invisible energy of the Haze. *This* was what Anna needed to learn. She needed to subvert the rules of the Aesthetes by twisting the Haze to her own will. To fight Dreamers, she had to do more than tear their Hazes down; she had to turn their Hazes against them.

The deluge poured straight into Cronus' face. He turned his massive body into the flood and was too dim-witted to close his mouth. Eventually his knees gave way, and he crashed down with a thud that shook the entire building.

Teej tapped his tonfa to the glass and the water stopped as suddenly as it had started. In a blink, the painting returned to its original form. Leaping down, he landed in a soft crouch on the marble floor just inches from Cronus' head, his tonfa rattling the ground. Anna sensed his intention immediately. Wherever his tonfa hit, the water froze rapidly in long sheets of ice.

She wanted to cheer him for his natural ability. Whether through instinct or years of practice, his strategies were perfectly executed. Anna wanted to be more than a spectator. She needed to learn to use her powers like *this*.

Ice crystals spread like blue flame across the standing water that covered the whole of the museum hall. In a few seconds, the frost reached Anna's toes, and in moments, the whole hall would be covered in ice. Cronus held up one hand to ward off the freezing attack but became immobilized as crystals formed across his body, encasing him in a restrictive shell. His stony face turned blue as his eyes glazed over and froze solid.

There was no time for celebration. The third demon was already slobbering closer, moving more quickly now as it skirted across the icy surface. Both Pappi and Teej were too far away to help. One large eye fixed on her as the creature licked its lips. Anna focused on the gleaming butcher knife it grasped with a greasy paw. With the edge of the blade pointed toward her, the weapon seemed small at first, but as the creature closed in, the rusty weapon turned sideways, and she saw it was large and heavy enough to cleave her in two.

This butcher intended to carve into her like she was a cadaver. *Don't let it get too close.*

Hoping her instincts would kick in, Anna tossed around ideas as the demon reared closer. What if she used the paintings like Teej? But they were too far away, and that wasn't how her Praxis manifested. She had to break things down rather than create or change them.

What if she burned the creature? But that wouldn't work either. Anna wanted to keep her distance, and she needed to figure out new ways of attack. Relying on the same methods made it too easy for Dreamers to predict and defeat her. She knew this was how Drowden beat her at Malamun and why she failed at the riverbank.

Looking at the water turning to ice beneath her feet, she bent to touch it as the creature lifted the heavy butcher knife over its head. Anna tapped her ring to the slush at her feet. Immediately, it started to form ice around her fingers, but she had a different idea. Heat. When she harnessed her powers, it appeared the easiest in the form of fire. Not wanting to create flames every time, she altered the water's temperature to produce steam.

You'll burn them all.

Her Praxis activated instantaneously, and the water evaporated with a thrum. Anna was momentarily blinded as jets of hot steam filled the air. The shockwave blasted forward, obliterating the fat demon from her view. She fell backward and hot, wet hair slapped across her face. Anna wiped frantically at her eyes, trying to clear her vision, her cheeks flushed and hot. *Careless!*

As the fog began to clear, she saw the results of her attack. Rising to one knee, she watched the demon butcher flail while holding its face and hissing horrifically. The air filled with the cloyingly sweet scent of seared meat. Anna had literally cooked the demon alive. Breathing in the vapors, she started to heave as the smell struck the back of her throat. Willing herself not to vomit, she held her breath. *There has to be a less disgusting way to fight.*

"Anna!" shouted Pappi. "Are you well?"

She suppressed a coughing fit, giving him a little thumbs-up gesture. Through the fading clouds of steam, it became clear Pappi had defeated the goat-headed demon. Legs were twisted at crooked angles, and the skull was shattered into pieces.

Pappi appeared at her side, and Anna began to panic. "Where is Teej?"

Pappi peered further down the hall where some of the lamps were snuffed out. Anna felt like the Haze was closing in on them.

"I'm fine," Teej groaned, his strained voice echoing from the far end of the hall.

Ringing out her clothes, Anna followed Pappi. Through her shoes she felt the heat lingering in the floor. Stepping over indeterminate chunks of fleshy matter, the stench from the cooked demon made her cough once more. Rubbing steam-filled eyes, she surveyed the carnage wrought by her own hands.

Cronos was a congealed smear of gray slime across the floor. Patches of bare skull where the flesh had been literally boiled off glowed white in the dimness. Beyond the mess, Teej writhed on the ground.

Immediately, Anna's heart sank. He was burned and holding his right leg with both hands. As soon as he saw her, he tried to smile.

"No need to worry. I'm all right. The big one was about to smoosh me. You saved me." Teej looked calm, but her Haze Sense and her eyes told her differently.

"*Smoosh you*? This is serious, Teej! We need to get you help."

Ignoring her, Teej gestured at a nearby painting. "Can you feel him in this one?"

Pappi lifted his Periapt walking stick and pointed at the painting. Turning to Anna, a soft smile illuminated his face through the perspiration on his brown skin. Even now, he looked utterly unfazed.

"Stay with our injured companion. Andre has used up much of his power. His stores of Vig, far more than we expected, have dwindled. You dismantled much of his power, Anna. It should not be hard for me to stop him, since I am faster than either of you. The best plan is for me to go while you stay with Teej. Do you agree?"

"I'm not useless!" Anna complained. "You don't need to leave me behind."

The Metik touched her arm gently and leaned in so only she could hear. "Does Anna speak, or her insecurities? What would you have us do next?"

Anna glanced at Teej critically. Even though he was grimacing, he patted the ground beside him. "Keep me company?"

"You're right, Pappi. Go after Andre. I'll help Teej."

It was her fault he was burned. She could keep him safe, or at least try. If something else attacked them, she would protect him.

Pappi stepped toward the broad canvas. It depicted a night scene of the desert with a rotting animal corpse framed in the center. He climbed into it, breaking through the surface like it was a still pool of water. This action reminded her of Andre's manipulation of his Art back in the security office.

When it was just the two of them, Anna was forced to witness the destruction her Praxis had wrought on her friend. Her world was turning nightmarish again. Garret's words rung in her ears now. *You'll burn us all. Burn us up. Burn the world out.*

As Anna looked into the shadows, she saw vague, undefined dangers swirling in the gloom. They huddled in a shrinking island of light, overlooked by horrifying paintings and a slowly descending doom.

Still, Teej didn't look worried at all. "You can relax. We have time to talk now."

Anna didn't want to talk. Heart beating fast in her chest, she held onto her Praxis in case something attacked them from the shadows.

"There's nothing we can do now. Pappi has got this."

Anna looked at his mangled leg, forcing herself to witness the suffering she had inflicted. "Teej, I'm so sorry."

He waved her over. "Just come here, would you? I'll show you how little you need to fear injuries like this. Remember what Lady Almeria said. *Less talking; show the girl?*"

"She didn't call me *girl*." Anna spoke with more malice than she'd intended. "Why are you so calm? There are monsters coming out of the walls and you're half melted. I fucked everything up again."

He laughed a little. "It's not as bad as it seems. There are no more monsters coming. You know that; you can feel it. We have a little time. I might as well explain some things. I think you're ready to hear them."

Anna edged closer.

fourteen

One by one, the lamps went out, and the light penetrated no more than ten feet into the gloom. Thankfully, the foul smells faded too. The carcasses of the slain creatures dissolved into pools of effluent. Mounds of gristly meat melted away into oil, creating rainbow patterns across the surfaces of the puddles. After these monsters were painted into creation, their short lived and fragile lives allowed them to step out of the canvas only once. Reverting to oil paint streams, they flowed into the cracks of the broken floor.

Anna knelt by Teej and felt like they were the last two people in the world. Their voices were the only sound, and everything they said echoed briefly before disappearing down the endless tunnel of night.

Still hyper-alert, Anna reacted to any noise by jumping to her feet and scanning the darkness for the source. Teej rolled his eyes each time.

"If you're so worried, you could bring down this whole thing right now."

"Bring what down?" asked Anna. "The museum?"

"Sure. The Vig in this Haze is running low. You could bring it to an end."

"How?"

"I'm not an Undreamer, but I guess you might grab the bottom of the walls and rip them back like wallpaper to reveal

Basine. Or maybe you could create a big tornado to blow the whole thing away."

"I never think of these things. How am I supposed to just *know* this?"

"Undreamers are famous for lacking in imagination, but you always find a way to survive when you need to. Just try not to overthink every decision."

Anna fiddled with her wet sleeves absentmindedly. She didn't want to argue with him because she felt guilty every time she looked at his burned flesh. But this really wasn't the kind of advice she needed right now. Thinking *less* didn't seem like a good approach when she had the ability to cause so much suffering. Perhaps if she made informed choices instead of acting on instinct, fewer people would get hurt. Rolling these ideas over in her mind, she didn't feel like it was the right time to tell Teej. Better to just listen to him for the moment.

"Well, I'm not sure I know where to *start*. I could try to summon a storm for a change. What do you think?"

"How about we just rest for a bit?" he suggested. "Look at this."

As he pulled back the leg of his pants, the material clung to his burned skin. Anna felt faint.

"Listen to me; we have to get you help. Those are third degree burns. Don't move too much."

Teej didn't seem worried. Rather, he looked at the wound with morbid fascination. "Nasty, right? Watch this though."

Awkwardly pulling a handkerchief from his pocket, he smeared a little red on the pristine white cloth with his dirty fingers. He laid it over the wounds, and it started to soak through with blood immediately. Teej waited for her reaction.

"What's that for?" she asked, unsure what was happening. He didn't answer.

Although the remaining Vig in the Haze was draining rapidly, there was a familiar tingle. Something was changing. At first, she predicted danger. Anna half rose to her feet, but Teej calmed her. "Shhhh. Look."

He rubbed the handkerchief back and forth briskly. Anna reached out a hand to stop him and then froze. Heat and a faint light leaked out from beneath the cloth. After several long moments, the cloth was covered in blood. When he pulled the fabric away from his leg, she caught a glimpse of intact skin. It was paler than the rest of his body, but his wound was healed.

"Not bad, right?" Teej seemed surprised and delighted with the results. He rubbed off leftover specks of dried blood with the back of his hand.

Anna tried to smile, but tears formed in her eyes instead. It was too much. She looked away, trying to hide her eyes from him.

"Oh, it's okay. Don't be upset."

Anna tried to talk, but all she could do was sob. She trembled as his hand brushed her hair, and before she knew what she was doing, she fell into his arms. He embraced her warmly, and she pushed her wet face into his soft shirt. He smelled sweaty and dirty and wonderful. This was a mistake. This was letting someone get too close. *They try to save me then they die.*

Teej laughed gently and kissed her forehead. "It's not as bad as it seems. It never is. These fights have gone on for thousands of years, and we can take the hits. Once you're Behind the Veil, there's *nothing* you can't overcome. One defeat isn't the end of the world. When you are a Metik, you have all the tools you need to pick yourself up and dust yourself off. In a Haze, healing isn't a process, it's a choice."

Anna shook her head gently. That all sounded too good to be true. She was conflicted. She wanted to believe he could heal everything, but she was also sure all suffering left scars, and those never healed.

Teej noticed the unconscious twitches as she tried to reconcile her feelings. He moved his hands down her body, resting his palms on her calf.

136

"What are you doing?" she asked gently, wiping tears from the end of her nose and sniffing.

"This hurts, doesn't it?" He rubbed her ankle gently with his fingers. He was right. Since Malamun, her ankle ached and it seemed to be getting worse with each battle.

"Yeah," she sniffed "A little."

"Well..." he trailed off.

She felt a burst of heat flash across her foot and up her leg. As the heat dissipated, the pain disappeared. Anna was sure it was some temporary trick or a subliminal sleight of hand, but she rotated her ankle, and the familiar shooting pains were gone.

Agape, Anna wasn't sure what to say. Was it wrong for him to do this to her body? Should he have asked permission? Was there etiquette for these situations? Considering everything that had happened to her, perhaps she should simply accept that occasionally, good things happened in Hazes.

Anna nodded politely as she continued to flex her ankle back and forth. "Thank you."

He leaned back and smiled. "You are most welcome."

"Teej, I—"

The headache at the base of her skull returned with a vengeance. That pain had remained with her since she'd left the Sump, sometimes fading into the background, but never truly leaving her. How could she ask Teej for help? How could she explain to him that some remnant of the Sump clung to her mind and wouldn't let her go?

Though the words caught in her throat, she forced them out. Her whole body rigid with fear, she managed to speak. "Teej...the Sump...I'm not...I can't..."

He looked at her with concern. "You are free of Avicimat, Anna. You got out. Put the Sump behind you and move forward."

Anna avoided his gaze. Her head thrummed with pain, and she struggled to catch a breath.

"Listen to me. I'm serious about this. You are not there anymore. Free yourself from these oppressive thoughts." He patted her arm softly.

Anna tried to respond, but she buried her face in her knees and put her hands over her ears.

"Anna!" he snapped. His desperate voice wasn't getting through. The Sump numbed her, and his words seemed weak and distant.

"This is important. You have to say it and you have to believe it. Say the words, 'I got out.'"

Her hands stayed over her ears.

"You got out. Say it!"

"I c-c-can't." The shivering would not stop.

Teej stroked her face. "Anna, you got out. Say it." His voice was insistent and compelling. It was a hand reaching down into the water, grabbing her, pulling her upward, but the surface was too far away. She started to wriggle free of his grasp, but he held on tight.

"Teej, my head hurts really bad! You're not listening to me!"

"Tell me that you are free of that place. Say the words."

"I am—"

The words wouldn't come out. For the first time, Anna felt like she allowed a piece of the Sump to cling to her. This fragment leeched her spirit until she was too weak to fight it. The remnant of the Sump had become malignant and swollen to the point that it was too late to excise it.

She shook her pounding head. "The words won't come. Something's wrong with me."

"Say it! You can do this. Come back to *me*. You need to say it. You're strong enough to take this step. *Make* yourself believe it before we enter Basine. Free yourself from the pain and doubt."

Even with his strength to help her, speaking the words felt impossible.

138

He kissed her cheek softly. "I know you can do it."

Anna steeled herself, summoned every ounce of will she had left, and spoke the words. "I got out."

As soon as she spoke, Anna broke the surface of the water, took a breath and was free. The relief was immediate, the pain in her head fading away. The change was so sudden and tangible that she felt light enough to float in the air.

I got out.

"I escaped, and I don't need to feel lost anymore." Happy tears flowed freely.

Anna hugged him and buried herself in his arms, squeezing him as tight as she could. He held her close, and they shared a moment of pure relief.

Was that all it took? To say those words out loud? Saying them here in the Haze with Teej made them true. Before this moment, a part of her mind felt dislocated, and the words snapped her thoughts back into place.

"What was wrong with me?" she asked.

"The Sump is a trap. Like I said before, you might be the first to escape. If there was a way for you to get out, there had to be a way for you to be truly free of it. Not just in body, but in mind too."

Anna rubbed her eyes then stretched her arms over her head. The Sump may come back to her at some point. The fear, the despair, the pain may not be gone for good. She didn't know. But for now, even though it was getting dark, the world had never seemed brighter.

fifteen

nna and Teej waited for Pappi to return to what had once been the Groven Museum, but was now a dark corridor with some empty frames hanging on the walls. They sat on comfortable red velvet chairs Teej had manifested with his Praxis. He tried to make coffee too, but there was too little Vig left, so the low coffee table sat empty except for a few candles. Anna's contribution to the ambiance had started and ended with lighting them.

"When we were emailing back and forth at the very beginning, how did you first sense my powers and find me?" she asked. "You never really explained."

"Haze Sense. You lit up like a beacon. Every time you were close to a Haze, even if you didn't realize it, you were exerting your Praxis. If I didn't seek you out, someone else would have. And I was alone. I needed a new partner. I needed you."

It felt good to hear him say that, but it didn't explain much. Anna motioned for him to continue.

"After Linda died, I felt the presence of another Metik. I felt *you*, but I was a mess. Moving by instinct, I detected one bright light in all that darkness. Your light."

"You sensed me after Linda died? Why not before that?"

Flickering candlelit made him look contemplative, but maybe he was just tired.

"I couldn't sense any other Metiks in the city until Linda's light went out. When Mott's Haze Spiraled, the winds of Vig rippled across the city and far beyond. I don't think it's an exaggeration to say it changed the world, but it can be hard to pinpoint exactly how. We're all still sifting through the aftermath. And the Spiraling Haze affected me too. I changed so much that I didn't feel like the same person any more. The old me, Donnel, was gone."

"Did my powers just appear when that Haze collapsed?" It seemed like a good explanation to Anna, and she wanted it to be correct, but he shook his head.

"I don't think it's that simple. Garret felt our meeting was serendipitous because he felt that extinguishing one light made another one burst to life. I found you so soon after Linda died that it seemed connected. But I think the spark of what makes you an Undreamer has always existed. Some little part of you has a firmer grasp on Basine than other people."

Teej's explanation was unsatisfying, and Anna frowned.

"Let me give you an example," said Teej. "When was the last time you were drunk?"

The strange question caught her off guard.

"I guess I don't get drunk easily. I feel dizzy when I drink, and it always gives me a headache, but it's not like other people."

"Have you ever been high? When's the last time you had a dream that you thought was real?"

Anna shook her head. "Why is that relevant? I've only tried weed once and it made me feel sick. I don't usually remember my dreams."

"See!" he replied, but Anna didn't see the connection.

"You're always present in the moment, never influenced by anything that warps your view of reality."

"That makes me sound a bit like the designated driver."

Teej laughed and she couldn't help but smile back.

"No, it's a good thing. Or it can be. You're always *here*, and by *here,* I mean *there,* in Basine. Even now, you're an anchor to that place and that's why you're such a powerful

Undreamer. You've got a tether back to Basine that is unbreakable."

Feeling ready to ask a harder question, Anna swallowed nervously. "Why didn't you trust me enough to tell me you were using Andre to get Drowden?"

He let out a long sigh and leaned back. "Can I tell a story? By way of an excuse?"

Anna nodded, wondering where this was going.

"About fifty or sixty years ago, Garret and I were in a really bad situation. I was young and green, but Garret was really at the top of his game. When he was sober, he was *so* skilled at changing Hazes that the Dreamer couldn't keep up. Garret was creative enough to pull something off you'd never expect. So many times, when we were trapped in a corner, I'd realize at the last minute that it was all part of his plan. He really was something.

"Anyway, Garret and I were on a merry adventure when our night took a turn for the worse. We came across an Aesthete who had created a Haze that was killing off homeless people in the city. This Dreamer was staging brutal street fights, conjuring Etunes of the greatest hand-to-hand fighters from throughout history. These legendary martial artists from every school and discipline massacred each other, and a lot of innocent people too, in rolling battles through the streets. We went in to try and stop it. As usual, I tried to talk to the Aesthete."

Anna smiled. "Ever the diplomat?"

"Yes, exactly. The 'negotiations' went really well: I was hanging in a cage, and Garret was thrown in the middle of a pit fight between a bunch of killers, ninjas, bear-wolves and ogres."

"Ninja bear-wolves?"

"No, regular bear-wolves *and* ninjas," said Teej with a completely straight face.

"The Dreamer was powerful and waiting for us. I was too inexperienced to help much, and Garret seemed to be in serious trouble. Crowds of baying maniacs surrounded him in this pit

142

screaming for his blood. He beat three guys in a straight up fistfight, one after another. These Etunes were incarnations of famous street fighters and known killers. Garret smiled through the whole thing. He was having fun!

"Then Milo of Crotan entered the fray. The announcer claimed that he was the greatest fighter who ever lived. Built like a tank and about three times bigger than Garret, he charged in like a bull, red-faced, pumped, and ready to smash this skinny old guy to pieces."

"Oh my God. What did Garret do? Did he use his Praxis?"

"In a very peculiar way, yes. He started this long speech. When Garret starts to monologue, his stories go on longer than—"

"Longer than yours?"

"Yes, his stories go on *even* longer than mine."

"What was his speech?"

"Oh, I don't remember all the details. Some nonsense about warriors and battles. It was very self-aggrandizing! Once he started, no one could interrupt him—literally. That's another one of his tricks. After his speech is done, Garret starts to strip off all his clothes. He's standing there in his birthday suit. Instantly, the crowd goes silent. No one, not even Milo, understands what's happening. Milo is screaming at him. I mean he's speaking ancient Macedonian and I think he's telling Garret to get dressed and get on with the fight, but he doesn't dare get near Garret. He's backing away."

Anna laughed out loud. It would have been amusing even if she didn't know Garret, but she thought it was funnier somehow when she pictured the old man's impish grin.

"Then what happened?"

"A very naked Garret just silently watched and waited. The Dreamer could not force the Etune of Milo to attack him. Eventually, the Dreamer started to run out of Vig. While everyone paused to see what Garret would do next, he shouted out to the crowd. He challenged the Dreamer to face him in person. Eventually, the crowd broke out in chant. *Fight him! Fight him!*

"And this isn't what the Dreamer wanted at all. He wanted a manly, violent fistfight, and it had all gotten a bit weird. He lost control, and that gave Garret the chance to win over the crowd. Now they're all cheering for *him*. And the Aesthete doesn't want to fight a naked Garret either. Everyone just wants this old man to put his clothes on. It all starts to wind down. Milo is walking out of the arena in disgust, and suddenly he gets a tap on his shoulder. He turns around and Garret is right there. He sneaked up on him, naked. And when Milo turns, Garret slugs him. *Pow!* One punch and Garret knocks him out cold. This naked, old man just smashes the greatest fighter of all time and lays him out. He's so unconscious, he doesn't spit out his teeth; they just dribble from his mouth."

"Gross. So, then what?"

"What do you mean?"

"What happened after that?"

"Oh," Teej laughed. "That's the whole story. The Dreamer was spent. Garret changed the tone of the Haze to ridiculous, so it broke down. When the Haze unraveled, we ended up under a bridge in the Bronx, one exhausted and defeated Dreamer and a butt-naked Garret. It was eye opening for me. Before that moment, I thought Hazes were too rigid to mock or disrupt. Garret just laughed and laughed. I didn't find it funny till years later."

Anna nodded. "Don't play by their rules, right? That's the moral. Don't let the Dreamer control the game."

"Yes!" shouted Teej. "That's what you're good at. In Malamun and in the Sump, you always find a way to disrupt the order. Even when people tell you the rules, you always break them."

He had a point. The story made her feel better. Being compared to Garret was a compliment, perhaps the highest compliment Teej could give her.

144

"But Teej—" she protested.

"I know, I know!" he said, irritated at himself rather than her. "You asked why I misled you. I was wrong. I thought you were the scared Metik hanging in the cage, but actually, you were the one brawling your way out of the pit."

"With my clothes on," said Anna. She grabbed one of the candles from the table and flicked it at him, splattering his shirt with hot wax.

"Hey!" he protested.

"That's for keeping things from me. And for the terrible apology via rambling story."

"I *am* sorry," he said sincerely, picking at the wax.

"I know you are."

"Enough old stories then. I need to tell you a little more about the Haze that Spiraled and killed Linda."

There was the barest tremble in his voice. This was hard for him.

"Go ahead," encouraged Anna.

"I don't remember much. There was a desert, a giant of sand and stone, the Apoth raving, Mott laughing, Linda crying out for help. It was a Fluxa Haze that took her life. You know about the other kinds of Haze already. Corpa Hazes are created by one Dreamer, and they only last a little while, and you've seen a few of those now. Staid Hazes are the ones linked to the Realm and they are more stable and immutable, like Malamun or the Sump. But Fluxa Hazes, well those are the ones that spread fast and change the world. Fluxas were always contentious amongst the Metiks because the potential for disaster was high. No Dreamers remain who are powerful enough to sustain one. There's probably not enough Vig in the world to make one successfully now, and that's for the best. Too many Fluxa Hazes have resulted in atrocity and death. Even the purest intentions can steal the souls of millions."

"What's it like inside one?" asked Anna.

145

"Like a hundred dreams layered on top of each other, the rules changing every few minutes, places (and even people) merging together, and there's no way out. And by their nature they require many Dreamers to create. That by itself can be the problem. I mean, it only takes one lemon to sour the punch, you know?"

She didn't. Seeing her confusion, Teej tried to explain. "Have you heard of Thomas Chatterton?"

Anna recognized the name but didn't know why, so she shook her head.

"He was a Dreamer and his ideas changed the world with a Fluxa Haze. They called him the Romantic, and his Haze made the world a better place. I mean, not for him *personally* since he took arsenic and died, but for everyone else."

"And that was all a Fluxa Haze? Romanticism?" she asked. The candles flickered low, casting nervous shadows across his face as he spoke. His eyes looked dark now.

"Yes, but that's an example of one that went well. Poor Princep. He thought his Haze would make the world better too, but that wasn't to be. The Mad Russian soured that plan and the world went to war. The whole world, because a bunch of Dreamers thought they had some big ideas and a little power."

"So, a Fluxa Haze created the World Wars?" asked Anna incredulously.

"Not created, but contributed, especially to the first one. There's not a single moment in history that's not intertwined with the schemes and machinations of Dreamers, sometimes trying to prevent disaster, more often making things worse. And that's when they actually work. When Fluxas fail, they Spiral and then—"

Anna made a whistling noise and pointed downward.

"Exactly."

She struggled to read Teej's expressions in the gloom. In a few minutes, they would be in complete darkness.

"Mott wasn't even calling himself the Midnight Man when he created the Fluxa Haze that killed Linda. His beliefs had a lot in common with the Apoth and Drowden. They'd feuded in the past, but Drowden pulled them together. Mott was the most powerful of them, but Drowden was the smartest and the most manipulative. Together with Ozman and the Apoth, the four of them conspired to form the Doxa. Their goal was to instantiate a Fluxa Haze, although they wouldn't call it that. Likely they would say they were 'Birthing a new God' or some such rubbish."

Anna was sure that if she could see his face, it would show disgust.

"Ozman and the Apoth are brothers. They worked together on some monstrosity they called the 'New Motive Power,' a misguided attempt to create a messiah formed of steam machines and clockwork parts. They were both powerful Dreamers, but together they were always less than the sum of their parts. They bickered constantly. Ozman was the more powerful, and the Apoth was the more ambitious. Something changed. I think Ozman may have developed a conscience. The Apoth's Pilgrims are abominations, and I expect Ozman would have hated them. He was ambitious too, but unlike his brother, he was not cruel. Cowardly and conniving maybe, but deep down, I think he was decent."

Anna thought back to Ozman. There had been a kindliness about the bumbling old man, but a remorsefulness too. Who knows what horrors he had seen his brother perpetrate, or what horrors he himself had committed?

"The Doxa found a powerful Idyll to increase their chances," continued Teej. "They collected all their followers into one group and formed a Choir: a collection of Muses who propagate and multiply the Vig they produce. Then they tried to create a Fluxa Haze. All four Dreamers saw it as a chance to change the world to suit them. Each of them hoped that their doctrine and dogma would become dominant in the chaos that followed."

"Where does Wildey fit into all this?" asked Anna. "And Rayleigh?"

Anna wanted to ask about Linda, but she held back for now. If she knew how Linda died, she would have a better idea if a similar fate was likely to befall her too. And yet she didn't want to ask him directly. It pained him to talk about her passing, so Anna would let him talk when he was ready.

"For a while, I thought Rayleigh had nothing to do with any of this. I thought the Doxa was just a bunch of rogue Aesthetes, and that was as far as this all went. Now I'm not so sure. Rayleigh is the most powerful Dreamer alive today, and he's the de facto leader of them all. He doesn't give orders, but he does forbid certain actions. For a hundred years, Fluxa Hazes have been forbidden. He hasn't done anything to stop the attacks on you, or the continued, and now exposed, plans of the Doxa. We have to find out why."

"And Wildey?" she asked.

Teej sighed heavily. "Ah, my old friend. You know Garret jokes that I'm a diplomat? Well, Wildey is *the opposite* of a diplomat. What would you call him in Basine? An anarchist maybe, or a revolutionary? He has a very strong sense of right and wrong. For him, kindness and compassion are not virtues. It's all black and white, good and bad, and when he decides to do something, he is uncompromising."

"He wants to meet us," said Anna cautiously.

Teej frowned. "I've tried to avoid thinking about him. I guess I just hoped he'd go away. I don't want him gone, but if some Dreamer killed him, well, I think my main emotion would be relief. I never want to see him again."

As the last of the candles fluttered out, they were left in twilight. A tiny sliver of silver moonlight shone through a high window and illuminated half his face and a patch on the ground.

"He said something about a Choir," said Anna. "Didn't he say they were children? Where are they?"

"Good question. I don't know."

"Are you mad at Wildey? Do you blame him?"

"Yes," he uttered through gritted teeth. "Yes, I blame him, but I blame myself more. For not knowing him better. For being naïve.

"Before we confronted the Doxa, we argued about the best approach. Wildey wanted to bring their Haze down. He wanted to make sure it Spiraled and killed all four Dreamers within. Most Metiks use a light touch with a change here or an adjustment there. They try to stop Aesthetes from causing harm by nudging them in the right direction, sometimes negotiating with them, sometimes convincing them, only fighting if necessary. But Wildey was always willing to skip to the finale. He was always prepared to go to war.

"I convinced Linda we could talk them down before Wildey made a move. Even I knew it was risky, but I was being idealistic. I'm not sure she believed in me, but she—"

Blinding light.

The real world flashed back, and the Haze was over. Bathroom stalls, sinks, a dirty mop, and the smell of disinfectant—they were standing in a bathroom. As Anna's eyes slowly adjusted, she noticed the distinct outline of Pappi holding the defeated form of Andre De Lorde by the back of the collar.

"It is over," said Pappi.

"Did you like my newest work?" asked Andre through bloodied lips.

"I wasn't a fan of this one," said Teej as he got to his feet and dusted himself off. "It's the kind of place where you wipe your feet on the way out."

sixteen

Anna would have preferred to reappear in the museum gift shop rather than the men's toilet. The white tiled walls were spotless, but she nonetheless had an overwhelming feeling that she shouldn't be here.

Teej and Pappi stood with the dejected form of Andre DeLorde between them. Pappi held the defeated Aesthete firmly, twisting his arm behind his back.

None of them looked like victors. Pappi was out of breath with bloodshot eyes, and Teej was filthy. Neither showed sign of serious injury. Now that the battle was over, Anna realized that she had escaped relatively intact. Indeed, she felt better now than she had for months. The guilt of her recent failures was erased by this success. The lingering dread of the Sump was excised from her mind, at least for now. Though looking ragged in tattered clothes with her hands smeared in blood and ashes, she finally stopped shaking.

Anna walked to the sink to wash her face, trying her best to avoid seeing her reflection in the mirror.

All three of them were caught flat-footed when Andre shook free of Pappi's grasp and moved suddenly for the exit. Panic gave urgency to his movements, and he made it to the door before any of them reacted. Teej gave chase, reaching out a hand to push the heavy exit door closed just as Andre started to pull it open

Pappi took a step backward as if he knew what was going to happen next, and Anna followed his lead. The two men were frozen in place, Teej holding the door closed while Andre glared at him. Teej was shorter, but they looked into each other's eyes. Andre's little beard and moustache, still immaculately styled, framed a scowl. They strained against each other, matching strength. Anna noticed with some apprehension that the Dreamer's hand was inside his jacket clutching something.

"Try it," Teej said in a low growl.

Andre pulled something out of his pocket and swung at Teej. It wasn't until the weapon fell from his hand that Anna realized it was a knife. Knocking the attack aside with his elbow, the weapon hadn't reached the floor before Teej landed three quick blows. Two solid punches to the chest and a straight right to the face slammed into Andre before he knew what was happening.

As they circled each other, Teej kicked the knife away. It slid across the white tiled floor, coming to rest at Anna's feet. She didn't know what to do. Help him? Tell them to stop? Pappi rested one of his large hands on her shoulder to reassure her, but it didn't help.

Holding his busted nose with one hand, Andre swore under his breath. Teej waited for him to make a choice.

"You don't hit as hard as the old man," said Andre with a cocky smile. "Garret would be pretty disappointed. Good thing he's dead."

Teej seethed. Anna had never seen him look so enraged. He stood stock still, arms at his side waiting for the Dreamer to come at him, his clenched fists white at the knuckle.

What was he trying to prove?

Andre sized Teej up and shuffled into a boxer's stance with his hands in front of his face. He took a few cautious steps toward Teej. Anna shook her head in disbelief. There was no need for this.

They exchanged blows, Teej quickly overpowering the taller man and knocking him to the floor. Anna shrugged free of Pappi's grasp and ran to break up the fight. Teej reared back to pummel a fallen Andre, but Anna jumped between the two men. At the last possible second, Teej pulled his punch and missed her face by inches. Her arms out to her sides, Anna looked in his eyes until the anger was replaced with shame.

"Dammit," he uttered under his breath. Panting heavily, Teej took a step back.

Anna guarded Andre's prone form. "Go stand over there till you calm down."

"There's no need for more fighting," agreed Pappi as he stepped toward them. "Let's try to be quiet so we don't attract the security guards."

Pappi gestured to Andre, who moaned as he stirred on the tiled floor. "Perhaps you can keep the noise down? We have no desire to hurt you further, but we know we would be dead if our fate was in your hands. If it is a choice between my discovery and your mortality, I assure you that I have strong feelings in one direction."

Pappi seemed to be the only calm one amongst them. Anna's heart beat loudly in her ears while Teej leaned against the nearby sink and panted. Running his hand through his hair, he pushed it away from his face as he struggled to regain his composure.

Andre gurgled as he tried to speak. Bending down to check his wounds, Anna noticed his nose was swollen and his lip was busted. His hair had fallen out of the topknot and hung down the sides of his face carelessly. Lucid eyes followed hers, although he looked thoroughly dejected. She wiped away the worst of the blood with the bottom of her shirt.

"Just let him finish me," he growled. He sounded inebriated with his swollen mouth.

"Why did you do this?" she asked with a tinge of compassion in her voice.

"You don't know anything," Andre spat. "Stupid girl. Your friends suspect Rayleigh is aware of the Doxa's actions and does not oppose them. The reality is much worse. Rayleigh *supports* the Doxa, and he has enforced a decree. Anyone who contradicts him will face the judgment of his new bodyguard. His command is simple: capture the Undreamer, kill anyone who gets in your way."

"Lies," said Teej without looking at Andre. "Rayleigh doesn't get involved like that. Who is this bodyguard?"

Andre sneered and spat once more. "You have not a fucking idea. He has enlisted Raguel as his enforcer and his assassin. Now, he can make any of us do anything he wants."

Teej started to protest but stopped himself, shaking his head in disbelief. Pappi seemed confused too. *Who was Raguel?*

"That can't be true," said Teej eventually.

Pappi put his hand on Teej's arm. "Sadly, there is some sense in this. I have heard whispers."

"Whispers of what?" cut in Anna. "I thought we were just fighting the last of the Doxa. Now *everyone* is after me?"

"You owe her some explanation," Pappi told Andre sternly.

Andre's face twisted into disgust when he looked at Anna. "You stumble into our most sacred Hazes, Malamun and Avicimat, and cause havoc. Then you kill a Dreamer and expect no one will take notice? Rayleigh will not stand for so much disruption. He called a Council and each Dreamer was given their instructions. We have no choice but to obey. Rayleigh is old and wise, and he always chooses the best tool to achieve his goals. Right now, that tool is the most dangerous being in existence. Raguel, the Green Knight."

"Great!" snapped Anna. "Every time one murderous asshole disappears, another pops up to take their place."

"This is nonsense," growled Teej. "Aesthetes don't hold Council any more. Not for a thousand years."

"Well, it was not what you call a friendly invitation," muttered Andre. "One by one we were called, and we were

153

instructed. If we harbored you or withheld information, Raguel would come for us. What choice did we have?"

Andre snarled his words through gritted teeth. Anna wasn't sure if he was full of hate for them or himself, but his demeanor had changed completely, and the friendly, charming Dreamer was long gone.

"Would it have brought you pleasure to see me dead, Andre?" asked Teej.

"Do not ask me what I think of you. I might not give the answer you want." With that, Andre turned away from them and slumped to the ground.

"What are you thinking, my friend?" asked Pappi as he pulled Teej aside. Teej didn't answer. He seemed rattled. Andre had really gotten to him.

Anna tried to fill the silence. "This Raguel is really so bad? And Rayleigh wants us dead. Didn't we already suspect this?"

"Feared it," replied Pappi. "And Raguel is the very worst opponent we could face. But it seemed far-fetched. Rayleigh was no friend, but he was far from an enemy. He can be reasoned with, or so we thought. He has kept the Dreamers in equilibrium for almost a hundred years."

"It doesn't matter," interjected Teej. "Andre's telling the truth about Rayleigh setting the Dreamers on us. There's no reason for him to lie. Look at him? He thinks he's already dead, either by our hands or by Rayleigh's."

Teej turned to the Aesthete again. "But there's one more thing you must tell us. Where are they? Where are Drowden and the Doxa hiding?"

Andre put his head down, covering his face with his hands.

Fearing Teej might get violent again, Anna spoke. "Why do we need to find the Doxa anyway? Aren't we in danger from all of the Dreamers now?"

"Indeed," replied Pappi. "The hounds are loosed, and the traps are set."

"Not for all of us," replied Teej. "Not for you and Alby."

Pappi smiled. "My friend, we have already chosen a side, and we are the prey. We will run with you and fight for you."

Anna was relieved by Pappi's presence. Teej's attack had unnerved her and the tall Metik was a calming influence on everyone. They needed friends right now, especially calm and competent ones.

"If I tell you," Andre muttered under his breath, "what will happen to me?"

"Either we kill them or they kill us," said Teej. "If we kill them, maybe it will create so much chaos that everyone just forgets about you. If they kill us, they probably tie off all the loose ends by murdering you, or worse, sending you to Avicimat."

Andre nodded. He looked at Anna. "You think him brutal, do you not? He is not. There is cruelty in this world you would not believe." Andre turned his gaze to Teej "I will tell you where they are, and I will hope for your success. Telling you will give me a better chance of survival, and I hate them more than I hate you. Still, your chances are slim. How will you face this savage army?"

"We have friends," Teej said simply. "And we will ask for their help."

Andre nodded. "Very well. Perhaps luck will help you prevail, but only if you avoid Raguel. Should you face him—"

"We will all die," finished Pappi.

PART TWO

Blood Moon Rising

seventeen

Anna could hear their voices but couldn't make out the words over the sound of the crashing ocean. The debate at the prow of Vinicaire's boat continued, but she had retreated to the stern. Instead of taking part in the heated discussion, she rested as she watched the cresting blue and white waves. The invigorating breeze was fresh and crystal clear as it slapped her cheeks. The tumultuous water fascinated her, perhaps because the sea felt completely different from the stagnant Black Water of the Sump. Or maybe it was because they were moving quickly away from trouble as the dock disappeared behind them.

After smuggling Andre out of the Groven Museum, Teej called Vinicaire to form a plan. The Aesthete told them to come to the docks, and they set sail immediately upon their arrival. However, motion wasn't always the same as progress, and they were no closer to agreement after two hours onboard. Sure, Teej had a plan, but none of them were convinced it was a good idea. Not even Anna.

Pulling her shawl around her shoulders to ward off the cold, she watched the men talk. Pappi spoke calmly, his body language open and neutral. Teej was a little more emotive, his voice rising and falling. He was telling another long story. Vinicaire interrupted frequently in a histrionic voice while strutting or gesturing wildly. From time to time Alby interjected, his voice gruff and demanding their attention while his eyes remained deadly serious. Though they were in conversation, they were all waiting for Anna to make up her mind about Teej's plan. She wasn't ready to give an answer.

Anna isolated herself at the stern for two reasons. The first was to get away from them all for a while. It would fall on her to decide if they went through with Teej's plan or not, and she needed some time to think. The second reason was even more frightening. Gathering her hair together into a loose ponytail, she pulled it up and to one side of her face and then the other, mimicking imaginary scissors with her fingers. Was she really going to do this? Anna lifted the ponytail high over her head before letting it fall from her hand into loose strands that fell comically into her eyes. She didn't know whether to smile or cry. This was why it had to go. From now on, it was either bangs or a bob. Anna couldn't burn up monsters with hair in her eyes.

Reaching into her bag, she found what she was looking for. She pulled out the gleaming silver scissors.

Why was this so hard? Her mom had brushed her curly mess of hair before school each morning. Half her childhood was spent at the kitchen table staring off into space while Mom battled a mass of knots. Her classmates had teased her about her wild mane, but Mom said the other girls were just jealous.

Anna lifted the scissors and let out a sigh. Monsters in a purple dessert, robots on the moon, zombies on an iceberg. If she could survive all of that, she could survive a haircut. Still, knowing it was the right thing to do caused a rebelliousness to well up in her. Why did she have to cut her hair for *them*? Anna wished she didn't have to do it alone.

"Not the curls!" The voice came from the bowels of the ship, echoing up the stairway.

"Elise!"

As her friend came up from the saloon and onto deck, Anna gathered her up in a tight hug.

Elise giggled and tried to wriggle free. "Get off me, ya goof!"

Anna loosened her grip but held her friend's arms, finding it hard to let her go.

Elise's wide eyes were locked on the scissors. "Oh, no! Oh! Wow! No, no, no. Oh my God. You're really gonna do it. And you were gonna do it without me. You *insane* person."

"I didn't know you were aboard. I'm glad you're here." Anna grasped a handful of hair and frowned. "I don't think I can do it anyway."

Elise smiled warmly. Her pixie nose and slender body made her look like the lead singer of a pop-punk band. Hopping onto the metal railing at the side of the boat, she balanced precariously on the edge. Her short vinyl skirt squeaked against the metal as her heavy boots swung close to Anna's hip. It was freezing, but Elise looked irritatingly scruffy and stylish at the same time. Her loose, off-the-shoulder white t-shirt was two sizes too big and fluttered in the wind as her green and pink braided hair flapped around her head.

Anna pulled her shawl tighter around her shoulders and looked at Elise's pale, exposed flesh. Not Anna's first choice for a comrade in war, she was nonetheless surprised at how much comfort she found in Elise's company. The pixie-sized girl was tougher than she looked. After all, she'd recovered (no doubt aided by her mentor Vinicaire) from an injury that would have crippled most people. She carried no obvious physical or mental scars.

"Do you think they're still arguing?" asked Anna.

"Manly men beating their chests. Circling each other, getting nowhere. Man. Man. *MAN*!"

As she spoke, Elise hopped off the rail, put her hands on her hips and puffed out her chest, imitating a man's voice. Anna completely lost her composure. After several long moments of giggling, she had to wipe away tears. By the time they stopped laughing, she had almost forgotten what had set her off. But when she looked up, Elise was in the same position, hands on hips, her face contorted into a stern frown, and it set Anna off again. Eventually, Elise couldn't hold in the laughter, and somehow Anna ended up in a hug with her friend once more. Pulling away and struggling to regain her equilibrium, she tried to change the subject.

"I'm so happy to see you. Of all the people I've met Behind the Veil, you've almost killed me the least."

"Thanks. They don't know how much they need us. They get caught up in their own worlds and they lose track of important stuff. When they're in Hazes too much, they get screwy in the head. You notice that? Garret was the screwiest of the bunch. Can you believe how he talked to me? He thought I was some Noop! Oh, and Vinicaire's not screwy. But the rest of them totally are."

Anna nodded and pursed her lips not knowing how to respond.

"So, your hair? Like, an undercut? Or just lop off the split ends?"

"Which particular split ends do you mean?" Anna pretended to protest, holding up a mess of curls and knots.

"It's not *that* bad," huffed Elise. "We can just cut around?"

"Nope, it's all coming off. Well, not all of it, but up to—" Anna held two fingers just below her ear. "To about right here."

Elise grabbed the scissors threateningly, pointing them in Anna's direction. The rocking of the boat made her hands shake, so Anna backed away.

"Whoa, maybe better if I do that to myself, don't you think? I've seen you with a sword."

"Oh, sure," said Elise. "But be quick. I need to borrow these soon."

"Why? Not the braids! I love the braids."

"What? No! No way. Vinicaire loves them too. He pulls them sometimes and...anyway. No, not like that! Oh, God!"

Elise was either blushing or pretending to blush. She covered her face and looked away.

"All right, calm down. What do you need them for?"

"Oh, right," Elise said, snapping back to attention. "I think we should tie Andre up. I need them to cut some rope or something. They say we don't need to worry about him, but we totally do. You agree right?"

"Well…" Anna trailed off.

"They think he's not dangerous. Maybe not to them, but what about us? And they always miss the details, you know."

"Actually, I think you're right," said Anna. "We need to tie him up. He's a Dreamer that paints and draws, so who knows what he can do if his hands are free."

"Right!" Elise beamed. "I heard them talking. I've decided I'm going to help you on your mission. I still have my sword, and after the fight with that robot thing, I keep a knife in my boot now too."

Anna frowned. Broaching the subject as gently as she could, she said, "Well, let me just sort my hair, then we can figure out something for our friend Andre. But are you *completely* set on coming? If something happened to you, Vinicaire would—"

"Don't you dare patronize me!" Elise cut her off. "It's my choice. *Mine!*"

Anna backed off. Elise was right. Anna was tired of being patronized, so she shouldn't do the same thing to Elise.

"You're right. Again. It *is* your choice. I'm just scared, and I'm not afraid to say it. I don't want you to get hurt."

"Pfft!" Elise said, rolling her eyes. "I don't want to get hurt either, and I'm scared too, but what else do I do? Stay here in this boat in the middle of the ocean? Drink the rest of the minibar? Go fishing? In this outfit? This is *not* a fishing outfit."

"The *rest* of the minibar?" inquired Anna.

"I only took some." Elise shuffled closer and took Anna's arm. "Annie, I don't want to be in the place where things aren't happening. You only live once, right? *Where were you when the boys saved the world? Oh, we were hiding in an old smelly boat cos we're just silly girls!*"

"Save the world?" Anna said incredulously.

"Well, maybe not *the world,* but what we're doing is still a big deal."

"Okay, okay. I'm already on your side. Now help me cut this hair."

"Yay!" said Elise, hopping from foot to foot. "Afterward you can help me find some duct tape or some rope for Andre."

Elise leaned closer, examining Anna keenly as she put the scissors up to her own forehead.

"A little lower," Elise advised.

Adjusting, Anna made the first cut, snipping away a whole handful of hair. Cutting with blunt scissors was surprisingly tough, and she had to saw through each bit. Holding a bunch of curls over the railing, she released the strands and they were carried by the wind over the ocean's swell.

"Cut less at once," Elise remarked.

She was right. Slowly, Anna cut and released her hair to the sea. With only one handful left, her thoughts returned to more pressing matters. "Do you think we should stick with Teej's plan?"

Elise sucked air between her teeth like she was thinking extra hard. "Vinicaire thinks the plan is good as long as he doesn't have to actually fight anyone. That tall guy doesn't think you are ready, even if he doesn't say much. And the kid doesn't think you perform under pressure."

For a moment there was silence then Elise finished, "But I do."

Making her last cut, Anna flicked her head left and right. *Not bad, not bad at all.*

"I do, too."

eighteen

Anna walked through the cabin, noting the ornate brass instruments at the helm of Vinicaire's boat, *the Gwenlee*. It was filled with modern flat-screen displays and touch screens. She didn't know much about boats, but she guessed this one was expensive, though somewhat opulent for her tastes. The interior was a touch gaudy, while the carved statues on the handrails crossed over into tacky. It was all very Vinicaire.

Opening the wooden door to the fore section of the boat, Anna was disappointed to see the same ring of people locked in the same circular discussion. Sitting on the right of the bow next to the winch was Alby. He looked serious, his youthful face at odds with his stern expression. Leaning on the mast next to him was Pappi, his expression neutral but his posture hinting at an undercurrent of tension. In the center of the group, Teej made a point with his hands. Vinicaire paced next to the galley entrance in an ostentatious faux-pirate outfit—leather waistcoat, bandana, waxed beard—perfectly mismatching the setting. He moved next to a gleaming jukebox and leaned on his cane. In the recessed radio enclosure, Andre sat with his head on the table and his hands curled into fists.

After a moment, everyone fell silent when they noticed that Elise and Anna had returned to the conversation. Elise slid over to Vinicaire's side, while Anna crossed the deck to stand in the middle next to Teej. Sighing, she said, "Let's go over it one more time."

Teej cast nervous eyes in her direction and looked at her expectantly. He gazed at each one of them in turn, and then paced back and forth for a moment before coming to stand by Anna.

"Here's what we've got so far: Andre has given us the location of the Doxa. The Doxa suspect that Andre killed us, or that his Haze at the Groven went wrong and we *all* died. For a small window of time, we have the advantage. You're the only people that can help me."

"We're the only people who *will* help you," interjected Vinicaire, his refined accent cutting through Teej's impassioned speech. "Everyone else is trying to kill you."

"We believe Andre speaks the truth?" asked Pappi. "And we are hoping that Drowden doesn't expect an attack? I'll only say this one more time: we are being too hasty. Why would he *not* expect our assault?"

Andre spoke quietly, but they all heard him. "Drowden thinks no one can get to him. Mr. D never guessed that *he*—" Andre raised his head and pointed dismissively at Vinicaire, "— Would be in your pocket. No one imagined the trickster would choose a side, far less the side of the probable losers."

"So, *this* Dreamer says *that* Dreamer is lying," said Alby. "But we know them *all* to be liars. They are all the same to me. Never trust an Aesthete."

Pappi rolled his eyes. "Come now, brother. That attitude won't help us in our current situation."

"All Aesthetes are equally bad to you, little fellow?" Vinicaire asked acerbically. Alby scowled back.

"I didn't ask you to come aboard my boat," Vinicaire responded. "Feel free to swim home. I welcomed Teej and Anna into my care to escape short-term threats, but I am not a soldier, and this is no army. I am helping you because I fear the

166

consequences of my fellow Dreamers falling into a civil war. I have no desire to start one."

"How does your Art manifest, Vinicaire?" asked Pappi.

"I am an actor." He stressed the last syllable.

"Perhaps you could *act* as someone a little more heroic."

"Dammit, I—"

"Stop this!" snapped Teej. He rubbed his eyes with forefinger and thumb like he was digging holes in his head. "Look, Drowden doesn't expect us to pull together. I know each of you, and I know that you would do anything you could to stop Drowden and prevent the Doxa from hurting anyone else. We just need to pull together. For what it's worth, *I* trust Vinicaire."

The Aesthete bowed to Teej, who went on, "Even Andre wants us to succeed. He's a loose end for the Doxa. Sooner or later, they will want rid of him. He has nothing to gain from our deaths and an awful *lot* to gain if we get rid of the Doxa."

They eyed each other suspiciously, like poker players running low on chips. Anna focused on Vinicaire. With her burgeoning Haze Sense, she could detect the strength of his Will. His colorful clothing made him look eccentric, but his piercing eyes were fiercely intelligent. He was playful, even foppish at times, but he was no fool.

"Very well, this is *your* plan," said Vinicaire. "We are all pieces on your game board. Explain how you need us to move."

Teej's voice went low, inviting them to listen closely. "Andre told us that the Doxa have taken refuge at Kanna Island. They think this stronghold is impossible to reach."

"Ha!" Vinicaire let out.

"*Almost* impossible," Teej went on. "Our easily amused friend here *can* transport us there on this fine vessel. Prepare yourself to engage the Doxa as soon as we have arrived. At Kanna Island, Vinicaire will stay here with the boat and guard our escape. He will hold the gateway open until our return.

"The Doxa should be easy to locate since their focus will be on their creations. They will have defenses, but with our combined strength, we should be able to overcome them."

Elise stormed up to Teej and poked a sharp finger to his chest. "I will be onboard with Vinicaire to guard the gateway as well."

Teej shook his head. "We will drop you off safely—"

Anna cut him off. "It's her choice."

Teej looked at Vinicaire for guidance. "Oh, I don't mind!" the Dreamer remarked with amusement.

"It's not his choice to make," said Anna firmly.

Elise winced at her mentor's flippant reply, but she hid it behind a swish of her knife. Sinking into Vinicaire's shadow once more, she offered Anna the briefest of nods.

"Getting back on track," said Teej, "The main problem with this plan is—"

"Raguel," Alby cut him off. "The Green Knight. Rayleigh supports the Doxa and Rayleigh controls Raguel. If he has sent the Green Knight to protect them, then this whole plan is suicide."

Vinicaire whistled. "*Raguel.* I hear he was responsible for the Bronze Age collapse. They say he had an army, but he didn't need it. They just watched."

"I don't think Rayleigh would send Raguel on an errand," Teej contradicted. "And this is no time for idle speculation. Rayleigh is cautious, and if he thinks we are any kind of threat at all, he will keep Raguel by his side to protect him. Kanna is not an easy location to reach. If Rayleigh sends Raguel to aid the Doxa after we have already launched our assault, he will arrive too late. We have time."

After listening to lengthy discussions about Raguel, Anna finally wanted some answers. The wariness mixed with awe in everyone's voice when they referred to this mystery opponent made her think he was some kind of bogeyman.

"Who is this Green Knight? At the museum, you said you didn't know anything about him."

Teej went back to rubbing his eyes wearily. This wasn't what he wanted to talk about, but she deserved real information about what they were facing.

Anna scanned the deck for someone who would answer her. Alby scowled, Pappi looked distant and Vinicaire had an expression of cruel amusement on his face. Anna addressed Andre. "Well?"

Pappi answered her question. "Hailing from ancient times, he was one of the High Lords of Gwinn. He was a Knight Errant, then later a nobleman of the Monarch's court, and he had his own kingdom within the Realm. In modern times, he has become a walking avatar of coldblooded death. This is why any of his names inspires despair in our eyes, Anna. The Green Knight would be the end of us."

Anna frowned. "Is he a Metik or an Etune? Or something else?"

Her questions echoed around the boat without answer. A single snowflake drifted on the wind to land on her sleeve. "Why won't you answer me?"

"Their answers would be conjecture," replied Vinicaire eventually. "Remember this: *run* if you see him. Run in a different direction than me. You are slow, and you might distract him long enough for me to escape."

"How do we know for sure that Raguel is helping Rayleigh?" asked Anna.

Alby responded this time. "Apparently we trust Andre now. This joke of a Dreamer made desperate claims to keep his head on his shoulders. Please, stop me if I am wrong. Anyone?"

"Why would I fabricate such a claim?" Andre replied curtly. "I *saw* Raguel when Rayleigh demanded my presence."

They all regarded him with suspicion.

"Look in my eyes! Do I lie? To Hell with you all. You know I am being honest. Metiks can sense the truth in a pack of lies." Andre was desperate and angry.

Elise stomped over to him. "We don't need to take that attitude from you. You almost killed my friend."

Andre dismissed her with a roll of the eyes and rested his head on the table again.

"I'm going to tie him up," said Elise. "So that he doesn't try anything."

None of them responded.

"I don't know what we can use. Will you come with me to find something?" she asked Anna.

"Sure."

Teej joined them. "I think there's rope in the hold. Let's go look. We could use a break."

The snow began falling in thick clumps, drifting silently onto the wooden deck as Anna followed Teej. Walking past Vinicaire and Andre, she noticed their eyes following her critically.

Pappi shouted after her, "Come back soon, Anna! Every time you leave the room, I fear all the sanity leaves with you."

Riffling through the dusty shelves in the hold, it was clear Vinicaire did not care much about this part of *the Gwenlee*. The storeroom was full of useless radio equipment, empty plastic bottles, gas canisters and assorted detritus. Anna was glad to be safe from the wind and snow, but it wasn't exactly cozy here. She rubbed her hands, trying to warm her numb fingers.

Teej pulled out baskets of broken metal and rusted tools, long frown lines framing his face. Anna had a sudden urge to make him smile, but she couldn't think of a joke.

Elise clattered through tins of paint and shifted mops and cleaning supplies out of the way as she moved toward the blocked-off lower section of the ship's hold. She forged ahead, giving Anna a moment to confer with Teej alone.

"I was thinking about when you fought with Andre. Why did you hurt him like that?"

Teej paused and grasped the metal shelves.

Anna went on, "They joke about you being a mediator or a diplomat, but isn't that a *good* thing? It's not a reason to mock you. Is that why you beat Andre up? Because of their opinion of you?"

It was clear now that Teej hid his feelings with a joke and an easy smile. He would shrug off negativity and avoid conflict, rarely opening up to her when he was in pain, but right now he was himself. He was raw, and more likely to share his true feelings.

"Being a diplomat hasn't really helped me recently. Too much talking got Linda killed, and I couldn't talk Garret into staying with us. Every time I open my mouth, things just seem to get worse."

"You still have friends, Teej, and you still have me. I know we're on Rayleigh's hit list now, but do we need to be so *desperate*? You always figure something out. Just give yourself some time to decide if this is the best plan. In the end, whatever you decide, I'll follow you. We all will."

A wave of relief seemed to come over him, and finally he smiled. "Thank you. You know, I keep thinking of Subotai."

"Oh yeah, me too," she joked.

"No, seriously. I have a story."

"Of course you do."

"Do you want to hear it or not?"

"I do," she said with a smile. Telling the story would help him more than it would help her.

"Guys, I found duct tape!" shouted Elise from the back of the storeroom. "But the roll is almost done. We need more. Or maybe some handcuffs *and* a straight jacket. Do you have those?"

"I don't think so, Elise! Not on this boat," Anna shouted back.

"Just keep looking," encouraged Teej.

Anna could tell he was itching to tell his story.

"Have you heard of Subotai?"

"Is that a type of car?"

"No," he said, carrying on without being fazed by her joke. "Back when Genghis Khan's armies roamed across the world and conquered every city, civilization and people they encountered, Subotai was their primary strategist. At the height of the Khan's power, every victory seemed a certainty and no army could stand against him. Every city that he came across was taken. Not just taken, it was *cleansed*. Subotai would kill every man, woman and child. Whether they surrendered, fought valiantly, or ran, their fate was always the same. If he was in a particularly bad mood, he killed the goats and camels too."

"Lovely story, Teej. *So* relevant to our current situation."

"Just stay with me for a minute. Subotai was a real monster, but he was a genius too. Most of his enemies were so terrified of him that they wouldn't fight back. At times, he took pleasure in personally beheading prisoners. He commanded them to wait in line while he slowly retrieved his sword. Do you know what they did? They obeyed and waited for death to come to them. They were too scared to run and too scared to fight, so they stayed on their knees in the mud in a line till he came back. Then he cut their heads off one-by-one.

"After the city was wiped out, his army stayed and ate all the food—even the goats and the camels—then plundered and pillaged until the smell of the dead was overwhelming, even for the Mongols. Then they burned everything and moved on to the next city."

"Does this story actually relate to something that is happening to us right now?"

"Not quite. Keep listening anyway. After Subotai had taken a hundred towns, the hundred-and-first saw his army on the horizon. What could they do? Fight? Run? Surrender? No matter what they did, their fate was already sealed.

"Frustration bubbled up in them anyway. That doom plagued their minds. How could they just wait? The tension was unbearable.

"Pretty soon two factions appeared. One side wanted to surrender and the other wanted to fight. The town square became a place of fervent open debate. Arguments escalated to protests and eventually, protests led to riots.

"The two groups clashed violently in the city square and a huge battle ensued for three days and nights. Eventually, the faction that wanted to surrender was victorious. All the while, General Subotai looked down with amusement as the city tore itself apart.

"On the third day, an emissary from the town rode to meet with Subotai. He explained how the city tore itself apart with more than half the inhabitants dead. Finally, a consensus was reached. They asked Subotai for mercy and then they surrendered."

"I bet Subotai didn't care, right?"

"He just laughed. Subotai was a serious man, not known for his sense of humor. On this occasion, he laughed and laughed. He laughed so long, eventually the emissary joined him. Everyone was laughing. Abruptly, he stopped."

"Uh-oh."

"Yes, exactly. As the laughter subsided, Subotai told the emissary, 'A city where the brave can be bested by the craven? Truly this is a glorious day for my brothers. We have the honor of ridding the world of your shame.'"

"And he killed them all? And their goats and camels?"

Teej nodded. "Even the hamsters."

"You should tell everyone that story."

Teej smiled. "I think you're the only one interested in my stories. They're all for you."

173

"I found some!" interrupted Elise from the back of the room. "There was a whole pallet." She skipped toward them, almost tripping over a bucket, her arms full of rolls of duct tape.

"What did I miss?" Elise asked.

"Just a history lesson," said Anna.

"Oh, thank God!" Elise smiled.

nineteen

The snow was still falling heavily as they huddled under warm blankets provided by Vinicaire. Anna pulled her shawl close.

As Elise scurried over to the corner mischievously, she unraveled a roll of duct tape and held it threateningly in the direction of Andre. "I won't let you hurt any of us. You could be planning some artsy dangerous thing to kill us all."

The Aesthete looked at her with bleary eyes and took a moment to process what was happening. "Oh, no," Andre said. "Keep away from me with that tape."

Walking over to them, Pappi glanced threateningly in Andre's direction. "Oh, *yes*. I think this tape will keep you from sustaining further injuries by me."

Andre sighed in defeat and that was all the encouragement Elise needed. With obvious glee she began the process of gagging Andre.

Pappi looked over at Anna and Teej in expectation. "Have we progressed to a less foolhardy plan?"

"Not yet," Teej responded. "I've been telling Anna a story."

Alby gestured to the sky. "Save it! This weather is not natural."

"He is right," said Vinicaire with a hint of panic in his voice. "And it is not of my making. We are discovered!"

"Calm down," said Alby. "Teej can sniff out the source of the storm with his keen senses. What do we face?"

Teej walked to the fore deck and looked into the distance. The prow sliced through thickening snow and mist, and there was little visibility. Sensing an opportunity for practice, Anna stretched her Haze Sense and followed Teej's example.

"Something has been relentlessly following us for a while," said Teej. " And it is not impeded by land or sea."

"Oh, this is fabulous!" said Vinicaire as he ran from one side of the boat to the other, looking out to the horizon. "Just wonderful. I am *so* glad to have you all aboard."

Anna inched toward the side of the boat, bit the skin at the base of her nails, and looked straight down into the waves.

"Why do you look into the water?" Alby interrupted her thoughts.

"Last time I looked into the ocean, it was full of dead people," said Anna, her voice sounding unfamiliar in her throat. Something was very wrong here.

Teej appeared at her side. He startled her as he squeezed her shoulder reassuringly. She touched his hand and nodded. "I'm okay."

"It's familiar," he whispered to her. "But it's not Drowden."

"Worse?"

"I don't know. Older maybe? It's searching for us."

"There!" shouted Alby. He'd moved to stand balanced on the bowsprit and pointed out to sea.

Teej nudged Anna. "Come on."

Together they joined Alby at the prow. Anna saw a vague form in the mist. A small green boat rocked gently among low waves while a man rowed lazily. Even though his back was to them, Teej seemed to recognize the man. The water was calm but Anna felt like they sailed close to an encroaching storm. Teej was grasping inside his coat for something he couldn't seem to find. Anna brandished her ring, ready for the fight ahead.

"What do we do, Teej? Are we vulnerable in the water? This feels bad."

176

When he didn't answer, Anna whipped around to find Teej frozen in place, his eyes unfocused and his mouth hanging open. "Can't be…" he mumbled under his breath.

The small boat floated closer, but the heavy mist obscured the passenger. The only sound was the splash of oars. And…whistling?

Pappi came to her side and let out a steady breath, prompting her to lower her Periapt. "No one to burn here," he said softly.

"Tom Collins is talking about you," shouted the boatman.

Anna recognized the voice.

"We only have rum," replied Alby, his expression softening for the first time since Anna met him. "And other pirate drinks on this funny little boat."

"Good enough."

Garret tossed the oars onto the deck, stood up in the rowboat, turned and reached out a hand to Teej, who didn't respond. After a moment Pappi stepped past him and took Garret's hand, and with creaking bones and a groan, the old man climbed aboard *the Gwenlee*.

"It is good to see you, old friend," said Pappi.

"And you, young man," replied Garret.

Alby waved, and Garret gave him a thumbs-up, but he walked past them all to get to Anna.

"Good to see you, hun." He gathered her up in his arms, and she squeezed him as tight as she could. He smelled like old-man sweat and the salty sea.

"The curls! I miss the curls."

"They'll grow back," she said with a shrug. "And my hair's never going to be as fabulous as yours."

"Shucks," he said as he pushed her away playfully. "Hey, it's the girl!"

"My *name* is Elise Beauchamp!"

"I know," Garret lied. "And Vinicaire. You're…also here."

"Indeed," the Dreamer replied coolly.

"Why are you back?" asked Teej. He was pale.

Walking across the deck to the galley entrance, Garret looked well. His simple black t-shirt and blue jeans were clean and crisp, and his hair was combed back from his face. His beard was as unkempt as ever, but he'd shaved around the sides and he didn't look tired. Despite the snow, he was unaffected by the cold.

"Retirement wasn't all it was cracked up to be," said Garret. "Hey, girly, have a drink! It will make you stop pretending you don't like me. And get me one, too."

Elise rolled her eyes as she stomped to the cabin to get him a drink.

"Been up to much lately?" Teej asked eventually.

"I met a gymnast. Twenty-two. Lots of energy."

"Is she coming?"

"Nah. She told me I was too immature. Left me for an older man."

"Older than you?"

Garret laughed and nodded. Anna was overjoyed to see him. She couldn't believe he was here, but she worried what his arrival might mean.

"Hey, hun. I see you've been up to your ol' fighting ways." He flashed his brightest smile.

"You keep popping up, Garret. Are you here to stay this time?" Anna asked.

He looked at Teej. "I'm here as long as you all need me. Or until the drinks run out. Speaking of which—"

Elise threw him a bottle, and he almost missed it. He wrenched off the cap with his teeth. Elise went back to binding Andre's hands with tape. Despite her protestations, Elise liked Garret. *Everybody* liked Garret.

"Welcome aboard," Vinicaire said stiffly.

Almost everyone.

"Uh-huh," replied Garret.

178

Wasting no time, he gulped the rum then pointed the half-empty bottle around the room. "What's the plan?"

An awkward moment of silence followed as glances were exchanged. Pappi shifted uncomfortably and leaned on the mast.

"It is not so simple, Garret," said Alby. "Our enemies may be protected by the Green Knight."

"Yeah, I know," Garret cut him off. "I saw him."

A ripple of surprise went around the boat. Even Andre turned to look at Garret, though he was now half-mummified. Vinicaire tried to hide his shock, but Anna sensed it.

"Explain," Teej said simply.

"My retirement ended prematurely because of a broken promise. I said I would never travel to the Realm again, but some events are beyond my control. Rayleigh pulled me off the Moonlight Road, and I ended up there."

"How is this even possible, Garret?" asked Pappi.

"No one has successfully walked the Moonlight Road for centuries," said Garret. "Everyone who has tried has disappeared, so naturally, we thought the road was in ruins. So much of the Realm is crumbling and closed off from Basine, it seemed that surely the Moonlight Road must have fallen to the same fate. But no!

"I trust you all know how the Moonlight Road operates? It's just like the legends say, folks. Once you find a gateway and begin walking across the light of the moon, every ten steps you appear in a whole new world. I walked for days, maybe longer. Each place I visited was stranger than the last, but as long as I stayed on the path, nothing could harm me.

"And that journey changed me. The Moonlight Road has a personality of its own, and it wants to be found. I think…I think it was glad of the company. Perhaps this sounds like madness, but the Moonlight Road was happy to no longer be alone. As I walked, it rewarded me. My mind felt less foggy and my old aches and pains seemed to fade. I'm sure the effects are fleeting, but even now that I'm back here, I feel better than I have in years.

"The Moonlight Road, *Mangata*, is waiting for more visitors. But walking the Moonlight Road makes you visible to some powerful people. Rayleigh watches the entrances and exits. He invited me to step into his domain. When I felt his call reach out to me, I decided to investigate."

"And?" Teej pressed him.

Garret pointed at Anna. "He wants to meet her."

"Well he can't meet *her*," said Anna instinctively.

"What exactly happened on the road?" asked Teej.

"The Road weaves in and out of everywhere in the whole Firmament, and each time you take a step, you never know where it will lead you. Walking through jungles of glass, ancient cities at the bottom of the sea, brushing past stars is like nothing you can imagine. As far as I was concerned, I was on a one-way trip and I would walk the road forever, or until it got tired of me. But Rayleigh is a powerful Dreamer and his influence seeps in. The Moonlight Road insulates you from harm, but a Dreamer like Rayleigh can still reach you there. He tantalized me off the road with promises of information. I could have evaded him, but curiosity got the best of me. I followed that rabbit down its hole."

"You *chose* to step off the road?" Alby asked incredulously.

"I did indeed, kid," Garret replied, "I knew my time on the road was limited. As I came toward the end, I felt him reach out to me. Rayleigh's Mimesis is familiar and old, and, Hell, we'll never be friends, but I didn't think he'd want me dead. Near as I could tell, I'd be dead soon anyway. So when Rayleigh offered a diversion, I took it."

"What *did* he want?" asked Teej.

"I already told you, he wants to meet Anna."

Garret turned his attention to her. "You're the first Undreamer that's appeared in a hundred years. Rayleigh is curious."

Garret waved them all closer. "Gather 'round friends. I'll tell you what I know."

They huddled around Garret.

"What makes a successful politician? There are a million different answers, but Rayleigh is the embodiment of pragmatism. He knows that an epic battle is coming. Rayleigh's only held his position as the big dog amongst the Dreamers because he's a politician. He has never been a fighter, but he's been able to rule for a long, long time.

"While watching Gwinn's decline, he formulated a plan many years ago. With Gwinn dormant, the Green Knight had no purpose, so Rayleigh gave him one. He recruited him with promises of a mighty battle to come with many worthy opponents. That was Rayleigh's first power play.

"His second move was his current position in the present conflict. Believing the Dreamers will clash at some point in the near future, he thinks this schism with the Doxa might be the spark to ignite a civil war. Do you feel in your bones how near we are to an all-out war? As the last of our people, we are in decline. There are fewer Metiks, fewer Muses and Idylls, and less Vig as the years pass by. Our resources are in decline, and the safeguards are relaxed. We're all circling the drain, and that means the Dreamers and Metiks will spiral into conflict. Rayleigh knows this, and he wants to secure what he can *while* he can. He wants useful resources to safeguard his future. Resources like a powerful Undreamer who hasn't yet chosen a side."

Garret sounded like Teej, or rather, Teej had always sounded like Garret. The old man spoke seriously of grave matters. Despite his calm words, Anna felt a sense of dread.

She looked to Teej for reassurance, but he seemed lost in thought. Since Garret's reappearance, Teej had barely spoken.

"I've chosen a side," said Anna. "I want to *end* Drowden. I want to make sure he can't hurt us or anyone else again, and I don't want to meet some *new* maniac. I don't know why he wants to meet me, but it can't be for anything good, right?"

"I am not so sure," said Pappi. "Rayleigh did not seem to be an enemy. Siding with Drowden and the Doxa is not in character for him. However, I agree that it's too risky to meet with him."

Alby interjected, "This is all pointless. We are left in the same position. We know the location of Drowden and the Apoth, but we still don't know if Rayleigh will offer them protection."

In a flash, Anna knew what she had to do. "Well, what if I go to Rayleigh and figure that out? If Raguel is there with him, then we know that he's not with the Doxa, right?"

There was complete silence. Scanning their faces, she tried to figure out if she had just said the dumbest thing of her life. When Anna looked at Elise, she shrugged.

After a long, uncomfortable pause, Pappi said, "This idea might work."

Alby nodded in agreement. "Anna should be able to gauge Rayleigh's intentions, and she may even find the Green Knight by Rayleigh's side. If that's the case, we will attack the Doxa at Avalon immediately. At Kanna Island, we might even prevail."

Teej and Anna locked eyes as everyone else faded into the background.

"You don't need to do this," Teej whispered.

Anna gave him a tiny nod. "Yes, I do."

"It is decided." Pappi clapped his hands together. "Anna will go and face Rayleigh."

"First, she'll need to find the Moonlight Road," chipped in Garret. "Rayleigh is expecting her. I can show her the way."

"On your wee boat?" asked Anna with a skeptical look.

"That's just how I came *off* the Moonlight Road. The entrances and exits are quite different."

"Then it's agreed," said Teej. "Garret will lead you to Mangata and you'll walk the Moonlight Road. When you get to Rayleigh, secretly send us a message—which we'll discuss later—and tell us if we can start the ambush. Vinicaire will transport us to Kanna Island, or Avalon if you prefer the old name, but we wait for your message before we make a move. And when we get it, Pappi, Alby and I will face the Doxa. Between the three of us, we should be able to overcome anything Drowden and the Apoth throw our way."

Elise was about to interrupt, but Teej acknowledged her complaint before she made it. "Elise stays with Vinicaire on the boat. They can protect each other and keep our escape route open."

As soon as the plan was set, Anna felt her insides churn with worry. They were putting their lives on the line, and this was all her idea.

twenty

The goodbyes were heartfelt. Elise hugged Anna fiercely, then kissed her full on the lips and ran off before Anna knew what was happening. Pappi hugged her close and told her to be brave but cautious. Vinicaire bowed theatrically and warned her "don't start believing." Alby, who she still didn't know well, stiffly wished her luck and shook her hand. Even Andre gave her a small nod of approval. He might have said something if Elise hadn't taped his mouth shut.

Only Teej and Garret would travel with her to the entrance of the Moonlight Road. Garret had to find the path for her, while Teej wanted to talk to her on the journey. He had some advice and a confession.

As Garret laconically rowed them toward the beach on the small boat, Anna waited for Teej to speak. She looked out at the water while little white waves rocked them sleepily. The snow had let up for now, and everything around them was gray. The beach wasn't far, maybe half a mile, but it wasn't getting closer very quickly.

The last time she had been on a boat like this, it was rowed by a giant monster in red. Refusing to let her mind linger on memories of the Sump, Anna focused on more pressing threats. Fidgeting with her ring, she concentrated on her Praxis: the Will, the Word, the Sight and the Sword. With practice, she had learned a little more of each, yet she still felt like a novice.

Anna edged a little closer to Teej and nudged him. It was cold, and she wanted to be close to him while she could. He hadn't been the same since Garret came back.

Should she rest her head on his shoulder? It would feel nice to have his arm around her. Once again, she was walking toward a challenge all by herself. Anna forced herself to remember that when she faced enemies alone, she came out on top. Charron and Mott hadn't been easy, but she had come out the other end. This time, she wasn't fighting only for survival; she was also fighting for her friends. For just a moment, she wanted someone to hold her and tell her everything would be all right, but Teej seemed lost in his own thoughts.

"It's a beautiful sight, even wrecked and ruined. You'll feel all your troubles and worries fade away in your rearview mirror."

Anna wasn't sure what Garret was going on about.

"The Moonlight Road," Teej explained.

"It really puts all your problems in perspective. When you're stridin' through that path of Moonlight, it's hard to care about all the small stuff in your life. The legends say it can take you anywhere. More accurately, they say it will take you *through* everywhere until you get where you *need* to be. And you can only ever walk it once."

"Could you take it to Malamun? Or the August Club?" Anna asked.

"Who knows? Maybe. If that was where Mangata decided to send you, then that's where the road would take you."

"Maybe you were meant to follow the road long enough to meet Rayleigh?" Anna ruminated. "Maybe you ended up where you were *supposed* to be."

"I don't think so," he said. "Afterward it brought me back here. I was supposed to end up right here, to help you."

They continued in silence for a while longer. Anna tugged on Teej's sleeve. "Where am I going to end up?"

185

Teej looked to Garret for advice, so it was the old man who answered her. He took a momentary break from rowing to stroke his beard. "Once you start to walk the road, you'll know what to do. I can't take the trip with you. Like I said, you can only walk the Mangata once, and Rayleigh wants you to come alone. When the road ends, you'll be there."

"Where?"

"With Rayleigh."

"It's not gonna be like—"

"It's not like Avicimat," Teej interrupted.

Anna nodded, reassured. Garret went on, "I don't know where exactly Rayleigh will meet you, but you won't see him. He'll speak to you through a proxy. It will make sense when you get there."

"That's all a bit vague, Garret," Anna complained.

"I'm afraid it's all a bit vague up here, too, hun," Garret said as he pointed to his head.

"Are you sure you should be rowing?" she asked with concern.

"Yeah." He smiled. "It's the mind that's foggy; the arms are still good. Besides, since I walked Mangata I feel much better."

Teej stared at the old man closely. Garret was right, though. His sinewy arms were like metronomes and the shoreline was approaching quickly.

"It doesn't really matter what the place looks like," explained Garret. "Rayleigh can make a Haze appear like an office or a dungeon or a space station. Just remember, the locale will be designed to intimidate you. You gotta be strong. Don't give anything away and don't lie to him, but don't share too much either. He doesn't want you dead, and he wants you on his side. You can't beat him in a fight, so he'll be prepared for anything you try. Just—ah Teej, you tell her! I sound like an old fart."

"I think she wants some actual advice. We're sending her into this blind. The least we can do is prepare her a bit."

186

"Yes, please do," Anna agreed.

"Rayleigh is dangerous," Teej went on. "You need to survive this *and* get a message to us. And then escape after that."

"Jesus, Teej," scoffed Anna, throwing her hands up. "Pile on some more pressure, why don't you?"

Anna knew the stakes. She needed practical advice, not dire warnings. "Can you tell me what this Green Knight looks like at least?"

"He's a big knight and he's green."

Anna glowered at Garret.

"Well, he is! Your Haze Sense will help you recognize him, although he is pretty obvious. Don't second guess yourself."

Turning around to look at the beach, Garret grunted. "Almost there. It's getting dark too."

"We need to find a place where the moon is very bright," explained Teej. "Minimal light pollution and far from civilization. Garret can take you onto the road from here."

They were exactly in the center of nowhere. The wind blew ocean spray in their faces. The snow had given way to rain, but then abated. Peeking out from behind the heavy gray clouds, Anna could make out the distinct shape of a full moon.

Scanning the shore, she saw no signs of life. Scrubby grasslands crested the hills and overlooked white sandy beaches. Shipwrecks littered the landscape with bright orange rusted hulls sprouting from the pale sands in the blue twilight.

"I'll go check to see if we can start the path here," said Garret. "I won't be long."

As they entered the shallows, Garret scrambled over the edge of the boat, swearing loudly as he stumbled and splashed into the water. Teej and Anna watched him fumble, both trying to suppress a laugh.

"Will he be all right?" Anna asked with concern.

"Who knows," said Teej, his voice distant. "He treats all of this like a big joke. He ran off before I could say goodbye, then came back before I could start forgetting him."

"I have to talk to you about something," said Teej suddenly.

Anna fidgeted with her ring and waited for him to speak. His eyes looked cold and blue, his slim face was a little gaunt and he looked nervous. "Go ahead."

"I never asked you what happened to you, before all of this."

"I know. I was glad you didn't."

"It's not that I didn't care, Anna, but what happened to you is not who you *are*."

Anna trembled. "I know it's not."

"I know you don't want to talk about it, but one day you might find that you can't."

"What do you mean?"

"When you go into Hazes, you tend to forget parts of your past life. You can't always choose which memories to hold onto or which ones will slip through your fingers."

There had been a time when her husband was always in her thoughts, no matter how she pushed them down. Now, she had to dig deep to remember him. The ring was still on her finger, but she couldn't picture his face. The suicide letter had been burned, unread.

Tears came to Anna's eyes, but she didn't want them. They were reflexive, since she didn't feel sad or angry. They were placeholder tears for placeholder emotions. She cried but she felt numb.

"I don't want to forget him, but I can't keep remembering either. It's too painful. I don't want to lose the memories of how he lived, but I hate remembering every detail of how he died."

"Those memories tend to stick, no matter what we do."

Together, they gazed through the dim light to the indistinct shape of Garret pacing on the beach. As she watched, Anna felt some measure of relief. She had dreaded the moment when they

188

would talk about her past. There were so many painful memories she wasn't ready to share: the accident at the river or holding his lifeless body in her arms on the shore. Now, if she didn't make it back, she'd never have to tell him any of it.

"Do you think it would have gotten better for you?" asked Teej. "If we never met and you hadn't been attacked by Mott. Do you think you would have made peace with everything that happened to you? Do you think you could have been happy?"

"I don't know," Anna told him matter-of-factly. She could have turned back so many times, either at Lady Almeria's house, at the Gisborne Hotel, or even when she first encountered him online. His messages had offered some vague promise of escape, and she realized now that she pursued that opportunity with fierce intensity to the exclusion of all else.

Teej took a deep breath, then gingerly reached out and took hold of her hand. She let him. "I have to tell you the one most important thing. No matter what happens, don't say your name."

"Why?"

"There's an old curse on the Green Knight. It has something to do with his origin. I don't understand exactly, but if he hears someone say their own name, he is compelled to kill them. No matter what happens, don't say your name."

"If I don't say my name then he can't kill me?"

"Oh no, Raguel can kill you just fine any time he wants. If you say your name, then he *has* to kill you. He won't be able to stop himself, and no one else can stop him either."

Anna wasn't reassured.

"They don't want you dead and they're not threatened by you, so they don't feel like they need to eliminate you. They're curious, so just play along. Whatever they ask of you, just do it. When they ask you to join them, stall for as long as possible. Tell them you need time to make a decision."

"Then what?"

"Then you come home. Head to Maxine's and wait there if you're back before us. You should be safe, for a little while at least. If we don't make it back in a few days…Well, then, you know it didn't work out for us. Keep moving, don't stay in one place for too long, and look after yourself."

"You really think Rayleigh will just let me go?"

"If he really believes you're considering joining him, I think he will."

"I won't ever join him. I'm with you till the end."

Teej squeezed her hand. "This is why you have to be better at lying to people. You have to convince them you might be an ally. But…till the end, I'm with you too."

His hand was strong and soft and warm. *Wait!* Teej still hadn't told her how to send him a message.

"Teej, how do I contact you? I'm guessing they don't have good cell phone reception there."

Teej didn't seem worried. Rummaging in his pocket for a moment, he took out the spoon.

"You have got to be kidding me. Shall I just call you on the spoon when I'm in a spot of trouble?"

"What did you expect, an App?"

"Teej, this mystical world of yours. It's—"

"Weird? Wonderful?"

"Low budget."

"Well, yes," he laughed. "But you can find wonder anywhere. Even in the cutlery drawer."

Teej placed the spoon into her hand and pushed her fingers closed around it.

"Think of me," he said.

"How? Like, think of you naked?" she joked awkwardly.

"No."

Was she flirting? Anna blushed, and for a moment, she thought Teej almost blushed too. It was the most adorable thing she'd ever seen.

"Just picture me in your mind. Think of my face and allow yourself to feel…whatever you feel for me."

190

Reluctantly complying, Anna closed her eyes and pictured his face, his smile and the funny voice he used when he was telling a story. The spoon quickly grew warm, and then hot. In a few seconds, she could barely hold it. Swapping it from hand to hand, she said, "That burns."

"Yes. When you think of someone, it heats up, and it's controlled by the last person who held it."

Teej opened his pocket wide and motioned for her to drop it inside. "You're the last person who touched it. I won't touch it again, so you control it. No matter where you are, it is attuned to you. If you think about me, it will get hot because it's already close to me. It's in my pocket and I'll feel it, even though my clothes."

"When I want to give you the signal, I just think of your dumb face?"

He mimicked offense but smiled almost instantly. "Exactly. When you think it's safe for us to attack, you think of my dumb face. That will trigger the spoon. Try not to think about me before then. If your thoughts linger on me for a little too long, the spoon will activate."

Mentally running through the checklist of everything she had to remember, Anna took a deep breath and tried to calm her nerves. On the beach Garret was waiting for her. Standing stock still, he seemed to have found the path.

"Let me go over this one more time. I go with Garret, the Moonlight Road takes me to Rayleigh, I find out if Raguel is there or not, don't say my name, then call you on the spoon-phone and come home. That's it, right?"

Teej smiled and nodded. "That's it."

Before she knew what was happening, she was in his arms. He hugged her closely.

"Good luck, Anna."

"Good luck, Teej. Please don't die."

Turning away before he saw her tears again, Anna clambered out of the boat and splashed her way to the shore through the surprisingly cold sea. She didn't look back.

Hope is coming to eat your heart.

That final stanza of the Midnight Man's epic poem had almost killed Teej and everyone he loved. It was the last thing Mott had said in the desert before Linda died, and the phrase rattled around in Teej's mind as he watched Anna climb the beach to reach Garret. Hope was a last resort. When your final handhold is hope, your grip is far too likely to slip.

And now all Teej's hope went with Anna. Sitting in the boat alone, he watched Garret show her the way. She was taking her first steps onto the Moonlight Road. Teej was sending her into the arms of the most dangerous man alive, and what had he given her to protect herself? Some vague instructions and a spoon.

It was too late to change course now. There would be no time for diplomacy when he faced the Doxa. That was going to be a street fight he needed to survive in order to help Anna. Teej hardened his resolve and prepared for the battle to come.

He craned his neck forward to see her take her first steps on this journey. Once more, Teej watched another person he loved walk out of existence on the Moonlight Road.

twenty-one

The Moonlight Road was a glimmer of diamonds on the dewy grass and a shimmering sheen of dappled silver that would disappear if you weren't standing in exactly the right spot. Anna struggled to find that spot.

"To the left, girl! It's right there!"

"Right where?" Anna shouted back at Garret. "I am not seeing it at all. Is it just the light on the sand here?" She pointed ahead at an indistinct glimmer. "Is that *really* it?"

"Yes!" he snapped back. "That's the path. Remember, wherever you go on the Moonlight Road, you can always find the moon. Now, don't move your feet. Don't even wiggle them toes."

Anna wriggled her toes into the sand, then grinned at him. She was freezing and she was antsy. Standing on the windy beach, they'd been walking around in circles for ten minutes now. She was ready to go.

"It shouldn't be this hard to find," said Garret. "That's the point. *No matter where you go, you can always find the moon.*"

"Well, it *has* been extremely hard to find!"

Patiently, he continued, "Now that we have it, you can start any time you're ready. Just stay on that spot. Don't lose it again. Remember what to do?"

"Yes, yes. Face the moon and start walking. It's not that complicated."

"Take a deep breath for a minute. Okay?"

Anna nodded and breathed out heavily. Chewing on her nails, she looked at the full moon, noticing how bright and clear it was tonight. She felt its light like an accusing glare. Her goodbye with Teej had been unsatisfying. There was more to say.

Too late now.

"How do you feel, hun?" Garret asked.

"Ready. Well, not actually ready, but, you know, I'm cold and I want to get going."

He smiled and nodded. "Attagirl! Now, remember I said you'll go through a different world every ten steps? For you, it will be every eleven or twelve with your little legs."

"My little legs aren't that much shorter than yours!" she protested.

"Your mouth is much bigger."

"Garret!" she snapped, but his grin got to her. "You're *such* an asshole."

"That I am," he admitted. "The worlds you pass through won't interact with you unless you step off the Moonlight Road. No matter where the road takes you, you will be safe. So, you won't feel the temperature and you will be able to breathe even if you are underwater. It's like a big, ole invisible tunnel that leads you safely where you need to go. Just don't forget not to step off until Rayleigh calls to you. Remember to walk slowly. The Moonlight Road is long, and the journey to its end takes time. As soon as you step on the road, Rayleigh will know your location, and he will try to call you off long before you get to your destination. He doesn't want to hurt you so just, you know, go with it. Don't be all '*Anna*' about it."

She rolled her eyes and bit her tongue on a sharp reply. Instead, she focused on her breathing to steady her nerves. "What happens if I don't let him take me?"

"What did I *just* say? You can try to avoid him and follow the road instead, but that's not really the plan this time."

"Okay, I'm ready to go."

Anna turned to take her first step on the road. With her Haze Sense, she felt the glittery path coalesce before her. Although she walked on an empty beach, she was about to step through a doorway.

"Anna," Garret interrupted her.

"What? We've said it all. I'm ready!"

"I know you are. I just wanted to tell you something about the kid."

"Which kid? You mean Teej?"

"Yeah."

Crossing her arms, she looked at him critically. "What about him?"

"Lots of women fall for him. I dunno why with that goofy face, but they do."

"If you say so. What's your point?"

"He's never had trouble finding women to help him."

"Is this about Linda?"

"Yeah."

"I know he feels bad for what happened to her, but it's not his fault. She was his partner."

"No, hun, Linda was *Wildey's* girl. She left him for Teej, and the kid didn't even realize it. When they had their disagreement, she chose to help Teej, and he went along with it. But she didn't help him because she thought he was right; she helped him because she was in love with him."

Anna shook her head. "Did he know?"

"Are you kidding? He's a good kid, but he can be real dumb when it comes to people."

"Why are you telling me this?"

"Be careful with him, Anna. He's broke up inside worse than you."

Anna turned away from Garret. "This isn't the time…"

"All right then. Just ignore me. I'm old and I tend to ramble."

195

Garret strode up to her, grabbed her by the hips, then turned her a little. "That way. You're ready now."

The path ahead was crystal clear to her Haze Sense. When she was a little girl, she'd spent hours on a beach just like this with Dad, digging holes in the sand and swimming. When she was with him there, she never wanted to go home. Standing at the entrance to the Moonlight Road, Anna felt that same resistance. But she had no choice; it was time to go.

"Goodbye, Garret," she said.

"I don't do goodbyes. See you later, hun."

Anna was already walking when Garret shouted after her. "By the way, I like the short hair after all. It makes you look like—"

Too late. The words were lost as Anna took one final step and crossed onto the Moonlight Road.

twenty-two

ight steps, nine, ten. Then eleven, and Anna was gone. This place looked like a damp beach, but it felt like skydiving into the stars. Anna's journey on the Moonlight Road began with inertia and exhilaration. This was different from all the other Hazes. They felt like a tickle, but this was a slap in the face. Her skin tingled all over, and there was a crackle of static. Pushing through this barrier felt like penetrating a slick membrane, and on the other side, everything was clearer and more defined. Once again, Anna stepped into a bigger, stranger world.

The Moonlight Road itself was almost invisible. It sparkled and shimmered from certain angles, but most of the time she couldn't see it at all. Anna was especially disconcerted when it started to carry her upward with each step. Counting those steps once more, she climbed into the air. *Three steps, four, five, six.* Soon she would cross into the next world.

Looking back, she realized the eleventh step on the Moonlight Road had already taken her out of Basine. Her surroundings looked similar, but there were enough changes to tell Anna she was somewhere different now. Garret had disappeared completely, along with the shipwrecks and the boat. She could still see the beach and the ocean, but everything was blurred, as if the level of detail in the world faded.

The Moonlight Road hovered four or five feet over the sand. Anna saw through the surface below her feet, but she wasn't sure how far it extended to her left and right, forcing her to proceed carefully and slowly. The wind no longer touched her, and she wasn't cold. It was exactly like Garret said. She felt safe and isolated from the world around her here. What would it feel like to step into the *next* world?

Nine steps, ten, eleven.

For the second time, Anna stepped into a new reality, but this time the barrier wasn't quite so resistant. The environment faded to black for a fraction of a second like pushing through theater curtains, then she entered a totally new world. There was no breeze, no change in temperature, but she looked around in astonishment to see books on all sides. Bookshelves surrounded her, stacked high above her head, stretching to infinity. The ground was so far below her she couldn't see it. Assaulted with sudden vertigo, Anna forced herself to look away from the black void under her feet.

Where am I?

Inside the cylindrical tower library, the dusty shelves were perhaps twelve feet away. The only focal point Anna could use to anchor herself and regain her equilibrium was a narrow bridge that stretched out from an illuminated doorway below her.

This strange library seemed both ancient and secret. She had stumbled into a forbidden vault. Examining the bridge below her closely, she realized it was made of books and only half-complete. Tattered pages fluttered in a breeze she couldn't feel. Her path led directly over that bridge, and she hustled onward, the dizzying vertigo making her eager to escape this impossible place. In another life, she might have lingered here, running her fingertips across the spines of dusty old books. But not today. Her friends couldn't wait for her to delay.

As she hurried along the nearly invisible bridge, she was aware that her path was no stranger than the one made of books. A ghostly passage of frozen moonlight took her through worlds she would never touch.

Eight steps, nine, ten.

A bright doorway opened at the end of the book-bridge and a girl appeared. She wore strange clothes, baggy and gray, and she looked sad. Anna didn't have time to examine the girl closely before she felt the pull of the next world once again.

Eleven.

A lake. Anna walked through—or, more accurately, the Moonlight Road cut through—the water. The road seemed to run a few inches below the surface, and waves on either side of the path couldn't penetrate into her little corridor of protection.

I'm like Moses parting the sea, but...less impressive.

Now she knew the Moonlight Road was about seven feet across. The little waves lapping at either side made her nervous, but there was nothing else to see here. Just water all around, a pale blue sky above and the Moonlight Road shining ahead of her.

Five steps, six, seven.

The gray clouds started to swirl into shapes. Anna stopped, and the clouds stopped too. Was her movement affecting the world around her?

Testing the theory, she took a half step, and as soon as she lifted her foot, the clouds swirled again, spinning into focus. Committing to a full step, she shuddered when she realized the clouds were not moving randomly. They were coalescing into the shape of giant horses. Ten of them, twenty, a hundred, filling the whole sky.

Anna pushed on, and the cloud horses became solid and real, their manes fluttering, their nostrils flaring. They surrounded her, each more than a mile high. Gray and roughly textured, they regarded her with fierce intensity.

"Hi," said Anna meekly, her words having no effect.

I'm a speck on a painting, a grain of sand on an infinite beach.

She continued walking under the gaze of the stallions of the sky. This place made her feel tiny, bringing back memories of Charron and the Sump, and the memory propelled her forward.

Eight nine ten eleven steps.

As the curtain lifted once more, the view rocked her back on her heels. Walking high above a city, massive spires started far below, then extended beyond and above her to scrape the sky overhead. Hundreds of creamy white towers, columns, and walkways crisscrossed the heavens with ridged ornamentation. Squinting, Anna realized they were shaped like bones. Long femurs for towers, tibias linking them, hip bones forming sloped ramps, and fingers as the supports for long, swaying bridges.

Anna's Haze Sense didn't penetrate outside the periphery of the Moonlight Road, but she knew this city of bleached bone was deserted. Still, she became queasy when she looked at the sight. The surfaces met at angles that didn't seem quite right, confusing her eyes. It was the grandest tableaux she had ever witnessed, and the view held such power that it made her retreat into her senses.

The bones ground together with a low, persistent groan echoing across eternity. Her vision swam as if the towers were melting together, the giant bones weaving a pattern that seemed to spin and cycle through different phases. Dizzy, Anna's knees began to buckle, a numbness creeping up her legs, and she desperately wanted to rest for a moment. It might feel nice to stay here a while.

I am in danger.

Five steps, six, seven.

Vision is just light hitting the back of the eye, inverted and incomplete. Or is vision composed of beams of thought sent out from the eye, streaming and pulsing until it is interrupted? Can the eye itself detect the disruption that sends the waves back into the mind, dissonant and disturbed, but incomplete?

The shape of the city meant something. The towers and spires formed a skeleton, but it was also a beating heart and a sign. Its shape created a word spelled in letters used before language existed. A symbol.

I am losing myself.

Eight steps, nine.

Anna escaped into the next world. She had miscounted. The city of bone had been dangerously seductive, filled with shapes that bewildered her senses. Just like the Sump, it was a trap for the mind as well as the body. She had to be more careful from here on. Thankfully, her legs carried her onward even when her mind betrayed her, unconsciously moving her into the next world.

Complete darkness. Anna stumbled into a black so absolute that she lost her balance and almost fell. For a moment she thought it was a residual effect of the symbols she'd seen in the city, but completely bereft of light, she realized that this was darker than black. Light did not seem possible in such a place. Holding her hand inches in front of her face, she could not make out any part of it. The path shimmering ahead of her was the only thing that seemed to exist, and even that light was faint. Aware that the next world might blind her, Anna squinted and moved on as quickly as she could, trying her best to follow the narrow path ahead.

Eight steps. Nine steps. Ten steps. Eleven.

It couldn't be. Anna was walking a few feet above city streets she recognized. It was a busy intersection close to her apartment. People hustled from the sports bar to the natural foods store to the Italian restaurant on the corner, splashing through puddles and carrying umbrellas to ward off the rain. Suddenly terrified that someone would see her, Anna tried to crouch low and sneak past.

Two steps, three steps, four.

A couple of men her age blocked her path. The older of the two adjusted his boyfriend's hood, fidgeting with the zipper before they shared a brief kiss and walked on toward her. Anna tried to dodge aside, but the Moonlight Road curved curiously, and they seemed to slide past her without touching her. Like they were mirror reflections in a funhouse, their forms stretched and morphed as they moved beyond Anna before reforming behind her. With a shudder, she hurried on. The Moonlight Road was impatient and lingering too long at any stop increased the risk of never reaching the end.

twenty-three

*O*ne step, two, three steps, four…
Nine steps, ten steps, eleven.

After what Anna guessed was about twenty minutes of walking the Moonlight Road, she had travelled through a graveyard, over a glassy desert, past a ruined castle on a hillside, through a skyscraper, and even under a river. While trespassing through the worlds, she remained detached and separate from each space, focusing on the trail of sparkles extending ahead of her. After more than a hundred transitions, she unconsciously wiped away tears. It was too much sadness mixed with beauty. Part of Anna wished the path would never end. What a glorious way to live—to simply walk the Moonlight Road forever, never worrying about anything, or touching anyone else's life, never staying in one place for more than a moment.

Eight steps. Nine steps. Ten steps. Eleven.

When she found herself over the Gray Sea, Anna's pace slowed as she stopped completely to stare over the horizon. The sky was a roiling mass of dark, almost-blue clouds. The ocean, perhaps fifteen feet below, was slate gray with white crests on the huge waves. It was primordially powerful and severe. Although her Haze Sense couldn't penetrate beyond the narrow corridor, Anna felt an instinctive dread and awe. This place made her feel like a tiny speck on a huge canvas. She had an overriding feeling that she shouldn't be here—that it was wrong to be here. On the margins of reality, a wrong step could send her off the edge of the Firmament.

Tempting.

Anna wondered if this was the *Endless Gray Sea* mentioned by Teej. Would it take her, if she was brave enough to traverse it, to the ancient beings Teej had been reluctant to talk about? The Provident?

Should I sit? Was it possible to sit on the Moonlight Road? Giving it a try, she bent at the waist. When her hand touched the sparkling surface of the road, it felt too cold for human skin. When she tried to pull away, the skin almost stuck, as if the ground was made of frost. The Road didn't welcome her as a guest, only as a traveler. There was no time for ennui on Mangata. She had to keep going.

Eight steps.

The hypnotic waves pulled her gaze toward them over and over. Since she couldn't hear them, they seemed engrossing more than ominous. Anna had a sudden desire to say something to hear how voices sounded on the Moonlight Road and to remind herself that she still existed.

"I can't stay here all day, right?" she said, testing her voice. It didn't travel far. There was nothing for the sound to bounce off, and the words drifted away from her to infinity. "This mystical, invisible moon tunnel might get bored with me and drop me in the sea!"

Was that what she wanted?

Receiving no response, Anna walked on, sad to leave the overwhelming sight of the crashing ocean. Those waves made her problems seem so small and transient. One day, maybe she'd come back to sail beyond this sea to find answers to the questions even Teej couldn't answer.

Nine steps, ten steps, eleven.

Anna pushed through a curtain of reality to reappear in a new world. Although the cold couldn't touch her on the Moonlight Road, the scene chilled her.

Clustered village houses with yellow windows and red chimneys were packed so closely together that there were no discernible streets between them. The village looked like it was from a few hundred years in the past. The buildings were red brick, and the roofs were covered with a thick layer of brilliant-white snow. The sky looked like a mosaic disintegrating around a setting orange sun. Strangest of all, the whole town sat atop rolling hills made of frozen ocean waves. The sea had become a series of ice hills and looked like a frozen moment in time, impossible and yet holding some internal logical consistency within its own strange existence.

Anna felt a twinge of familiarity, as if she'd seen this place in a movie or a poster. It took her a moment to realize where she's seen this scene before. *Oh, Moonlight Road, what a playful sense of humor you have.*

She remembered the moment her dad hung the painting over the old, brown sofa in their little summerhouse by the lake. Mom called it kitsch, but Dad was much less snobby about art. Anna noticed it every time she sat down, but she had never looked at it carefully. Curiously enough, as a child, all the abstract imagery seemed normal. Even more curious was how she was seeing it now. Surely it wasn't coincidence. Mangata had access to her memories, almost like a window into her soul. For a moment, she was grateful that out of all the moments from her past, it chose this surreal image to craft a whole new world around.

Was that too simple an explanation? Garret told her the worlds along the Moonlight Road were real and not hallucinations from her own mind. Did that mean she could step off the path to explore this frozen ocean town? Was the gauche, cheap painting secretly based on a real place, created by a Dreamer whose work had been reproduced and sold in a bargain supermarket home décor section? What came first, the Dreamer or the dream?

Suddenly worried she might be getting distracted again, Anna started to move more quickly. Had she gone too far? Was this where she was *supposed* to be?

"No. Keep going. Keep going for Teej."

Thinking of him for only a moment, Anna dragged her legs, now weary with the long walk. She watched the ocean-village speed past below her.

Nine steps, ten, eleven.

Sad to leave a familiar place, Anna pushed into the next world. She had finally arrived at her destination. Ahead of her Mangata continued onward. For the first time, there was also a narrow path leading off to her right. The Moonlight Road split, and Anna needed to make a choice. Should she continue straight ahead or take the side path to Rayleigh?

Anna didn't hesitate.

twenty-four

"All ashore!"

Vinicaire stood at the prow of the boat like an animated hood ornament. He gestured theatrically for them to disembark, then clumsily stepped off the deck onto the rickety pier. As he hit dry land, he spent a long time adjusting his cape and waistcoat. The low sun, just beginning to set, cast a long shadow that emphasized his ridiculous attire. A top hat and tails were not appropriate choices for sailing on rough seas, but Teej dismissed the Dreamer's idiosyncrasies. Despite his bravado, Vinicaire was just as nervous as the rest of them. He might not be taking part in the fight, but merely coming here could be enough to mark him as an enemy of Rayleigh and a target for the Green Knight.

Avalon, Kanna Island, and The Island of the Dead were all one and the same. The island was a knuckle of rock in the middle of a roiling sea. A strong swimmer could reach the mainland if the seas were calm, but at this time of day, the dying light made it look distant and remote. Waves periodically crested so high that the mainland disappeared from view completely.

Vinicaire's opulent boat seemed delicate amidst the severe spikes of broken, twisted rocks lining the shore. In front of them, the rotten pier became a snaking staircase that curled around the hillside and out of view. The whole structure looked likely to topple into the waves at any moment with fragmented steps peppering the climb. They would probably have to jump or scale across the gaps in the path, making the whole journey a daunting prospect.

Following the stairway to its zenith with his eyes, Teej examined the lighthouse on top of the hill attached to a crumbling outpost station. These two structures were surrounded by a small patch of grass and scrubby wasteland. Far above and to the right of the outpost, a tree dangled precariously over the ocean, curled branches reaching out as if it was mid-fall.

Behind them, the sun was inches from setting on the water. The dying light painted the cloud-daubed sky in a thousand shades of red and orange. If it weren't for the cold spray from the sea and the omnipresent wind, it would have been tranquil. Instead, Avalon held an austere beauty. The waves urged them to get out of the boat as quickly as possible.

The trip hadn't been long, but it had been rough. Vinicaire knew the way to every secret backdoor in the world, and the journey to the island wasn't very pleasant. Teej's heaving stomach thanked him when he set foot on solid ground. Pushing out a tiny amount of Will to calm his heaving guts, he waited for everyone else to join him on dry land.

"You're sure it's safe?" Vinicaire asked, his nonchalant tone at odds with the question he asked.

"We haven't been detected yet," Teej replied. "And if we are noticed, we will have time to make an escape before we are caught." He sounded more confident than he felt. Although Teej had no concrete evidence about the Green Knight's location, he felt something tug at the edge of his senses. It was something familiar but *broken*. His Haze Sense had tingled at first when they found Garret out at sea, but afterward, it continued to niggle at him. It felt like they had pulled something through with them when they came here, but the feeling was vague, and Teej admitted to himself it could just be nerves. Or déjà vu.

Garret joined him on the pier. "I don't think we have been detected. Far as I can tell, the Doxa are in the outpost. Though *something* is in the lighthouse too."

"I feel it as well," Teej agreed. "Something bad."

"Ohhhhh, a big mysterious bad thing," Elise said as she clambered ashore. "How specific."

Vinicaire reached out a hand to help her up. "It's not our problem, my little protégé. Our job is done. The sea is conquered."

"My hero," Garret drawled before winking at Elise. "She's too good for you, Vinicaire."

"Do you want to adopt her?" the Aesthete inquired.

"I don't want to deprive you of your bodyguard. Should she ever get bored of guarding that body though, she's welcome to join the men as we save the day."

Elise rolled her eyes.

Turning to the Aesthete, Teej offered his hand in friendship. "You didn't have to do this. I don't know why you've helped me—twice now—but thank you."

Vinicaire didn't shake his hand, but he gave a slight bow. "Sometimes rational self-interest grows tiresome for a gentleman of finer tastes."

"All right then," said Teej. "I hope I see you both again."

"Could happen..." Vinicaire trailed off.

Elise hesitated, then gave Teej a nod of reassurance. "It's gonna be okay, Teejay. Anna's gonna be okay."

He nodded in return. It was what he'd needed to hear.

As Vinicaire and Elise walked back to the boat, she turned and waved. Teej waved back, then they began the ascent.

Pappi and Alby were already on the stairs with Garret following close behind. Teej hustled to keep up. The rotten timber pier creaked ominously underfoot. Allowing himself one last look back at the boat and his two companions, Teej swallowed down his growing sense of dread.

His companions wasted no time and were already partway up the stairs that wound around the mountainside, but the niggling presence bothered Teej, and he kept looking back. His Haze Sense told him the presence wasn't malicious, but it was ubiquitous on Kanna Island.

Shaking the thought from his mind, Teej pushed on. The climb was steep and precarious, and he kept losing focus to gaze at the setting sun as it kissed the horizon. This wasn't the time to appreciate the aesthetic beauty of Kanna Island, but the ragged, burning skyline reflected the ocean in a deep blue and daubed the sky with yellow and red and even splotches of purple. It was a breathtaking sight.

Garret shouted back, interrupting his reverie. "Keep up kid. In Avalon no man has time to look back at his own footprints."

"Do you sense anything different now that we are getting closer?" Teej asked Pappi as he caught up with him. The Metik's Haze Sense was almost as keen as Teej's.

"I sense someone hiding in the lighthouse. And below us, I detect a rumbling from their creation stirring in the caves."

"What form will their Fluxa Haze take?" asked Teej. "I remember the Apoth once tried to create a creature from crude science and eldritch energies. It was an abomination. He called it the New Motive Power."

"I doubt this new creature will be different. Whatever form it takes, it is the result of Drowden's and the Apoth's Art, and both have souls that are now ugly and cruel. We must be ready to face all flavors of nightmare."

Alby narrowed his eyes and frowned.

"What concerns you, Alby?" Teej asked.

"I suggest we avoid the front door. I can create an entrance for us. Over…there." The boy pointed at the top of the stairs. At the summit of the incline, the path passed close to the side of the outpost. It was a long walk from there to the center of the island and the front of the house, but Alby could create a side door rather than using the front one.

"Sounds like a plan." Teej glanced at Garret to gauge the old man's opinion.

"You're the boss," Garret agreed.

As the path wound up and around the hillside, it doubled back on itself. The climb was difficult, and Teej wiped his brow with a handkerchief while his legs powered on. Underfoot, each plank shuddered and seemed on the verge of collapse. By this point, the wooden slats had mostly rotted away. When Teej looked through them, he saw the high waves and the two figures in the boat far below. Elise's green and pink hair stood out brightly amongst the dark ocean. Vinicaire's face was upturned and watching them.

Teej felt a pang of vertigo and the height made his head spin, so he forced himself to look straight ahead. What an ignominious end it would be to simply fall in the sea. Vinicaire would probably find that more amusing than tragic.

His right hand on the rough rock face and his left on the shaky wooden handrail, Teej let his mind drift to thoughts of Anna. Would she be able to withstand Rayleigh? She was tough and resourceful, and in truth, she'd done as well on her own as when he was with her. Charron and Mott were not easy opponents, and she'd prevailed over each. When she was with him on the frozen river, anxiety and the lingering effects of the Sump overcame her. Still, she'd picked herself back up. At the Groven, even wracked with self-doubt, she'd fought as best she could and had saved him from Andre's Etune creations. Mott, Charron, Andre, and Drowden. She'd faced them all and survived, yet still she wasn't comfortable in Basine or in a Haze. Until she allowed herself to face her own past, she'd never be able to truly master her Praxis. Behind the Veil, the most powerful Metiks and Dreamers were those whose minds were clear and confident.

Their awkward goodbye niggled at him. He should have thought of something better to say. Though he had helped her escape her old problems, he'd sent her into danger, and with no real words of encouragement or support. Those dark brown eyes of hers had seen too much horror, and likely they would be seeing more very soon. Rayleigh could show her all the treasures in the world to sway her to his cause, or open her mind to unimaginable terrors. Teej staked everything on her resilience.

Though unlikely, he hoped she might already be on her way back to their old hideout in Maxine's. Perhaps she should just disappear for a while and go into hiding, like Andre. They had allowed the Dreamer to escape and find a hidey-hole to recover. Perhaps Anna could do the same. Maybe in ten years, Teej would run into her in some safe corner of the Firmament. She'd have some new friends, and she'd be confident, secure in her abilities, no longer afraid, her past resolved and her future bright and beckoning.

While his attention drifted to thoughts of a safer world, a few moments passed before Teej noticed the spoon in his inside pocket was burning hot.

"Garret! Anna is trying to send a message!"

The old man balanced precariously between two wooden steps at the summit of the stairs, while Alby and Pappi waited at the top after already completing the ascent. Garret waved Teej forward.

"Does it look safe up there?" asked Teej, still distracted by the message from Anna.

Garret nodded solemnly. "I guess. This is your rodeo, kid."

"We are found out!" shouted Alby. His jaw was set, his eyes serious. "Our enemies mobilize their defenses. Prepare yourselves; I feel that any moment they will—"

The wooden steps detached. One-by-one, like a line of dominoes, the staircase unfurled from the mountainside. Garret jumped to safety, and Teej leapt after him. Too slow.

The old man shot out a hand but grasped thin air.

Hurtling to the ground, Teej shouted for help, but it was too late.

twenty-five

Much like the beginning of a nightmare, Anna couldn't remember exactly how she got to this place. Her eyes were locked on the orange and yellow lights that bled out into the night from the stained-glass windows of the church at the top of the hill. Against the dark-blue and black backdrop of the surrounding hills, it was a beacon. This was her destination.

Still, she lingered in the darkness. The night air chilled her while a strong wind swept through her clothes and penetrated her bones. Standing at the outskirts of a village, there were no streetlights or lamps to illuminate the night. Rather, a few torches flickered in the darkness. Looming trees seemed charged with intentionality as they towered over her in the gloom, their shadows corralling her toward her destination. Their very reason for existence was to block her route and narrow her choices down to one option: climb the hill and enter the church.

Her Sense wasn't yet refined enough to find Rayleigh's exact location, but she knew she was in a Haze. When she'd stepped off the Moonlight Road by choice, there were no more invisible walls to hold back the chill and the glimmering path leading the way had disappeared. She was in the world of a Dreamer again, and the Moonlight Road was far behind her.

Pushing her Haze Sense outward, Anna felt a saturation in the air. It was like a sponge full of water, but the substance here was Vig. Her Praxis crackled like static across the tips of her fingers, looking for an excuse to force itself out into the world. Something pushed back, equalizing the pressure. She was unsure whether the resistance came from the very nature of the place, or the Will of an Aesthete.

The bright windows of the church lit up a few scattered alcoves and statues across the architecture, but most of the vast structure was lost to shadow. She could make out the shapes of spires and towers, but the overall outline of the building was obscured. It rested on top of a jagged rock cliff, and the walkway to the entrance wound through a dark forest before being swallowed by a bright orange doorway. It looked vaguely warm and inviting, in stark contrast to the biting cold around her.

Hundreds of people marched in a procession up the slope. Leading the group were a handful of individuals in black ceremonial robes. As they moved past the dim torches, she could make out more details of the shuffling men and women. Their pace was slow and deliberate, full of pageantry. Anna estimated she could reach them before they got to the church.

In the dim light, Anna picked out the faintest outline of a paved path lined with scrubby bushes and trees, and set off as fast as she dared. Nearly tripping twice on dark roots and branches that spread like tendrils across the road from rotten old trees, she made her way up the steep incline.

Her raspy breathing became as loud as the rustle of the trees in the wind. The people ahead moved in silence. Anna paused when she reached the first torch, wondering why it looked so dim even up close. The flames were a faded orange and cast weak beams of light into the unnatural blackness. Realization slowly dawned on Anna that there were no stars. The sky above was like a flat piece of black fabric. The moon was gone too.

With aching legs as she pushed up the steep hill, Anna turned a corner in the snaking path to see the pilgrims hadn't gone far. Now that she was closer, they looked less threatening, but also less human. They walked like marionettes, shuffling and unnatural, and very slow. If she hustled, she could catch them, but what would she do when she reached them? Talk to them? Reason with them? Perhaps it would be best to blend in with the crowd.

She figured it would be better to enter the church with the crowd than enter alone when they had all taken their seats. If this was Rayleigh's Haze, it might be impossible to hide, but it was worth a try.

Despite the heaviness of her legs and the burning in her chest, Anna accelerated from a brisk walk to a run. Her eyes adjusted to the dark. Another torch. A twist in the road. Chest burning. A dirty puddle. Leap over it. Mouth dry, cold sweat. Anna could almost touch their black robes. Desperately out of shape, she gasped lung-fulls of cold air as she slowed from a run to a walk. Teej was right; she needed to hit the gym.

Edging close enough to be discovered at any moment, Anna tried to make out more details. Just formless black robes and metronomic steps that pulled them toward the glowing gateway of the church. After watching the dragging feet for another minute, Anna came to a disturbing realization: this felt like a death march.

Stretching out her Haze Sense, she tried to determine the nature of the procession. The air hummed with Vig as she got closer. Shuffling toward the back of the pack, her legs trembled nervously. Expecting them to spot her at any moment, she held her breath, but they shambled on, heedless of her proximity.

When they were just moments from the entrance, Anna stumbled. She clamped a hand over her mouth to stifle a curse, worried she might alert those around her. Checking to see what had caused her to trip, she saw a fallen woman's body sprawled across the path.

She bent to check on the woman, pulling the black hood to the side. A haggard face stared at her with blank features. The woman reached out a shaky hand to touch Anna's face, her toothless mouth making a wheezing, cracking sound. Grasping the woman's cold fingers, Anna felt life fade from them.

"Hold on. Please stay with me. I'll get help." The words sounded pathetic as they escaped her lips. There was no succor to be found here. The woman's hand fell limp. Touching her mouth, Anna felt no breath and then no pulse. It was the first time Anna witnessed someone's life leaving their body with her Haze Sense.

With shaking hands, Anna reached down and tugged off the woman's cloak. Turning the frail body over, she untwisted the garment to remove it from the now-naked corpse. At the back of the crowd, no one turned to watch or stop her.

After donning the cloak, Anna touched the woman's face again. In movies, they closed the person's eyes when they died, but these eyes were already closed. She allowed herself a moment to feel guilty about how little guilt she felt, then walked quickly to the back of the group, catching them just as they reached the doorway to the church. They didn't react when she gently nudged herself into the middle of the group.

With a throng of other lost souls, Anna walked through the bright entrance of the church, out of the cold night and into a fresh nightmare.

twenty-six

The church hall was vast and filled with echoes and whispers. It took a minute for Anna's eyes to adjust to the glowing braziers and sconces around the atrium. The flickering flames illuminated the pilgrims' blank faces, highlighting their unfocused eyes and gaping mouths. Anna pulled her own hood over her eyes to remain anonymous and tried to match their expressionless gazes. They milled in the middle of the entrance hallway, waiting for something or someone. She took the opportunity to scan the surroundings for danger.

The disorientating architecture had long, distorted curves and a lack of clean edges, tricking the eye into misinterpreting distance. The alcoves and cornices radiated from a long spine across the ceiling, giving the impression they were inside a ribcage.

Bone-white columns converged hundreds of feet above them, and the main hall branched off into smaller rooms at either side. The large gateways were so far away that they seemed tiny and were blocked with solid wood doors. Two fifty-foot stained glass windows flanked the central hall. Benches wide enough to fit almost a hundred people in each row sat on either side of a long passage broad enough for the pilgrims to congregate with plenty of space to spare. A multitude of brass dishes held hundreds of candles nestled in sand. The smell of incense and cloyingly sweet herbs filled the air but did not mask the mustiness.

Tapestries and murals filled with iconography littered every available space, but none of the imagery was Christian. There were no depictions of saints, angels, or Jesus. Instead, Anna was surrounded by imagery that evoked subtle nightmares. Every surface was covered with images of monsters and scenes depicting anguish, fear, and despair. The tableaus were charged with symbolism, but Anna did not have the knowledge to decipher their meanings or significance.

They were intensely fascinating though. Anna remembered the first time she'd been in a chapel. The depiction of the broken man on the cross haunted her, even as a young child. *Why did they do that to him?* she'd asked her dad. Now she felt that same sense of wonder anew.

On her left a mural towered over all the others. The scene portrayed a heavily armored king standing on a cliff overlooking a city full of spires. The perspective made him giant sized, and he looked ready to crush the buildings. The sun made a halo behind his head, and he held a massive black sword in one hand and a limp woman's body in the other hand. About half his size, she was gripped by her neck while blood flowed from her wounds to the ground, creating a lake around the city. At his feet, a circle of armored knights gazed at the king, each seeming as big as a castle.

Anna glanced to the other side of the hall at a mighty tapestry draped loosely from the wall, depicting a cast of a hundred characters. They were kings and knights, bearded men and musicians, layered on top of each other and stretching as far as she could see. The fabric depicted some sort of feast, and as Anna looked more closely, she saw dozens of anachronisms. One of the old men wore a watch, there was a car in the background on a hill behind a castle, and an ancient knight held a modern automatic rifle. The effect of a pop culture mash-up crudely painted in an archaic style was disturbing.

Oh no.

The nearest image was horribly familiar. Toward the bottom of the tapestry, a gigantic figure stood on an inky black boat, holding a hook in one hand. Charron. How many more figures would Anna recognize on these walls if she had the time to examine them?

Focus. The cavernous hall was filled with distractions purposefully. She had to look past the curiosities and stay focused.

Anna stretched her Haze Sense. Raising her hands in front of her body, she waited to feel a tingle in her fingertips. After a moment, she felt the distinctive thrum of Vig above her, resonating back as a rippling breeze across the surface of her skin. She let her eyes follow her Haze Sense upward. Far above the altar, she spied a mezzanine for the massive church organ. The pipes varied in scale from smaller-than-she-could-see to bigger-than-a-truck. Using her Haze Sense to penetrate the instrument's inner workings, she discerned this organ was not intended to play music. The Dreamer from this Haze would speak to her through this set of pipes.

And this Dreamer was unlike any she had met so far. The air was syrupy with his swollen Vig. It caught in her mouth and made her sluggish and disorientated. If every other Aesthete she had met was a flickering flame, she was now staring into the sun. The potency of this Haze and its creator was almost too much to bear.

Anna instinctively pulled the heavy black cloak tight around her shoulders. Trying to avoid discovery, she shuffled toward the middle of the crowd only to realize she would soon have to make a choice. The congregation split into two groups, one moving to the left and the other to the right. She was momentarily exposed and alone as the groups parted. Realizing how much she stood out, she made a choice and stepped hastily to her right. Blindly she followed as they formed into single file and moved around the side of the hall.

Biting her fingernails, she shuffled with the crowd toward a side door that was opening. Suddenly, clanking footsteps echoed loudly through the space. A knight stepped into view, and Anna glanced away lest she catch his attention. At the same moment, a different knight appeared through a door on the other side of the hall.

The knight closest to her was all shiny steel with glowing blue seams between the metal plates, his ornate armor decorated with metallic wings that stretched from the back of his helmet. The engravings of lions and dragons on the breastplate almost seemed alive as he moved with clockwork precision.

Two more knights appeared from both sides and waited for the line to move toward them. They joined the others to make six in total. Each of them carried long, curved halberds while two captains hefted kite-shaped shields taller than Anna.

She tried not to look nervous as she shuffled toward them. Suppressing her desire to flee, she fidgeted with her ring self-consciously, aware that she might need to use it at any moment.

At the start of the line, two of the knights swung a censer of incense on the end of a long chain. The clouds of scented air spread quickly, becoming a wall that swallowed the congregation in gulps. Each person leaned their head back and inhaled deeply before being consumed by the thick mist. As the congregation moved past the knights, they reappeared beyond the cloud on a set of stairs and gathered on a little wooden walkway about eight feet off the ground.

The final knight, garbed in the same armor, but with a wolf's pelt hanging over his shoulders, stood at the top of the balcony, apparently waiting for them to reach his position. The organ played a single, long, plaintive note and then fell silent again.

As the man ahead of her moved toward the knight, he tilted his head back and breathed in deeply with no hesitation. Anna was next in line. Should she do the same? She turned her head to the side and recoiled from a glimmering halberd blade just inches from her face. The knight would not allow her to turn back.

The decision was made.

Stepping forward, Anna lifted her head and opened her mouth wide while holding her breath. When her eyes began to sting and her lungs demanded air, she let her head drop and walked forward. The knight ignored her, apparently convinced by her subterfuge. As she cleared the clouds, she breathed in a little of the vapor. It was sweet and cloying. Rubbing her eyes, Anna followed the line and started to climb the stairs. Was stealth still an option? She decided to remain with the group. The longer she remained hidden, the better prepared she would be when she was finally noticed by the Dreamer.

Anna climbed the wooden staircase to the platform. An arm shot out, missing her by inches. The knight grabbed the woman next to her by the shoulders and tore off her robe. Anna backed away, almost falling off the platform. The woman shivered as he looped a noose around her neck. Tying additional ropes around her wrists and upper arms, he then bent low and looped coils between her ankles. The woman was sent to her doom with a lazy shove.

Drop, crunch.

The rope snapped tight.

For the first time, Anna heard someone try to speak. The woman wheezed and gasped, begging for help as she swung back and forth rhythmically on the thick rope. Anna tried not to react, but when she saw the woman's eyes roll back in her head, she stifled a scream.

Don't look away.

Forcing herself to remain calm, Anna watched the horror. The ropes were pulled toward the ceiling, transforming the woman into a macabre marionette. Her hands strained against the bonds and her bare feet curled up as she writhed and spasmed. After what seemed like an eternity, she went still. The knight nonchalantly prepared another noose for the next victim.

Anna numbly stepped away from the wooden platform, climbing down the stairs and retreating to the middle of the hall. To her right, one of the knights turned to look at her, but didn't move in her direction.

With sickening efficiency, the executions continued. One by one, the victims were stripped naked and pushed to their deaths. Their complicity was shocking. *Why aren't they fighting back?*

The complex pulley system carried the victims through the air toward the altar, forming a gruesome congregation around the sides of the church. Four twitching bodies were brought to the front. The ropes tied to their arms and legs animated the bodies to look like they were walking through the air, controlled by an unseen and cruel puppet master.

The horror overwhelmed Anna. *Why don't I stop this? Am I frozen?* By the time she pushed herself out of her stupor, almost half the people on either side were already dead.

"Stop this."

Her words didn't go anywhere; they fell from her lips but could not penetrate the stale air of the Haze.

"Stop this!" she shouted. This time her voice was amplified by her Praxis. Becoming a weapon of Will, her words spread into the Haze, disturbing the design of the Aesthete.

The knights on their podiums froze, but their potential victims portrayed little reaction. Milling around, the poor souls showed no sign of relief and barely noticed that their lives had been prolonged. Three of the hanging victims continued to kick and struggle, until there was only one. Finally, there was stillness and silence.

The remaining congregation turned to face Anna. She sloughed off the black robe and stood firm, exuding as much confidence and strength as she could manage. *I am an Undreamer, and I will not accept any of this.*

"Do you know who I am?" she shouted as loud as she could. Her voice shook, but she continued. "I am an Undreamer, and this will stop immediately. I came like you asked, now what do you want?"

Her words seemed to end the performance and the atmosphere deflated as the knights backed away from her and filed from the hall. Without looking in her direction, the people shuffled past her. One by one, they ghosted out the large doorway, and it took a long time for them to leave. Anna tried to catch their eyes as they passed, but they avoided her gaze.

All the heavy doors, including the main entrance, closed with a simultaneous slam.

Beneath the altar, a twelve-foot-tall solid oak door creaked open. Bending low to fit through the passage, a green-armored knight entered the hall. Remembering their plan, Anna thought of Teej. This was why she was here. She had to let her friends know they were clear to attack the Doxa.

Decked in ornate armor with ancient symbols and runes, the Green Knight was implacable in polished steel. He moved with a confident, smooth gait and made no sound despite his heavy armor.

Little details stood out, like the gleaming spikes at the knees and elbows. The armor was charred, more black than green. Blue flames flickered from the joints in his metal frame. Within that suit, Raguel perpetually burned, never free from pain.

In his right hand he carried a longsword. He placed it carefully in front of his chest, resting both arms lazily on the pommel. On his back, a shield swung as he moved, secured by loose leather straps. Anna's Haze Sense thrummed with overstimulation. There was simply too much Vig to process.

Anna closed her eyes and brought Teej to the forefront of her mind, readying herself to send him the message. She pictured the fine line of his chin, the gentleness of his blue-green eyes, the tone of his storytelling voice, and the lightness of his laugh, always warm, but sometimes melancholy. Her thoughts lingered on the strength in his hands when he pulled her out of the Sump or when he held her close in a comforting embrace.

She would help him now by letting her mind go to him, when so often she chased those thoughts away as though they were frivolous.

The Green Knight waited. He shifted his posture and regarded her with curiosity.

Anna's eyes moved past him to the bodies that started to wiggle at the end of their ropes again. One male and one female puppet swung awkwardly into position in front of her and the Green Knight.

The male puppet's hand went up to his face in a horrifying facsimile of a salute. "Shall Mr. Rayleigh give you away this time?"

The mouth moved but the eyes remained rolled back in the head. The ropes made the cadaver gesticulate wildly with exaggerated movements that were utterly unnatural. Anna recoiled. Rayleigh was talking though the dead man.

"Greetings, Anna Cassidy. Mr. Rayleigh is happy you came. Better late than never!"

Cassidy? No, that name died with her husband.

The voice crackled with reverb like an old guitar. It echoed around the hall, amplified by the curves in the architecture. This new enemy was the opposite of Drowden's bestial demeanor. Rayleigh's surrogate sounded like a talking doll with a busted speaker.

"There are two reasons you should heed what Rayleigh has to say. Rayleigh possesses the two qualities that you do not have: age and wisdom."

Modesty too. Anna took a moment longer to fasten Teej in her thoughts. She had to make sure he got the message.

Teej would have mocked the arrogance of Rayleigh's opening lines. Trying to ease the tension, he would have joked to Anna, whispered a sly aside, and then he would have confronted their enemy, unbowed.

"Do you know why you are detained?"

The puppet's mouth hung open while a rivulet of spittle and blood dripped from the corner of its lips. His question hung in the air. What answer was he expecting from her? Was this all a test? Both Garret and Teej had warned her about Rayleigh's persuasiveness. This nightmare wouldn't persuade anyone. *Never play their game; their game is always rigged.*

"I'm…an Undreamer. And I came to hear what *Rayleigh* has to say."

The longer she kept him talking, the more time Teej, Garret, and the rest would have to get into position. At that moment, she made up her mind that she was willing to sacrifice herself for their mission. If she died here so they could live, she would have no regrets.

"Rayleigh is going to ask you something. When that happens, you're going to say yes. We think agreeing would be best." The brittle voice crackled with static.

Below the hanging bodies, the Green Knight stood completely still.

Anna remained in motion, subconsciously preparing herself to make a stand. Why did her legs have to shake so much? "Just get on with it."

The latches of the large wooden door *thunked* as they locked behind her. She didn't turn around to acknowledge the threat.

"Since you got here, we've had such fun! But have you made a single *choice*?"

It seemed ridiculous that she was having this conversation with an animated corpse, but she had to treat the Dreamer like he was in the room in front of her. Since this was his Haze and he was present everywhere within it, Anna didn't have to try hard to imagine his presence. He used the cadaver to intimidate her, so she would treat it like a normal person—like a bank teller or someone trying to sell her car insurance on the phone.

Anna waited for him to continue. Long minutes stretched out uncomfortably.

The ropes uncoiled suddenly, and the body of the man fell to the ground with a wet slap. Anna turned away and leaned her hands on her thighs. She looked down at her feet; little red specks of blood dappled her white sneakers. With her insides heaving, Anna swallowed hard and tightened her fists to gain control of her clenching stomach.

"Please answer our questions. It prevents unnecessary mess," said the female marionette. The voice was still a singsong nightmare, but it was a woman's now. The puppet pointed at her with a floppy arm. The mouth opened and closed automatically and the head lolled backward. "We are happy to see our guest, but we have much to discuss. No time to be silly; we are not here to play. Do you know how we will make you listen to us?"

Anna took some time to compose herself and prepare an answer. Her body was still seized with a kind of numbness. "I'm going to guess threats to me or to my family."

"No," the body said as it threw up its arms.

Anna winced, expecting it to fall, but it remained upright. On the ground, the broken body of the man was splayed across the front pew, a broad pool of blood forming on the floor.

"Rayleigh knows you speak of family to mislead. You are not worried about your family. You are worried about your friends."

Anna felt the need to lean on something for a moment, but she didn't want to appear weak. Shuffling uncomfortably, she tried to keep her expression blank. This was like poker, and she'd never been any good at bluffing.

"You think you have a very clever plan," the voice whined. "You chose to face us alone, and you think this choice was brave and honorable. In truth, you have not made a single choice since you came here. Rayleigh always says that when you control a man's options, you control their choices."

"Obviously! If I had a choice, I would not be listening to this shit!" Anna's snappy response might have been a mistake, but the words came to her lips easily. This pomposity was unbearable.

Creak, rattle.

The ropes unfurled, and the woman's body fell too. This time Anna closed her eyes instead of turning away. The corpse landed on the tiled flood with a heavy crunch. Two more bodies were drawn across the hall, the ropes animating them in a crude facsimile of a walk, their legs bobbing up and down while the arms swung back and forth at the end of their strings.

"Oh, come on!"

The woman on the left had red, curly hair, the length Anna's had been until she'd just cut it. As her black robes fell away, she was wearing clothes that matched Anna's too. The male corpse had loose, tousled brown hair and now wore a baggy shirt and jeans with sneakers, just like Teej. When they reached the center, they both spoke in chorus.

"Rayleigh *made* you listen. He set you on a path a long time ago without you realizing it. A loooooong time ago."

Anna shook her head. It was hard to endure this nonsense. She had a big mouth, and she'd always been bad at pretending to like awful men. She tried to focus her Haze Sense and see past the puppets, but she couldn't seem to find Rayleigh.

"When your husband went in the river, did you *choose* to leave him behind and swim out of the water?"

"Stop this!" she shouted. The Word came easily when she was angry. The puppets fell silent, their heads dropping to their chests. "I'm not doing this again! I've spoken with monsters before, and underneath all *this,* you're just another little man."

"Oh, come now, I'm a bit more than that." It was his real voice, smooth and calm with a low rumble. He sounded like someone selling expensive coffee in a radio ad. The words reverberated around the hall, but she couldn't locate him. His voice emanated from the organ pipes.

"Do you think you chose to come here?" Rayleigh went on. "I used Garret to bait you into this. And do you think you *chose* to help Donnel? He is more manipulative than I am. At least I do not attempt to hide my ambition to control another's fate. The truth is that even he followed a narrow path with no branches. He lost his former partner, and he needed another to achieve his goals, and you were there. In a day, how many choices do you really make? How much of life is walking a narrow path?"

"I don't have time for this," she said, stalling him while simultaneously impatient for it to be over. "What do you really want?"

"Do you seek to rush me?" Rayleigh's tone was suspicious. "Or the opposite? No matter. I have kept everyone on the end of my strings for a very long time."

A blood red moon slid from behind the clouds and appeared in the stained-glass windows. With its appearance, a sliver of red light shone into the hall. Anna wondered why Rayleigh put it there. She assumed that everything was intentionally placed by Rayleigh in his own Haze.

Considering his words, she found herself leaning on a nearby pew for support. The fact that he wouldn't face her angered her. "I don't know what you want from me. Why you want me and my friends dead? Why did you—"

"Why did I help those mad Dreamers?" he interrupted. "You don't want to talk about them either, do you? You want the conversation to move away from them, but you can't help yourself. They are foremost in your mind."

Dammit. This was a game, and she had to make better moves. Anna had to maneuver the conversation sideways without giving away more information. Still unable to locate where he was hiding, Anna looked to the ceiling and the rafters.

"Why do the Doxa draw your ire, Anna?"

"Because Drowden sent me to the Sump! I'm going to kill him."

The mouths of the dead chattered for a moment in an utterly inhuman imitation of laughter. Three more slid across the railings to the front of the church, one with green and pink hair, one with ridiculously foppish clothes, and one with a long, straggly gray beard.

"You'll engineer Drowden's death, will you? You won't even consider another way to resolve your problems?" mocked Rayleigh.

"I have no choice! Everyone wants me dead, including you."

"I don't want to kill you." There was a mock solemnity in his tone, like he was hurt but sincere. Anna didn't need Haze Sense to know it was an act. "I don't want to kill *anyone*. This group of Dreamers and their religious dogma is *distasteful* to me."

"Distasteful?" Anna found herself shouting. "I'm speaking with dead bodies in your mystical murder church!"

As Anna shouted, the Green Knight straightened to attention. It was an implied threat she understood. This conversation was taking a toll on her. Her legs wobbled as she lost her temper.

"I didn't murder anyone," replied Rayleigh evenly. "No lives were lost here. And is this church not familiar? I did not choose it for my own benefit. Was it *not* the happiest day of your life then?"

"No," she said with a tremble. "I don't know this place." Anna wasn't sure if she was lying.

"Good!" he said with genuine warmth. "It's a *good* thing when we forget, even if we lose the important days. The memories that teach us nothing must be left behind, or they drag us backward. If not the ceremony, then perhaps we could have relived your reception instead. You danced with him, did you not? I could dance with you, Anna. I could wear his face, and you could pretend you were back with him. Would you like that?"

"Fuck you," she said, her voice quivering. A spasm shook her body, like a nervous twitch she could not suppress. He

229

shouldn't be *allowed* to talk about those memories. This wasn't fair. She was coming undone.

Desolation.

"This was all just to control your *choices*, Anna. Not only to lead you to this moment and to *prepare* you for our meeting, but to make sure you were receptive. As I told you, when you control someone's options, you control their choices. Your path had to be narrow enough that you would breathe the poison without resisting."

Of course! The smoke she'd breathed—it was poison.

These victims weren't real people; she could feel it now. They were Etunes: illusions created by Rayleigh. He had conjured them to fool her into breathing the incense without resisting. Anna felt the poison numbing her and slowing her reactions, causing her body to gradually fail from the bottom up. In a few minutes, she would collapse and this fight would be over before it could even begin.

Anna looked at the Green Knight suspiciously as he stood motionless.

"They are *my* puppets, whether they are alive or dead. Someone always pulls the strings. Right now, Teej pulls yours, but I pull his. This kind of life need not continue. You pulled the strings of your husband, did you not? He didn't smile very much that day. You rushed him into a life he wasn't ready for, because you thought marriage would save you both. When he went in the water, you wouldn't let him drag you under. Quite the opposite, in fact. Now you'll survive, while your friends will surely die."

One by one, the puppets fell to the ground.

Elise. *Crunch.*

Garret. *Crunch.*

Teej. *Crunch.*

Each time, Anna wanted to jump away, but there was too much numbness in her body to react. Cracked skulls, pale white bones jutting through flesh, blood everywhere. This was all a trap.

No. Oh no.

A suspicion formed in her mind, and there was only one way to test it. She had to find out for sure.

"My name is Anna."

The knight didn't move. She waited a moment, took three deep breaths, four, then said it again louder. "Did you hear me, Green Knight? My name is Anna!"

No reaction. *That isn't the Green Knight.*

Anna gasped in alarm as her legs slid out from under her. Her hands grasped the wooden bench nearby, but her legs were dead weights. The numbness crept up slowly but inexorably. She could no longer command her own body.

"We have plenty of time to talk, Anna. Please, let your worries melt away. There's nothing you can do. Let all of the fear go. When you can't make any choices, your path has narrowed to a point and all you can do is *be*. No need to fear. No need for your blood to burn so hot."

They would all be killed unless she could warn them somehow.

Anna pictured Teej as her world went black. She thought of the fine line of his chin, the gentleness of his blue-green eyes...

twenty-seven

"Teejay, wake up! Annie would kill me if anything happened to you!"

Anna! Where was she? Where was *he*?

The words penetrated the fog in his mind and became a focal point for Teej to reconstruct his equilibrium around. It wasn't Anna. This high and shrill voice belonged to Elise.

Black shapes moved across his field of vision. Teej's head thrummed with waves of pain. Memories came back in chunks, and he struggled to put events back into order. Anna was walking the Moonlight Road to meet with Rayleigh. He let her go alone, so they could launch this desperate assault on the Doxa at Kanna Island. When Anna sent him the message that it was safe to attack…

He'd fallen.

Teej squinted against the painful light. The sun was low on the horizon again. The sun never set in Avalon.

"Sit up slowly, my friend," said Pappi. "We are in no immediate danger."

Pappi was wrong; they were in danger. This was their only chance, and their time was limited. Anna had sent the all-clear message, but they were back on the beach where they started.

Wait a minute! Teej was getting another message. The Fetish was hot in his pocket *again*. What did that mean?

"Another message from Anna. How long…" Teej struggled to get the words out. His vision doubled, and the light burned his eyes. He had a concussion, and perhaps some bruised ribs, but this place was rich in Vig and Teej was the best healer of all of them. Calling upon his Praxis, he focused on a healthy image of himself, and Willed his own body to conform to it and eliminate his injuries. The pain eased in his chest as his ribs reknit themselves. Torn muscles snaked back into place. Cracking open his eyes, he looked around.

The sky was a palette of muted pastels fading to gray as the sun set. The soft sand was beneath his head, and he sifted some between his fingers. The smell of the sea filled his lungs. As Elise bent over him, her green and pink hair and soft features were at odds with the harsh rocks behind her. She shivered, her loose-fitting top exposing one pale shoulder to the wind and drizzling rain. Garret leaned over him as well, the old man's gray mane blowing in the breeze. Pappi's angelic face showed only the merest hint of concern. Teej marveled at his friend's ability to look unperturbed at all times. Only Alby looked worried about possible threats. The boy scanned their surroundings farther down the beach, his Periapt readied in front of him. The hockey stick thrummed with energy. Alby was ready to fight.

Sitting on a nearby rock adjusting his hat, Vinicaire said, "I wonder if you're less clumsy than you seem. Perhaps you've been practicing falling off cliffs for a while now, for you landed in precisely the right spot you'd be aiming for if you wanted us to accompany you into battle. Your medal-worthy dive certainly got us all exactly where you wanted us. It appears that I may be assisting you after all. I'm here now with nothing better to do."

Elise jumped up to stand by Vinicaire. "I'm ready for this. I've practiced everything you taught me, and I told Anna I'd keep Teejay safe."

"Quite..." Vinicaire trailed off.

Sitting up slowly, Teej assessed the situation. He was on a patch of scrubby grassland by the beach. Directly above, the broken slats poked out of the cliff face like splinters. Most of the wooden walkway lay in ruins around him, rotten timbers embedding themselves in the soft sand.

"How did you get down?" he managed to ask.

"The air is rich with Vig," said Pappi. "We swim in a soup of miracles. Together, we floated down the mountainside."

"That sounds like fun." Teej rubbed the back of his neck.

"The cliff collapsed, and you almost fell on my boat," Vinicaire commented, his eyes filled with mirth.

"*The hills, they tumbled to the ocean*," Teej chanted.

"Come again?" said the Dreamer.

"Sorry. Got a song stuck in my head. Never mind. I got another message from Anna. How long was I out?"

"Ten minutes," said Alby. "If there's another message, it can mean only one thing. We are done for."

"Nonsense," said Vinicaire. "If she sent a *second* message, she is merely reaffirming the *first* one. She is willing us to haste. That is surely the long and short of it."

Teej shrugged at Pappi. "He could be right. We don't have enough information to know what the message means. If Vinicaire's keen sense of danger is not disturbed, we need not be afraid."

"Yup," drawled Garret. "Like he says, if this lily-livered jellyfish is brave enough to press on—"

"You are such a dinosaur!" snapped Elise.

Teej held a hand up to silence them. "Enough. I know things aren't exactly going to plan. Something doesn't feel right. But here we are, and there's no going back."

Elise tutted and skipped away, while Garret shook his head. Alby gazed off into the distance with a troubled expression.

Teej glanced to the top of the cliff where he could still see the outpost and the old lighthouse, but there was no easy path to the top now. Pappi was correct about the amount of Vig present. The air hummed with it. There was so much potentiality in the Haze that every surface took on a hyper-reality. Selmetridon might be grander, the Moonlight Road might be more wondrous, the House of Ware might be more intoxicating, but no place was more *vibrant* than Avalon.

This is too beautiful a place for a battle.

"Did I bounce when I hit the ground?" asked Teej with a grimace.

Elise burst into giggles. Garret heaved Teej to his feet before slapping him on the shoulder roughly.

"You didn't make it all the way to the ground," replied Pappi. "You landed on a ledge, then the girl ran up to help and we all carried you down here. It took a while. Vinicaire took the longest to climb up the beach. Those doubts and fears are heavy to carry."

"Your friends are distasteful, Donnel," said Vinicaire.

"They'll grow on you," murmured Teej. "Alby, what's the situation? What do we know?"

"When our enemies became aware of our arrival, they helped the walkway fall. They have not escaped yet, but perhaps they can't. Kanna is peculiar, full of secret routes and ancient doors. I fear they have not left because they feel there is no need. They are not afraid to face us."

"Perhaps our appearance helps them?" Pappi offered. "We are fuel to their fire?"

Vinicaire nodded. "If they seek to create their Fluxa, our presence will not calm the situation. I suggest we do our dirty business quickly."

Pappi gestured to the lighthouse. "The house of dynamite waits for its guests. Come in, little sparks."

"No time for flowery words brother." Alby scowled. "Teej, we need your keen Senses. Do you detect anything?"

Teej was relieved that Alby was there. The boy would not feign sympathy or wax poetic. His conviction to stay on task was what they all needed now.

Narrowing his eyes, Teej eyed a shadow in the cliffside. A passage from the beach snaked toward the cleft as it became a cave. It might be a dead end, but it might also be an entrance.

Garret noticed the cave, too. "That looks like a terrible idea. Let's do it."

Elise frowned. "We can't go that way, can we?"

"My dear," said Vinicaire, "I think that is the *only* way we can go."

Teej guessed the murky, wet cave connected with the pristine white lighthouse far above, but the connection was labyrinthine. From the outside, the island appeared tiny, but Teej's Haze Sense told him it was far larger inside.

Something else niggled at the edges of his Senses. There remained some vague splinter he could not dislocate. Something *had* followed them there, a mysterious presence that stayed out of sight. Something prepared to wait for the proper moment to reveal itself.

The only consolation was that there was no taint of Drowden's mysticism yet, nor was there any trace of the corruption of the Apoth's creations. It was all masked by the power of this island. Teej wondered if the nature of Avalon would benefit his enemies or his allies. *Cui bono.*

Alby gestured in readiness. "Awaken from your daydream. We must venture into the cave with haste. No reason to hide our intentions now."

Teej turned to Vinicaire. The Dreamer spoke before Teej could ask a question. "Yes, I'll come. I'm ready to wash my hands of this whole situation."

"Look after Elise and help however you can," said Teej.

"This is really happening?" Elise shrieked.

Garret led the way. "Where the knife meets the bone, Elise. Where the knife meets the bone."

twenty-eight

Anna fixated on the wooden doorway of the church. Only twenty or thirty feet away, it remained solid and locked. She did not see a way to escape, and she couldn't move her legs anymore. She was running out of options. Rayleigh's words wormed their way into her consciousness even when she tried to close him out. Although she couldn't oppose him or escape, she hated having to listen to him.

Pushing her limp body off the wooden bench, Anna flopped to the ground and crawled across the marble floor toward the back of the hall. She moaned in frustration as her limbs failed her. Her numb legs were dead weights, and all the muscles below her chest refused to obey her commands. Pulling her body with the power of her arms, she struggled until they burned and ached. Her breathing was getting shallow. How long would she last?

"I assure you, the poison is for my protection only. The substance in your blood is called '*eitr*,' and it is both the source and the end of all life. It is fast acting and, if I wished it, lethal too. If you try to get away from this place, your heart will snap like an elastic band. I am doubly insured of my safety because your infusion is also a paralytic. You must realize that I could not live this long by taking risks. I am sure you cannot harm me, but you do seem to have a habit of getting *out* of predicaments: Mott and Avicimat are no small feats."

"I'll add you to that list!" she snarled. It was an empty threat, but maybe the bravado could keep her spirits up for a little longer, or perhaps her words of defiance could feed into her own Praxis and help her fight the poison in her body.

"Fret not, Anna! You *will* make it through this predicament. It will take a while for everything to play out in Avalon. We should talk while we wait. Will you tell me what you saw on the Moonlight Road? I have never walked it myself."

Anna wanted to scream, but she could barely breathe. Teej and Elise could be dying right now, and she felt powerless.

"Fuck you!"

"There's no reason to take this treatment personally. I promise, you will survive this day, and none of your enemies will threaten you again afterward. This is a very turbulent time for our community, but it *will* come to an end. Sometimes it takes one night of knives to make a hundred nights of peace. If I hadn't intervened, you would most likely be dead by now. I've saved you many times before. I am the *architect* of your survival.

"Do you want to know what will happen next?"

Anna *did* want to know—she *needed* to know—but she dreaded what he would say, so she continued to crawl in silence. After a few sluggish moments, she rested her head on the cool floor and focused on her breathing, trying to pull air into her constricted lungs.

"Tell me!" she croaked.

"It's all about the anarchist. I *need* to find him."

"Wildey?" Anna's mind raced.

"It's unusual that I can't find him. It's time for him to die. I know that your boyfriend can locate him. Despite the bad blood between them, they maintained a bond. Did you know they used to be close?

"I thought it might force him out of hiding if you were in trouble. Then, I could follow you to his location. Why didn't you go to him? Where *is* he?"

Anna remembered Andre talking about Wildey while she ate pancakes. That meal led them to this dark path. The wrong path. While her mouth was full of pancakes.

She almost laughed. "I don't know," she lied.

Her breathing eased a little. Momentarily, the poison relaxed its grip on her so her panic receded. Starting to plot, she glanced around desperately. Could she still push through this Haze and out the other end?

"Why are you doing this?" she asked.

"Cleaning house. What a mess! I cannot overstate the importance of tidiness. When you leave crumbs, the kitchen fills with rats. The Occultist is foul. You call him…Drowden? What he did to you was nasty business. And the experiments of John Murray Speare are even worse. The Doxa's nonsense needs to stop, and I am confident your friends will fix that.

"The cleaning won't stop there. I need to remove more filth. A fine, old gent like Garret is a decent Metik, but his mind is gone and he is ready to die. As for Donnel, he is too naïve for my tastes. Naivety is the worst mental vice. There's a place for the naïve Behind the Veil. It's cold and it's under the ground."

As Rayleigh droned on, Anna seethed. A fire burned in her and her ring flared for a second, straining against the power of this place. Both palms on the ground, she pushed herself halfway up, then fell hard. Her cheekbone cracked down on the cold marble with a crunch. Her fire went out.

"Raguel will clean everything. Anna, you are the only one from your whole troupe that matters. All of them became redundant when you appeared. An Undreamer. That is something special! Although you are weak and clueless, you can be taught."

Anna didn't want to say the words, but they came out through clenched teeth, "Just… let them go. Please don't kill Teej."

"It's all out of my hands, and I agree it is upsetting. Before too long, you will look back on this moment and consider your attitude childish. Your boyfriend's time is up and there's nothing you can do about it. In a few hours, all your friends will be gone and everything will be a good deal better for you and me. Only then can our community *heal*. Afterward, you *will* help me track down the anarchist.

"In a way, Wildey is most responsible for your boyfriend's fate. I see now that perhaps sending my Green Knight has been a mistake. I would call off Raguel if I could. I really would. Alas—"

"You're lying!" Anna screamed. "You just told me you planned this all along."

She concentrated on her ring but was too weak to summon its power. She had failed Teej, and their plan was doomed.

Anna savored the memory of his healing touch in the Groven. She remembered resting her head on his shoulder on the boat. There were so many times he had chased her fear away and made her glad to be alive. Anna had protected him from the Midnight Man and nursed him back to health. They had gone through all of that together, and now they would die apart. Teej was going to lose his life because she was too weak to stand up.

Rayleigh continued to grandstand. Every word burned away more time.

"Someone must be willing to make changes or the Firmament will fall to stagnation. While the Green Knight is stoic and loyal, Gwinn sits in front of a mirror, lost in his own reflection. I went to Selmetridon, you know? Can you *imagine*? I tried to talk with him. I think I talked *at* him. He is lost to the world. Gwinn has fallen into Torpor. Even the mighty can be claimed by that silent, smothering assassin. When I approached the Green Knight, I did not expect him to be so receptive. After languishing so long, he needed a *purpose*, so I gave him one and now he is with *me*."

As Anna lifted her head, pain raked her face like a clawed hand. Weakness saturated her arms, and she shook with strain as she tried to lift her dead weight of a body. The more she struggled, the faster the poison in her blood circulated through her in a thin stream of corruption. If the Eitr made her powerless, why was her Will straining to combat it?

Because I can fight it.

Tensing her whole body, Anna summoned the strength to fight. Meanwhile, Rayleigh continued to goad her.

"I helped your enemies, but only to give them sufficient fire to burn each other up. You know of the Choir? Perhaps not. A group of Muses work together to enhance the potency of an Aesthete. They are a mighty resource, perhaps one that is *too* useful and *too* powerful. I sent them to help make the Occultist's portals more deadly, to make John's clockwork Pilgrims more resilient, and to help the Doxa craft their little paper deity. I gave them just enough spark to get their little project started. And there is a new way to use that power. I gave them a hint simple enough for them to follow. A monstrous thing, but a necessary one: the blood.

"When this Fluxa Haze of theirs Spirals, everything will be cleansed. Everything. Except Wildey, I suppose. The Choir is gone, Garret will find peace, your boyfriend will pay the price for his naivety, and this little schism will be over. Yes, very tidy indeed. And long in the planning I tell you. I—"

For the first time, Rayleigh stopped talking. When he momentarily paused, it signaled to Anna that her intuition was correct. He didn't want her to burn herself free.

In the past, before Anna used her fire, she felt it strain to be loosed on the world. When she burned the werewolf, the spark threatened to become a flame, and when she burned Mott, the flame demanded a conflagration. But she always pulled it back. Garret's words stayed with her. *Your pain will burn them all. Burn the world. Burn us all. Out.* It had been a warning to her to temper that flame, but she couldn't constrain the fire any longer.

In a world of dwindling light...

Anna stoked the bonfire within. Her Periapt ignited and scorched the skin around her finger black, and then spread from there. She sent the flames into her infected veins instead of into the world. Targeting the poison alone, it flowed through her blood and wrapped around her heart before coursing through her whole body. The toxins fizzled and popped within her. She *saw* the black, sticky tar in her blood. Her back arched as pain overcame every one of her senses. Glowing, ragged lines of orange and red burned so brightly they could be seen through her skin.

Her heart stopped, and for a moment, Anna was an avatar of pure flame. Then, with a thump, her heart beat once more. The poison broke down from black sludge to powder until the links between the atoms split.

The Eitr was obliterated, and she was free.

No exertion of Will so great came without cost. Fighting against the poison and the unrivalled power of Rayleigh in his Haze, Anna let out one final burst of flame, then passed out.

twenty-nine

"Just let Alby do it."

Teej nudged Elise away from the heavy wooden doorway. She seemed to think she could pick locks, but they'd humored her long enough. Sulking, she threw the bent hairpin aside and tutted loudly.

"Don't worry, hun, the kid isn't any better at lock picking than you," said Garret. "He's just gonna hit it with a big stick"

Ignoring them all, Alby stepped forward and ran his hand over the door. Stepping back, he nodded gently as if he'd found what he was looking for. He swung his Periapt into the wood. The impact made a barely audible thud, but he let out a little groan and held the stick in place. Cracks spread out from the point of impact, and then the wood transformed to flakes of thin ash, falling to the floor like a carpet of dead leaves.

Elise's frustration disappeared, and she gasped. "That was amazing."

Without looking at her, Alby simply said, "Thank you."

Together, they huddled to look through the doorway. Inside, the gloom was hard to penetrate. Even this close to the entrance, Teej's Haze Sense detected no details, but something of great power lay ahead.

"Come on," he said, stepping inside as confidently as he could manage. The rest filed in behind him.

They squeezed through the crevasse in single file, the light from the beach fading behind them as they entered the purple luminescence of the cave. As Teej expected, it was much bigger inside than it looked from the outside. Stalactites and stalagmites subdivided the space. Bare rock, slick with slimy cave water, reflected the light from torches and braziers located around the edges in the shadows. Teej's first steps reverberated around the interior of the huge space. He traipsed through puddles of sulfurous water. The whole place reeked of brimstone and burning oil. Teej's Haze Sense tingled with the occult energies and ancient thaumaturgies that filled the air. The Doxa created this place for old, dead Gods and terrible new ones. It was an ancient catacomb used for secret ceremonies, blood rituals, and human sacrifice.

Pressing forward through the cavern, Teej stayed in the front while the rest filed behind. The farther they went, the more the labyrinth opened up before them. At first, they stepped around the stagnant pools, but eventually, the brackish water came up to their ankles.

"Ruined," declared Vinicaire as he examined his sopping shoes. Everyone ignored him.

They followed a line of torches and glowing fungi that set out a path through the widening cave. Teej couldn't see the walls anymore, just the trail ahead and the water beneath them. The air smelled thin and stale, and the dripping stalactites made an occasional plop in the silence. Eventually, the path looped around to the right, and as they cleared a narrower section, they came into a huge central chamber.

"Beyond this point, we enter the Fluxa Haze," warned Pappi. He touched Elise's arm. "Do not lose yourself."

"That goes for all of you," warned Teej. "I've been in a Fluxa Haze. It's different from anything you've experienced before. Even a Metik's mind can be affected. Your memories, your emotions, even the essence of your personality will be open to the Haze. Remember who your friends are and remember why you are here. Do not let this place turn us against one another."

"We'll be careful, kid," said Garret with a slap on Teej's back.

They trudged deeper into the cave until they came to the end of the path and saw the opposite end of the sanctum. Bare rock was sculpted to form a mighty, empty throne.

"I was expecting some big demon thing," said Elise. "And maybe lots of little demon minions."

"As was I," said Vinicaire, laying a hand on her shoulder.

"What should I do when the fighting starts?" asked Elise.

"Stick close to me, girl," said Vinicaire. "Though these Metiks can change and influence this Haze, I have my own means of protection. I cannot Dream a little Dream here in someone else's domain, but I possess some enchanted items of protection that I have always wanted to try. I'm sure they will suffice."

"Shush!" snapped Alby. "Something stirs." Inching forward, his hockey stick glowed as he held it in front of him like a makeshift torch. Suddenly, he froze.

"We're in the middle of it," whispered Pappi.

"The middle of what?" asked Elise.

Teej stretched out his Haze Sense and immediately understood the concern of Pappi and Alby. In the cave all around them, a violent Haze whirled like a storm, but in this spot in the center: nothing.

"So…what now?" asked Elise. Her question was met with silence.

"Welcome to the abiogenesis of a new divine being!" They heard the Apoth before they saw him. Then he stepped into view from behind the throne. A long crow mask, like the ones worn by plague doctors in the seventeenth century, covered his face and muffled his voice. Above a beak and behind thick glass goggles, two bulging eyes gazed out at them. A long, black leather overcoat covered his tall, thin body, and his scarecrow arm pointed at them as he spoke.

"They do not see your wonder. Yes? No? My Lord, they are blind to the New Motive Power."

The voice was high-pitched and manic. Garret leaned in to whisper to Teej, " He won't stop us. Do you see the madness in his eyes? We should eliminate this threat quickly."

The Apoth was in a state of Torpor. For a moment, they were in the eye of a storm, but any second, it could Spiral. Muttering incomprehensibly under his breath, the man was distracted.

"Alby," Teej waved the boy over. "This Haze is precarious. You must be ready to act quickly. If this creation of the Doxa, the New Motive Power as he calls it, makes an appearance, strike quickly and decisively."

Alby looked resolute with his hockey stick grasped firmly with both hands. Confident the boy was ready, Teej turned to address his enemy. He put his arms out to show he wasn't a threat then cautiously stepped forward.

"John, you know me. I am a Metik and I've brought some representatives of my order. This Fluxa Haze must *stop*. We have judged you in violation of the tenets of our creed. You have broken the rules of the Aesthetes and created a Haze likely to Spiral. If you step down now, your punishment need not be severe."

The Apoth's head wobbled to the side like a confused animal. That was a bad sign. The long beak of his mask made him look inhuman, but it was the eyes behind the mask that worried Teej the most.

"Shall I just cancel the scheduled birth of my theological father? Shall I tell the ether to formulagate at a later date? Is it best I tell my messiah his new dawn should wait till nighttime?"

The ranting paused for only a moment.

"Shall I just check with the custodians of the Firmament, hmmm? I assume Enkidu has requested an extension. What of our current overseer? Does Siegfried demand that I step down?"

"Those are old names." Garret's voice was commanding and firm as he stepped to Teej's side. He sought to pierce the Aesthete's madness. "Words from before my time, so old they mean nothing. You've seen what happens to Dreamers that try to create Fluxa. Meddling with old legends and myths leads to madness."

The Apoth jumped back as if struck, stumbling on his own black cloak. "Wisdom there was in those old thaumaturgies." The Apoth pointed and twitched as he spoke. "Age does not bring wisdom. You are proof of that. Yes? We have succeeded where many others failed. Things are made better for everyone. Prices, worthwhile prices, were paid. You will see. In the end, you will all see."

"What of Ozman?" challenged Teej. "Was the price of losing your brother to the Sump worthwhile? And where is Drowden now? The Occultist has left you to face us alone."

"Ozman made a valuable contribution to our work. I forgive him for being too weak to see its conclusion."

In his peripheral vision, Teej saw Vinicaire back away. Was the Dreamer considering retreat? Teej hoped he would maintain his nerve for a few more minutes.

"You don't understand," the Apoth went on. "You don't know how the new blood economy works. Rayleigh shared the revelations of the new dogma with us and it makes us strong. I do not need my fine companion any more. Not to kill all of you."

Teej shuddered as he felt a familiar breeze, an old smell from a distant memory. Sand in his eyes, the glare of a distant sun...*I remember this.*

He tried to shake off the feeling, but the Apoth lifted his arms and the braziers and torches went out. Total darkness.

thirty

Teej stood in a desert. Yellow sand stretched out in every direction, and overhead, the raging sun beat down, surrounded by a swirling nebula of glowing stars. He pulled down the hood of his cape, put his hands on his hips, and waited for the giant in front of him to speak.

A creature of stone and dust rose from the ground. Over forty-foot-tall, it was just a chest, arms and a head with indistinct features like an unfinished sculpture. Time seemed to reverse every few seconds as its hands crumbled to dust, then the fingers reformed in an endless loop of entropy and creation. The giant didn't move, but Teej felt sure it was aware of him.

"Where am I?" asked Teej. "Who are you?"

"What did you expect me to be?" asked the giant. The words didn't come from his lips. Rather, Teej heard them inside his own head.

"Something more familiar, more personal," said Teej. The words came from his mouth without his volition.

"I have been waiting for you," said the giant.

"Since you took Linda?" asked Teej. Again, he tried to say something different, but the giant controlled his words. Teej's mind was clouded. He was a prisoner, and unable to resist, he slowly fell to one knee and bowed.

A grinding stone hand stretched toward him, and his knees buckled under the weight of the heavy palm on his head.

"Abandon your burdens. In this desert, you lost Linda. Now you can rest here with her forever."

"Yes," said Teej. He felt his own mind drift away from him, his consciousness dissolving.

"Welcome home, Donnel."

"I am home." Teej's flickering resistance faded. A tear streaked his cheek despite the smile on his face.

"Be at peace, son."

Son? No, this wasn't right. Where was he?

Shaking free, Teej righted himself and looked at the giant. "You are the New Motive Power," he said with his own words.

"I am," it replied.

"Get out of my head," he commanded. Instantly, the fog obscuring his thoughts cleared. Although his surroundings looked like a desert, he was in the Doxa's Fluxa Haze. For just a moment, it infiltrated his mind, but now he was free.

Or was it just a moment?

Urgency pushed him on, and Teej pointed an angry finger at the giant.

"Take me to my friends," he commanded with the Word, and a door appeared in the giant's chest. Through the deep sand, Teej trudged forward as quickly as he could.

"They are already lost," said the New Motive Power.

"We'll see about that," said Teej as he walked to the door and peered inside.

The atmosphere changed to the acrid scent of petrol fumes and blood filling the air. Through the doorway, Teej saw a gas station at night. Bright spotlights shone on the forecourt while the rest of the parking lot was swathed in darkness. A silver Dodge was parked by a rusty gas pump. Someone stood at the counter looking out to the deserted road. A buzzing, purple neon sign flickered on and off over the door. Teej tried to read it, but the letters were in Cyrillic.

Teej closed the door behind him, yellow sand leaking into this new dream. Behind him, the door disappeared completely.

As he passed the car on his way to the gas station entrance, he noticed the keys were in the ignition, but there was no driver. The engine idled. With a sense of dread, he lingered outside the storefront.

The assistant at the cash register looked at Teej, and his form shimmered like a mirage. He gestured for Teej to walk in the door.

"I am Peter!" the man called out with a wave. Before Teej could respond, the man screamed as he shook violently then disappeared.

Something about this place didn't make sense. Feeling a familiar hum of Vig, Teej turned quickly with his Periapt in his hand to check the road. When he saw Alby, he breathed a sigh of relief.

"We are the first ones to awaken," said Alby as he stepped out of the darkness, hockey stick Periapt in one hand and his clothes stained with dirt.

"Are you—"

"I am fine," said Alby. "I thought I would find Garret first."

"His mind is already foggy," said Teej with concern. "I fear this form of attack may be his weakness. He seems okay now, but before the Moonlight Road, he was barely able to button up his shirt. Wait, why are we at a gas station?"

"Because this Fluxa brings forth our worst memories," said Alby. "And my parents died on this road."

"Oh God, are you—"

"I am fine," interrupted Alby stoically. "We have to keep moving."

Teej nodded solemnly as he agreed with the boy. The two of them had escaped the mental prison, but not the physical one. They were still in the Fluxa Haze and threatened by whatever the New Motive Power really was. They had to find their friends and get out completely.

"This way." Alby pointed his stick at the car. Teej headed for the passenger door, but Alby cut across him and opened the trunk.

"Good instincts," said Teej as he saw the lights peeking out from the next portion of the Haze in the trunk. Without hesitation, Alby jumped inside and Teej followed, stepping into the back of the car and falling through the portal.

They fell for a few feet before landing next to some stone ruins on a hillside. Alby landed in a crouch on the rocks, but Teej fell face first onto a patch of scrubby grass.

"Ouch," he complained, picking himself up. The air was thin, suggesting they were high in the mountains. Thick clouds made their surroundings gloomy, but a small bright patch overhead suggested it was midday here, wherever they were.

Ahead of them, a man in smart clothes sat in lotus position in front of a mighty bronze statue that looked like the Buddha, but with a sinister, upturned smile. Leaving Teej behind, Alby set off at a run. As he closed in on the man, he shouted out. "Brother!"

Pappi did not respond.

"Alby, wait!" called out Teej. Running up the hill, he leapt over broken rocks and closed in on his friends. When he reached Alby's side, he saw the boy's dismay. Pappi was in a trance, his eyes a milky white.

"Listen to me," pleaded Teej. "I don't think this is who you're looking for."

Teej's Haze Sense blazed, and he perceived the form of Pappi outlined with a hazy aura.

"I know my brother," snapped Alby, his eyes wide and his hands shaking. "Something has a hold of him."

Teej turned to the statue. "There was a giant similar to this in the desert."

"I saw it too," said Alby. "At the gas station we were observed by a figure in the stars. I believe it was the spirit of the New Motive Power."

"How do we wake him up?" asked Teej.

Alby held his brother's hand while their foreheads touched.

"They shout to scare us off," the boy whispered under his breath. For long moments, it seemed like the words didn't reach Pappi. Eventually, he blinked and cleared his eyes.

"Confidence is quiet," he said finally. "And refuses to bow to fear."

Pappi shook himself, slowly stood, and turned to face them. "I am glad to see you both. I was…very far away."

"We have three more friends to find," said Teej. "The New Motive Power seems to have no problem clouding the minds of Metiks."

"But we can shake ourselves free," said Pappi as he clasped Alby's shoulder. "Or we can be brought back by the love of our companions. We must remember that we are still in the caves beneath the island in Avalon. The Apoth is still here, and we must find him."

"Where now?" Teej asked Alby.

"I sense no more doors."

"The best route is the one that confronts our enemy," said Teej as he walked toward the bronze statue. Before he reached it, a door appeared in its chest. Together, the three of them walked through.

Teej covered his face against a flash of light. When he opened his eyes, he found himself lying in a puddle of water on the cave floor. He struggled to rise. Pappi and Alby were already awake, although they hadn't quite recovered their equilibrium yet. Ahead of them, an unconscious Garret was guarded by Elise, who stood over him clutching her sword.

"About time you all opened your eyes!" she said as she brandished her weapon fiercely.

Teej assumed she would be the last to awaken, but she was the first. "Why isn't Vinicaire ready to fight?" he grumbled as he gestured at the unconscious Dreamer.

"Great question!" shouted Elise. "I'll ask him when he wakes up."

Noticing her eyes were wide with fright, Teej followed the direction of her sword point with his gaze. The giant from their collective dreams was in front of them. This different version contained the combined features from all their visions, merged into a fresh nightmare.

The New Motive Power sat in the throne that was empty before they entered the Hazes. It was perhaps eleven feet tall, so it towered over them even while sitting. Wearing a human form, it had sandy skin covered with wiry, cord-like muscles. Its hands and feet looked more like hooves with three sharp claws on each. Although tightly wound white bandages covered its thighs and belly, its arms were shining brass. Long streaks of dripping crimson ran across its arms and legs, as if veins and arteries were on the outside of its body. Wearing a corroded metal mask, it sported a tattered red and black cloak with a hood that partially obscured its face. A perverse, bleeding grin stretched the mouth along the sides of the skull beyond the mask. Gums and teeth, visible through the space where the cheeks should have been, were a mess of fangs and ripped flesh. Through two small slits, the eyes twinkled like stars.

"Remember, we are still in the Haze," said Pappi grimly, his calm demeanor disturbed. "This thing cannot exist outside the Fluxa. We must destroy it to end this madness."

Teej nodded and readied himself. Though he could see the horror of the thing, his Haze Sense provided insight into its nature. He sensed the mix of human bloods within the creature that gave it power. The New Motive Power was repulsive, like an infected wound in the fabric of reality. While most of the body was formed by the Apoth's crude pseudoscience, the skin was tattooed with symbols and runes, hinting at Drowden's involvement.

Garret stirred, and Elise helped him to his feet. "You do not want to know where I've just been."

"It cannot be worse than here," commented Pappi.

"Look to the right." Alby tugged Teej's shirt and directed his attention.

A copper tank hissed as steam escaped from the seams and joints across its surface. Bolts looked ready to explode as pressure built within the gleaming shell. It was distillation equipment, but several of the output pipes connected, incongruously, to a chunky beige box that looked like an old mainframe computer. On a platform stretching above the creature's head, a chunky computer monitor hovered. The seventy-inch screen glowed green and pulsed like a heart monitor display. A network of cables and wires tangled outward and connected to the creature's right arm like an anachronistic life support machine sliding inside the bronze skin above the wrist. The whole cluster of junk machinery whirred and beeped in a poor simulacrum of scientific innovation. The dreams of madmen made into real nightmares.

"Jeeeeeesus Christ," said Elise.

"Not even close," replied Teej. "That is one *disappointing* messiah."

The creature seemed aware of their presence. It breathed in and out heavily, its mighty chest heaving as if it was in pain. The Apoth raised his arms and stepped out of the shadows.

"I offer them as a sacrifice!" he raved. "They have escaped your geas, but you may yet devour them here, in your true form. Feast on them and swell, my beloved New Motive Power."

As the Apoth slinked back into the blackness and disappeared, the New Motive Power got to its feet. The Dreamer had gone into hiding, but there was no time to search for him. The cave rumbled as his monster stomped clumsily but purposefully toward them. A flickering, neon light surrounded its body in the dim light. The deceptive size made it seem closer than it really was, but it would still be on them in moments.

Pappi's walking stick Periapt came to life as a makeshift torch. Holding his cane aloft, the yellow light partially

254

illuminated the cave. Teej saw the tension on the faces of each of his friends. They gathered together into a defensive circle.

Awake at last, Vinicaire fumbled in his pocket and pulled out a watch. It looked benign, but Teej felt the Vig stored within. Vinicaire spun it around on the end of a heavy chain like a slingshot, ready to release at the right moment.

Holding his staff high over his head, Garret whispered a few words until it lit up with a ragged, white flame, illuminating the whole cave. The intensity and scale of Garret's power eclipsed Pappi's and Vinicaire's by several degrees of magnitude. Squinting against the old man's flame, the New Motive Power stumbled backward a little, temporarily vulnerable.

"Boy, now!" shouted Garret.

Taking two steps forward, Alby whipped his body around and threw his Periapt with all his strength. Spinning like a discus, the hockey stick flew past Teej with so much momentum that he involuntarily ducked. Pappi pointed his own Periapt at the streaming hockey stick, marking its path with a beam of light. The Periapt followed the light as if on rails. Pappi changed the stick's fundamental properties in mid-flight to blast the creature with the force of a truck.

Boom.

The cave shook as the New Motive Power took a blow to the chest no living creature could survive. Alby and Pappi were a perfect partnership, the power of each supplementing the other. Teej almost cheered.

"Go now, brother!" shouted Pappi, and Alby started running at breakneck speed.

Stepping past Vinicaire, Teej motioned for Garret and Pappi to join him. Huddled in the middle of their group, Elise kept her head down. The best way to keep her safe was to end this fight quickly. If they could bring down the monster, the Haze would fade.

"Metiks!" Teej shouted. "Cover Alby!"

Garret and Pappi understood. Drawing in Vig and focusing their power, the three of them attacked in unison.

Pappi smashed his cane into the ground and sent a shockwave rumbling through the floor under the dark god's feet. Cloven hooves scrambled for balance on the cracked rock.

At the exact same time, Garret threw his staff. It arced through the darkness before exploding into a thousand points of white light that showered down on the creature. The hailstorm of burning sparks targeted the eyes and face.

Teej synchronized his attack with the other two men. Spinning his Periapt in a tight loop, he expelled his Will as a blade of fast-moving, invisible air. The accurate gust flew over Alby's head and found its target by slicing into the creature's upper chest. The three attacks knocked the dark god off balance. Losing its footing, it fell backward with a heavy crunch. As it dropped, the New Motive Power unplugged the computer cables connected to its chest, then hurled the wreckage at Alby like a mace.

A mass of metal as heavy as a house flew toward the boy, exploding in the air to create a shower of cogs, gears, sparking cables and razor-sharp shrapnel. Alby disappeared from view as the explosion moved through the cave toward the rest of them.

At the last moment, Vinicaire threw his pocket watch into the wreckage. A wide bubble of fractured light formed from the blast. The energy field, about ten-feet high and twenty wide, suspended the debris in the air. Everything within the bubble continued to move in slow motion. Teej grimaced. When the metal shrapnel left the energy field, it would return to its former momentum and get them anyway. Now they had enough time to see what would tear their bodies apart. They had nowhere to hide.

"Find cover!" shouted Vinicaire.

Dammit, no time!

Grunting, Teej grabbed Elise's arm and pulled her close. Trying to triangulate a safe location where the spinning debris would miss them, he angled his own body to protect her. He tensed and waited for the metal to shred their flesh like tissue paper.

Expecting one of the heavy cogs to hit at any moment, Teej focused his Haze Sense on finding Alby in the chaos. The boy had evaded the explosion and now vaulted over the New Motive Power, grabbing his Periapt from its steaming chest as he leaped clear. Pirouetting gracefully, he brought the weapon down on the creature's skull with momentum and power.

Yes!

The New Motive Power's head split open like a ripe pumpkin beneath an axe. Teej felt its Vig burst free of the diseased body as it ruptured.

Whoosh. One by one, pieces of metal flew over and past Teej and Elise. Some clattered into rocks with percussive, metal-shattering explosions while others disappeared into the shadows soundlessly. Just as Teej was about to breathe again, he felt a tug at his side. Pulling his right hand free, he glanced at his shirt and saw smears of red. As a ragged sliver of metal shot past, it had taken a chunk of flesh from above his hip.

"Oh shit."

Elise pulled her head away from his embrace to look at him, slowly realizing what had happened. "Teej!"

"Are you…?" he asked.

She put her hands on his chest in concern. "I'm fine, but you…"

Relieved, he clamped his hand over the wound to slow the bleeding. He felt no pain, despite not knowing the seriousness of his injuries. No pain at all.

"I'm all right. How is—"

"I'm fine," said Garret as he joined them. "And the boy is fast!"

"Almost as fast as Vinicaire!" Pappi smoothed down his jacket and breathed out a sigh of relief. "Our Dreamer friend moves quicker than the wind when he is making a tactical retreat."

"Good job, Alby!" Teej shouted.

"How can we help you?" asked Alby when he noted Teej's wound.

"You just saved us all. Try giving us a smile."

With an almost imperceptible nod, Alby, for the first time, smiled back at Teej.

As the New Motive Power bled out, the effects of the Fluxa Haze faded. Once, it had been a being of blood, but the Apoth's thaumaturgies changed its shape. Its blood drained away, and the other horrors in the cave disappeared. Even the light returned as the braziers and torches stoked themselves anew.

Around them, the gloom lifted as rock walls slowly morphed into wood panels and neat bricks, the space becoming a rustic, open-plan living room. The irregular floor slid into square stone tiles and water drained away as the cave was replaced with the interior of a lighthouse and they transitioned back to Avalon.

But Teej became only vaguely aware of the changes. His head was spinning, and his vision was blurry. Clamping his hand deeper into the wound at his hip, he tried to slow the bleeding. Focusing his Praxis into his abdomen, he couldn't grasp enough of the dissipating Vig to fully heal himself.

Elise's big eyes teared up and she covered her mouth. He must have looked bad.

Teej squinted at his companions, scanning each of them for injury. Garret hustled over to stand by his side, his expression even more grave than Elise's. Farther away, Pappi poked the remains of the New Motive Power with his cane while Alby still seemed ready to fight. The boy walked past the carnage but stopped at the foot of the stairs.

From the doorway at the top, the Apoth stepped into view, limping and hunched over in pain. No longer able to conceal himself, his distress was obvious. His failure had taken a heavy toll on him—the collapse of the Haze imbued with so much of his own Will.

"Had enough deicide for one day? Great and sudden is the reckoning that shall fall upon you; I'm here to tell you that."

Alby didn't hesitate. Taking three steps at a time, he closed the distance to his enemy in seconds. With his Periapt ready, Alby jumped toward the stooped Dreamer. When he was less than a foot away, however, the Apoth reacted quicker than any of them expected. His apparent weakness was a ruse. From beneath his calf-length, leather coat, he produced a small blunderbuss with its horn-shaped barrel pointed directly at Alby's chest. At point black range, John Murray Speare pulled the trigger.

The Apoth's arm shot back with the recoil of a cannon, and the thunderous blast shook them all. Teej held his breath. *Please, no.*

As the smoke cleared, Alby lay flat on the ground with a smoking crater in the middle of his chest.

"Brother!" shouted Pappi in dismay.

"Don't come closer!" the Apoth barked and brandished the gun threateningly at the boy's immobile body. "If I shoot again, there won't be enough left of him to save. You'll have little bits of him here, and here, and here…"

The Apoth clawed at his mask with one free hand while he wielded the weapon unsteadily with the other. Eventually, he peeled off the mask and dropped it by his feet.

Teej was weak, but he forced himself to look at John Murray Speare's face. Pallid skin and blond, disheveled hair framed deep-set, hollow eyes. His manic gaze darted around with dilated pupils. The mask was off, but he looked no more human.

Struggling to stay on his feet, Teej knew he had to distract the Apoth. Forcing himself to ignore the warm blood flowing over his fingers, he addressed the mad Dreamer directly. If he could gain his attention, perhaps Garret or Pappi could do something. He tried not to look at Alby's body.

"John, this is over. This has all happened before. Do you even remember? Is this really what you want? Mott has died from all this madness, and Drowden will too. You needn't. Stand *down*!"

There was conflict in the Apoth's eyes. His mouth was twisted into a grimace, but his expression was fearful and desperate.

Teej needed to show him that pulling the trigger would doom him.

To his left, Teej could feel Pappi's fear and rage. He hoped the Metik would not fall into despair before hope was gone.

The Apoth's weapon weaved back and forth threateningly over the prostrate form of Alby. Teej took one more step. Staying calm, he tried to catch the Apoth's gaze. If he could just look him in the eye—

"Too late," muttered the Dreamer. "It's too late for us, for you, for him."

Deliberately and callously, the Apoth aimed at Alby's head. Teej's failure was about to cost another life.

Wait.

From the dark corner of the room, someone approached the Aesthete. It was the same strange presence Teej had felt since he arrived on the island. Even as the Apoth brandished his weapon threateningly and retreated closer to his concealed assailant, he was oblivious.

Teej peered at Garret's clenched fists, Pappi's eyes filled with sorrow, Elise's trembling bottom lip. Teej gave them a tiny nod. He hoped it conveyed the need for them to stay back and keep calm.

The Apoth's blue eyes darted manically from person to person. His weapon weaved little spiral patterns as the barrel pointed at Alby, then them, then back to Alby.

Teej tried to freeze him with a gaze. "John, we're just going to back off. My friends will leave this place. Just let me take the boy and you can—"

As the hidden stranger stepped out of the shadows, words caught in Teej's throat. Instead, he watched the imminent attack with slack-jawed horror.

Patches of ruined human flesh clung to a metallic frame. Pistons and actuators animated the Pilgrim like a marionette, its movements jerky and awkward. As it closed in on the Apoth, the gleaming skeleton within started to glow, causing the air itself to distort with a heat haze. In a rib cage of metal and broken bone, swollen human organs undulated back and forth with each step. A withered heart, connected to the flesh and metal endoskeleton with wires and tubes and sparking electric cables, oozed with each slow beat.

The face still held some façade of humanity. The Pilgrim had repaired its visage somewhat. The right side looked human, while the left was a mass of exposed red muscle fiber and metal. And there was consciousness in the eyes. Those eyes were clear and full of sadness and righteous rage.

Let your ruined soul be a flame that burns only him.

John Murray Speare froze in terror as the Pilgrim's right hand clamped down on his shoulder. The Dreamer instantly fell to his knees and dropped his weapon, the creature's immense strength overpowering him with ease. He tried to speak, perhaps attempting to command his creation, but it was a mistake. The Pilgrim's hand swallowed his face from behind as it hooked three fingers inside his mouth. John Murray Speare screamed once, his last words a gargle, before his head was ripped apart. The flesh and bone snapped like stretched elastic. The upper half of the skull was ripped free, then tossed aside with a wet, crunching noise as it hit the ground.

Redeemed, the Pilgrim closed its eyes in satisfaction.

Standing in stunned silence, Teej was interrupted by Garret's hand on his shoulder. "The boy."

He was right; they had to help Alby. Pappi was already running up the stairs to his brother. Eyeing the Pilgrim cautiously, Teej followed his friend to the fallen boy. The bloodied creature stood motionless, frozen in place. As Teej reached the top of the steps, the creature mouthed thanks from malformed lips. Teej gave it a tiny nod in response.

Pappi fell to his knees in despair. There was no sign of life from Alby.

They were too late.

"We have another problem," said Garret.

"Out of the mist rides a Green Knight with a black heart," replied Pappi, his head still bowed in sorrow.

"Not now," muttered Teej. "Not now."

thirty-one

Anna snapped back to consciousness and bolted upright. She was lying on the scorched tiles of Rayleigh's church. Nearby, the crackle of burning wood reminded her of the flames she had unleashed. The scent of scorched timber was in her nose and mouth, and the heat from the burning benches washed over her in waves. She remembered the flames scorching through her body as they burned the poison out of her, before they burst outward in an expanding solar flare to ward off her enemies. Her fire had both shielded her and forced the knights away. But since it had been too much too fast, her limbs were now leaden. The poison that had numbed her was gone, but she was exhausted.

Anna noted with some alarm that her skin was exposed in the hot air. Her clothes were scorched. As she shuffled to her feet, little wisps of cinder and ash fell off her body. It wasn't enough that she was trapped in the Haze of the most powerful Dreamer alive, but she was now facing him naked too. *Great work! What a job well done.*

All around her, the church burned with hot orange flames, but little smoke. Testing her balance, she cautiously got to her feet. Although wobbly, she was able to stand. Her head remained clear enough to face any remaining danger, but it wouldn't be hard for them to simply poison her again if they wanted her docile. Anna clutched her ring, ready to engage her powers at a moment's notice if anyone came close.

"Hope is the buoyancy of the soul, often too cruelly deflated." Rayleigh's disembodied voice drifted close. He was still right there. *Great.*

"All this fighting is pointless. Where do such theatrics lead? Raguel has already engaged your friends, so there is not a single thing you can do. Can we try to talk sensibly? I won't move against you again. I can see you are no threat to me."

The tone of his voice angered her. Though he was out of sight, Anna readied her Praxis. Breathing in slowly, she imagined herself as a strung bow, a loaded gun, or a bomb primed with the fuse lit. Anna pictured all the Vig in the Haze flooding into her, and then she made that feeling real. She would kill him if she could, even if it meant killing herself too. Anything to save her friends.

"You are directionless and weak, but your hurt fuels you. I've seen pain before Anna, but nothing like yours. No one alive has ever burned like you burn."

Anna's Haze Sense tugged at the edge of her perception. Some vague intuition was just beyond her grasp. A cool breeze flowed into the room, cutting through the scent of burning wood. The fire was spreading, but the smoke parted to clear her view. Near the organ that relayed Rayleigh's voice through the valves, the blood moon shined through a high window. It stood out, bright and unnatural.

Why had Rayleigh chosen a blood moon?

In a flash of inspiration, Anna realized the importance. Rayleigh warped the moon into a threatening presence since it couldn't be hidden here. To Anna, the moon meant hope. She hadn't finished her journey because Rayleigh's diversion wasn't her final destination on the Moonlight Road, so that meant…

That was it! Anna had discerned a path through and out the other end. A way back to her friends. Back to Teej.

Rayleigh anticipated her thoughts. "Do not even think about it, woman!"

Instead of confronting her, he cloaked the moon to hide it from her. She had figured out a way to see through his lies. Anna now realized she was a serious threat to him and grew in confidence. She felt him exert his powers. From behind the flames, his knights started to file into the church again. From all sides, they sought to block her escape.

"This is not where I am supposed to be. I didn't complete my journey on the Moonlight Road, so you can't stop me getting back on." As she said the words aloud, she felt the truth in them. This place was a trap, but not a physical one. It was a conceptual trap, and she was snared in its lies. No more.

Ignoring the knights with their swords and halberds, Anna lifted her ring into the air and pointed at the blood moon. As she released her Will toward the sky, she allowed her consciousness to expand beyond the world she observed. Since this wasn't Basine and the walls weren't made of stone, they could be manipulated. Everything around her was made of the Vig exerted by Rayleigh. This wasn't the church where she got married, but a crude prison decorated with cruel imitations of her genuine memories. The bright, red moon wasn't a sphere of rock thousands of miles away, but only existed as a symbol.

She recalled Garret's words: "There is always a moon. You can always find a moon." Although Rayleigh tried to hide the moon with the bloody veneer, he could never remove it completely.

Anna concentrated on that red veneer and then drained it with a turn of her hand. Breaking apart the illusion, her ring burned hot as the crimson gave way to familiar silver light. The transformation was complete and the pale moon returned.

Rayleigh's voice held a quiver of uncertainty, "Why bother? Mangata brought you to me. This is where you are *supposed* to be!"

"No," she replied. "I am supposed to be with Teej."

"Do not do this. You must heed me or you will die!"

"You don't get to decide anything about me, not even how I die. I don't have to listen to you anymore."

Anna needed to focus. The knights were almost on her. The nearest sword was less than a foot away.

Taking a tiny step to the right, Anna saw the sliver of sparkling diamonds that signaled the Moonlight Road. Closing her eyes and hoping with all her heart that she could walk the path once more and get home to Teej, she stepped forward. Suddenly her bare skin was bathed in moonlight.

Rayleigh shouted after her, "The Dreamers will never stop hunting you! You will spend the rest of your life running from us. It's in the blood. Anna, that's what you must know. It's in *your* blo—"

It was too late. Anna didn't hear his words. She was already gone.

thirty-two

With a puffy face and eyes filled with despair, Vinicaire burst through the doorway into the lighthouse. His smart clothes were ruffled, his hat sat at an unfortunate angle on his head, and his sardonic wit was gone. Everyone waited for him to speak, but he couldn't get any words out.

"I assume we can't escape that way?" said Garret.

"I…was a fool…to follow you here!" wheezed Vinicaire.

"When we die, they'll sing songs about your bravery," replied Garret.

Nervously, Elise walked toward Vinicaire. "You're back! I thought you…Were you just going to leave me?"

"Be silent girl," he snapped. "The adults need to talk."

Chastised, Elise slumped in rejection. If they escaped the island, she might feel very differently about her relationship with her mentor.

"The Green Knight blocks our escape," said Vinicaire. "Perhaps we climb the tower? The topology has changed, so maybe we can jump to safety? We must be swift, he will be here any moment."

Teej still couldn't believe the Green Knight was real. He had been a legend amongst lies and a whisper of warning to unwary Metiks for hundreds of years. *Though the foe you face may be but a foot soldier, prepare as if you face the Green Knight.* The proverb was so ancient it had fallen into cliché.

"We'll make for the tower," said Teej. "But I need to help Alby first."

Pappi left his brother's side to stand with them. His expression was blank. Teej felt the tall Metik's hand fall loosely on his shoulder. "No, we must keep moving. My brother's wounds are mortal. We cannot undo them in time."

"Elise!" Teej shouted. "Come with me. Follow me up the stairs."

Elise's eyes were like saucers. Mirroring their nervousness, she appeared just as unnerved as the rest of them. Teej wished there was a way for her to escape, but the best he could do was stand between her and the danger. There was probably no escape for *any* of them now.

"That's it, girl," Garret encouraged as she nervously shuffled past them. "Ignore the cyborg and the dead demon. Nothing to see here."

She moved beyond the Pilgrim, making for the bright doorway at the top of the stairs

"Isn't Drowden up there?" Teej asked Garret. "In the tower? I sensed him before."

"I think he's made his escape," said Pappi. "I'll go with her. Maybe I can find an escape route." Pappi didn't look at Alby's still form as he stepped away from it. Teej winced, imagining the pain the Metik must have been feeling.

"Are you sure?" Teej asked.

"I'll go," Pappi repeated with finality, and Teej gave him a nod of appreciation. "If we encounter the Dreamer, I will not be overcome. Elise will be protected."

"The best we can do is slow him down," said Garret. "Perhaps buy them some time to find a way out of here."

"Slow him down?" whined Vinicaire. "Why not punch a mountain or pick a fight with the sky? Mayhap we challenge him to a friendly game of chess, best three of five?"

"*Mayhap* we try our best and—" Garret stopped talking as the Green Knight burst into the room.

It was too late.

Someone shouted, "Run!" Pappi and Elise disappeared through the doorway just as the battle began.

thirty-three

Peter was at peace. The blood of his creator trickled down his face, a cool sensation on his remaining patches of flesh. The Inductive Regress Chip in his skull whirred and hummed a happy tune. At one time, it was his antagonist, a commanding presence and a virtual dictator within his own brain, but now, it was a friend and a brother. It gave him advice and occasionally asked for guidance.

What shall we do next, Peter?

The question made him pause. He hadn't planned on existing beyond this moment. The end of his creator was an event that had not made it into his calculations. Emancipated from his final executable function, Peter idled as his internal procedures cycled wastefully. *What a guilty pleasure!*

Setting aside his own plight for a moment, he looked around the lighthouse. The dim light illuminated the worried faces of the Metiks. The Metik looked pallid from the serious wound at his side that dripped constantly, staining his jeans crimson. Peter should help him. He owed more to this injured savior than he could ever express.

The Arabic Metik next to him was wracked with grief. He tried to hide his sorrow, but it was written in every move he made. Everyone avoided the dead boy at the foot of the stairs. Even now, residual smoke rose from the black wound in the center of his chest.

For Peter, time passed differently than the others. His Inductive Regress Chip continued to divide each moment into executable slices. Potential actions filled each millisecond, so the moments seemed to pass more slowly. When the powerful green enemy entered the room, he had more time to observe its nature.

The information from his data sources was conflicted, but the Knight was a ruthlessly efficient combatant in each scenario. Compared to Peter, who used every possible microsecond of time efficiently to achieve his objectives, this enemy was fast.

Dark green armor covered every inch of the Knight's body. It looked and smelled burnt. The metal arm and leg panels were curved and organic, while blue, electrical sparks and smoke flickered out of the joints between the plates. On the shoulders, spikes curved and poked out of a tattered, ashen cape that hung to the floor. A hood framed the helmet that contained dark slits for eyes and a mouthpiece that was smooth and flat. His cruel, metal fists curled around two long swords. The straight-edged blades, meant for dueling and penetrating heavy armor, were made of clear, polished crystal.

As he scanned the Knight, Peter decided he would try to help. Under normal circumstances, he would be a formidable foe. Even in his diminished state, he could aid the exhausted Metiks. The Vig-infused blood in his veins healed him at high speeds, which was the reason he was able to stand after his last ordeal. Combined with the Inductive Regress Chip in his head, he was still a deadly weapon. Not deadly enough to defeat this opponent on his own, but perhaps he could slow it down. Perhaps he could delay his savior's demise.

Peter looked over at the Metik. *Teej.* Even injured, Teej had beaten Peter. Teej might survive this day, but he would need Peter's help.

As the Inductive Regress Chip spun into action, Peter evaluated the potential outcomes. Attack from the left, strike at the head and torso, then kick at the legs? Negative. The Knight

271

would cut him down quickly. Attack from above, jump to the roof, grab him from behind? Negative. The Knight would dodge to one side and strike with both blades, cutting him in two at the waist.

Going through every situation took too much time. He needed to rely on his human intuition rather than his machine logic. Peter jumped forward. This was how it would end. Peter wanted to save some lives.

He would try to die better than he had lived. For Sarah.

Raguel's storm of swords swept through the room, and nothing could stand against him. Vinicaire's cloak twisted around his body as the crystal blades flashed toward him, and he fell in a pile by the fireplace. He cast some sort of shield, an ephemeral green energy wave, but it was a weak attempt to protect himself from the dual swipe that cleaved through his body. There was no time to guess whether he was still alive. The Green Knight moved past him.

Teej summoned his Will and reached for his Periapt. He gripped the tonfa till the wood creaked. A vague plan formed in his mind while he pushed Vig into his weapon. His power seemed to flow glacially. He was too slow to match Raguel's speed. This felt like falling toward disaster.

Stepping to meet his enemy, Teej tried to intercept the Green Knight. His friends all moved at the same time. Elise and Pappi burst out the back door, leaving the lighthouse tower. Garret held his staff in both hands and stepped up beside Teej, his stance defensive and stalwart. Alby twitched at the foot of the steps, a flicker of life clinging to his body.

The Green Knight charged, and Teej felt like a sand castle about to be hit by a tidal wave.

At breakneck speed, the Pilgrim ran past them toward the Green Knight. The creature existed somewhere between a joke and a nightmare, its human skin flapping as it left bloody footprints with each step. Nonetheless, the damaged body was quick and agile. It vaulted over obstacles and leapt into the air ahead of Raguel, using its own burning metal skeleton as a weapon.

The Green Knight pivoted on his front foot. Teej exchanged a panicked look with Garret. They wanted to help, but both the Knight and the robot were too fast for either of them. The first round of this battle would be fought by the swiftest soldiers.

It was over in seconds. Dropping down on his right leg and spinning, Raguel rotated his body completely and came back around just as the Pilgrim was about to strike. For a moment, it looked like the burning fist of the robot might find its target. The Pilgrim's powerful blow harnessed all its momentum and Vig into one swift attack. At the last second, Raguel flashed the blades through the Pilgrim without resistance in one impossibly fast motion.

The two pieces flew past Raguel, spraying the knight in oil and a spattering of sparks. Raguel took five more steps before the pieces of the Pilgrim hit the ground.

Teej's Vig swelled as Raguel bore down on him. He swallowed deeply and swung his Periapt into the space where his opponent would soon be.

The battle was savage. Teej parried and blocked by instinct. The crystal blades flashed faster than his conscious mind followed. All he saw was Raguel's implacable metal faceplate beneath the hood. His Haze Sense bolstered his peripheral vision and his reaction time for each attack, but every time he blocked, the unbelievable strength of Raguel shook his bones and strained his muscles to breaking point. Each time his Periapt deflected one of those crystal blades, he invested it with enough Vig to ensure its safety. Anything less and it would have smashed to pieces. He deflected five or six killing blows a second. Each parry happened at the last possible moment, and any one of those blows could end his life if his timing was off.

The worst fights he'd experienced were always like this—physical and personal with no time for tricks or surprises. Teej conjured nothing, and there was nowhere to hide. Will powered each blow with extra strength drawn from the world around them, every swipe steeled with the strength of his very soul.

Wondering why he wasn't dead yet, Teej felt the familiar twinge of Garret's Vig. Unbelievably, the old man was fighting Raguel from the *other* side. Even as one arm and one blade undid Teej's defense and threatened to overcome him, the other blade was fending off Garret. While Garret's staff crushed uselessly against the Knight's perfect defense, Teej was being pushed back. Identifying Teej as the weaker of the two, Raguel sought to eliminate him first. Each swing inched closer to Teej's jugular.

Teej stumbled. The sudden lapse in balance allowed a near lethal riposte to rustle his hair. Half an inch lower, and he would have been undone. Regaining his feet, Teej assumed an attack stance, steadied his breathing and prepared to weather the storm once more.

The tonfa and staff were good general-purpose weapons for Metiks. Against armor or a skilled swordsman though, both were at a disadvantage. A tonfa excelled when used for defense or close-range combat in tight spaces. A staff was good for keeping enemies at a distance, but even when wielded proficiently, it could not penetrate a skilled swordsman's guard. Worse, both Metiks constantly imbued their Periapts with Vig to prevent them from breaking, while Raguel was not similarly constrained. His crystal blades, invincible and lighter than air, whistled as they danced.

With some desperation, Teej realized he was running out of space in the room. Pushed back to the stairs, he fended off lethal attacks while getting trapped in the corner. Blood ran from the wound at his side. The Will to hold his own body together was failing. Garret weakened beside him as he struggled to capture the Knight's attention.

In a moment, Raguel would defeat Teej single-handedly. When he turned both blades on Garret, the old man would fall just as quickly.

Anna.

With the image of her smile in his mind, Teej countered a downward swing that turned into a feint. He raised his tonfa too slowly. A sword swung toward his exposed neck. Twisting too far, he lurched to the side. The killing blow would come from above.

Just as Teej started to close his eyes, he caught a glimpse of Garret on the other side of the Knight. During the sliver of respite gained as Raguel invested all his attention on killing Teej, Garret made his last, desperate move. Taking advantage of the distraction, he planted his staff onto the ground. He invested all his Vig into the bare rock floor in a brutal exertion of power. The explosion hit all three of them equally.

Teej's body was blown backward, through the wall of the lighthouse and over the beach. As he spun through the air, floating soundlessly amongst rock and debris, he closed his eyes and waited for the ground to meet him.

thirty-four

Wet sea spray tickled Teej's face. He imagined himself lying in the sand with the sun beating down on the top of his head.

Get up.

Trying to take a breath, he coughed in spasms that wracked his body with agony. Spitting up dust, each breath filled his head with pain. He rolled over and the feeling slowly returned to his arms and legs. An unpleasant stickiness dripped down one half of his body. As his consciousness phased back in, he remembered the mortal wound just above his hip. It was a miracle he was waking up at all. Perhaps it would be better if he stayed unconscious.

He couldn't give up yet. Pappi and Elise were reason enough to keep fighting. If he could get to his feet, even for a moment, he would force the Green Knight to take his soul before it found his friends.

Cracking his eyes open, Teej was amazed at how far the blast had thrown him. The explosion had propelled him through the wall of the lighthouse and he rested on a pile of rubble. How had he survived? His best guess was that Garret had exerted some measure of protection for him in the blast. Had he been thrown clear of a fight that continued without him?

There should have been more pain. Although some feeling returned to him, numbness lingered. He'd lost so much blood that he felt the coldness seep into his bones. For Teej, this fight should be over.

Pushing his legs under himself, he managed to half-stand. He was weak, but he exerted a little Vig to hold himself up. Residual Vig still swirled through the air, and he sucked in the particles like he was swallowing little snowflakes of renewal. Though his body was failing, his Metik abilities took the strain. His Will was the crutch his failing physical form could lean upon.

The summit of the lighthouse caught Teej's eye. The lamp turned slowly, casting a beam out to sea. Through a massive hole in the wall, he could see the curling steps of the interior of the lighthouse tower. The heavy metal staircase was deformed by the blast, but still mostly intact. From inside, he heard clattering rubble and movement, but he couldn't identify the source. Casting out his Haze Sense, he detected Pappi at the summit, but everything else was blurry. Teej struggled to focus his Haze Sense properly, a residual effect of Garret's blast.

Staggering across the dirt path toward the lighthouse entrance, Teej glanced up to see his friend walk past the hole in the wall twenty feet above him. Garret strode confidently up the ruined staircase. After Teej took four more halting steps, the green, battered armor of Raguel passed the same gap. Teej tried to call out, but his words were lost in the wind.

Gritting his teeth, he forced himself onward, although he was falling forward more than he was running. Teej scrambled over broken rocks to get back inside the lighthouse. As he cleared the rubble and extended a shaking hand onto the twisted metal railing of the stairway, he heard the battle ahead intensify.

Teej started to climb the spiral stairs, each step harder than the last. The clatter of weapons echoed down to him. Frantic energy powered his shaking legs as he forced himself upward. As his strength failed, he closed his eyes, held his arms out, and pulled Vig into himself once more, refreshing his muscles, knitting together ripped tendons in his arms and legs, and partly healing the smashed ribs at his side. Nearing the top, he saw the flutter of Raguel's cape. After one last rounding on the spiral stairs, the battle came into view above him. It was drawing to an end, and he wouldn't reach them in time.

Garret and Raguel stood on an unsteady portion of the staircase. Behind them, the wall had fallen away so the wind blew Garret's wavy hair across his face. An orange light burst around them. With one hand, he beckoned the Knight to come at him. Garret looked like he was smiling.

"Come down here, Knight!" Tecj shouted up. "I've not finished with you."

The Green Knight looked at him briefly, then turned away dismissively. Teej wasn't a threat.

Heaving himself upward, he knew he would be too late.

The explosion had robbed Raguel of one of his swords and had battered his armor, but he clutched the remaining blade confidently. He moved quickly and efficiently, maintaining full control of this battle and still looking unstoppable.

Raguel's sword swung low, but Garret's staff smashed the blow aside. The reverberation of Vig made Teej wince. Raguel's swings pushed Garret back. The Knight held his remaining sword with two hands, his grip transitioning from low to high smoothly as he adjusted his style from moment to moment. Garret's feet were planted firmly, and he knocked the blows upward, stepping around to his enemy's weaker side. Raguel's attacks increased in intensity, and he blocked flawlessly. Garret's own swipes stalled.

For a single, desperate moment, there seemed to be hope. Raguel over-extended a lunge, and Garret twirled and smashed the Knight's sword downward with this staff. With his opponent's weapon momentarily pinned, Garret pivoted and cracked his staff heavily into Raguel's inner knee with an explosive crash and a flash of blue sparks. It buckled, and the Knight almost fell. Teej felt like cheering.

Slowly the knee straightened itself and Raguel reared up again, his blade slicing across Garret's face. Garret crumpled soundlessly in a pile of rubble. Splayed across the debris, he looked like a pile of wet rags.

"Dammit, no!" Teej fumbled up the remaining stairs, keeping his eye on the Knight.

Before he could get close, Raguel jumped across the gap to snatch Teej off his feet, slamming Teej into the bricks. There was no resisting that kind of strength.

Raguel's metal forearm squeezed against his neck, making it hard to breathe and impossible to move. Teej's feet dangled uselessly below him, scrambling and kicking for something solid. He looked deeply into the dark eyeholes of the Green Knight's faceplate.

"Ha!" choked Teej. "Your sword. Look at your sword, you miserable bastard."

Head turning slowly, Raguel glanced at the blade. Smashed. Garret's final blow had shattered the unbreakable sword of the Green Knight. For a second, Raguel quaked with anger. Pulling his arm back, he prepared to ram the broken shards through Teej's skull.

Resigned to his fate, Teej went limp.

"Stop!"

Raguel froze in place. The razor-sharp, broken blade hung in the air. Behind him, Garret stood slowly, a diagonal cut across his face stretching from cheek to forehead. Though blood ran down his face, he smiled.

"In days long past, I was a warrior,
Wars were my life; blood was my wage"

Garret's words held Raguel in place.

The speech—or what sounded like a quote—charged with Vig and Garret's last reserves of Will, could not be interrupted, not even by Raguel. Garret's poetry penetrated to every corner of Avalon.

"When the wars were done, they made me a general,

Then the currency was the lives of young men,
And I spent freely.
When the status of my career diminished, my skills fell out
of favor,
I became a storyteller,
And the audience craved the details
Of each soul I had taken,
And each dead man's final words.
Now I am old,
My career is at an end,
And only one story remains to be told.
The story of how I went to the grave,
And how many souls my enemies spent,
To send me there."

"Who…wrote that?" Teej croaked. "Wasn't it…?"

"Yeah, I wrote it." Garret responded with a tired smile, wiping blood from his brow. "I'm quoting myself. Take care kid. Garret's proud of you."

As the words left his mouth, Garret casually stepped back through the hole in the wall and fell out of view. A fraction of a second later, Raguel leaped after him, compelled to chase even though it led to oblivion.

It was nicely done.

thirty-five

Nine steps, ten steps, eleven.

The glittering surface of the Moonlight Road stretched for thousands of steps. Each one seemed to carry Anna farther from Teej. She didn't know how long she'd walked that road. Whether minutes or hours, she dutifully followed the path and wondered whether it might take her somewhere even worse. She had escaped for now, but would she get back to Teej in time to help? Garret told her the Moonlight Road was capricious. It would take her where she *needed* to be. Right now, it took her on such a long, twisting route that it seemed she might eventually stumble upon Teej through random chance.

Through deserts, forests, ancient cities, ruins, wastelands, swamps, towns and tundra, she trudged ahead on the smooth path. She passed cities in the sky, fields of blue snow, and towers of frozen rainbows shimmering under a green sun. Swaying castles built from the stuff of ghosts passed before her view.

Keeping her pace steady, Anna never deviated from the path. She held her memories of her friends close and kept moving forward. She refused to linger in her own fearful thoughts. No more talk of *desolation*. No more self-pity. No more self-destruction. If Anna sacrificed herself for anyone now, it would be for him. For Teej.

"Can you hear me Moonlight Road?" Anna shouted. "Take me to him!"

Six, seven, eight, nine, ten, eleven steps.

Anna ran.

Drained of emotion, drained of energy, and literally drained of blood, Teej climbed the stairs because he didn't know what else to do. Those spiral stairs to the sky seemed to go on forever. The higher he climbed, the quicker hope died.

Below him, the wind whistled through the hole in the wall. The same hole Garret fell through to his death. He couldn't forget the sight of the two shattered bodies broken on the rocks hundreds of feet below. Locking the memory away, he promised he would find time to grieve later. For now, he was cold. Cold to his friend's death and cold to his own fate. *Just. Keep. Climbing.*

Though the wound at his side knitted back together, he had repaired his own flesh poorly. The muscles were ripped and tangled and the skin was taut. Losing pints of blood weakened his body further. Pausing to pant through a spell of dizziness, he looked at his blue hands curled tightly on the handrail. He was a mess, but his Will helped to push him forward.

Close to collapse, he noticed a shadow ahead. With a sudden sense of dread, he rushed onward, his own pain pushed to the back of his mind by concern for his friend.

Pappi stood outside a solid, wooden door barred with iron deadbolts. Teej joined him at the top of the stairs. Finally, he'd finished the climb to the top of the tower, but his Haze Sense tingled to warn him that something was wrong.

Pappi didn't react to Teej's presence. The tall Metik stood in a trance, his gaze fixed in the middle distance.

"My friend? Are you hurt? Where is Elise? Drowden?"

Pappi looked at Teej with distant eyes, lost in despair. "Elise is within. She rushed ahead and was caught by the

Drowden. I was locked out. I was not strong enough to break down the door. If Alby were here, he would have known what to do. After feeling the loss of Garret, my thoughts went to my brother."

Teej observed his friend's profound sadness. "Don't lose hope. There is still a chance."

Pappi didn't respond. Teej grabbed him by the shoulders and shook him gently. Slowly, the Metik returned his gaze. "Raguel has been stopped. Escape is possible. Go back!"

"Where? For what purpose?" asked Pappi, a note of frustration in his voice.

"Go back to your brother! Raguel is gone. We may yet save *them all*! Have hope, my friend."

"His wound was—"

"Yes, severe. You know what they say, though. *Until the blood runs cold, there is a chance.* With the residual Vig left from the fight, there is a chance to save him, but you must be swift!"

Pappi's expression changed to grim determination. He looked back at Teej and nodded. "Yes, we can try. But Elise…and you are wounded."

"Let me worry about Drowden and Elise."

"What will you do? You are weak, my friend. Too weak. If you can't fight, then what?"

"Parley? I'll think of something. Now go!"

Before he'd finished speaking, the quickest Metik of them all was already on his way to tend to his brother.

Alone now, Teej turned to face his fate. He hoped for a moment to compose himself, but the door was already opening.

"Come in," the guttural voice growled with malice.

Teej stepped inside as confidently as he could manage whilst barely able to stand.

Drowden sat at a simple table. The Dreamer was just as Teej remembered him. Straggly black hair and beard, ill-fitting coat over a dirty waistcoat, scruffy clothes over an ape-like body that bulged with both muscle and fat, and clear blue eyes filled with thunder. Drowden was like a beast that had learned civility to survive in the human world but hated the imposition.

He gestured for Teej to sit in a plain wooden chair opposite him.

Above them, the huge lamp of the lighthouse revolved slowly, casting a blinding light across the room every thirty seconds or so. The bulb was replaced by a floating ball of energy, but half of it was black with darkness while the other half burned like a white-hot sun. The whole room thrummed like a power station.

On wobbling legs, Teej propped himself upright on the back of the chair and feigned nonchalance. Slowly, he lowered himself to sit opposite his final adversary. Once he let himself sink into the chair, the light turned to illuminate Elise in the corner.

Gagged and tied securely, Elise was barely able to move in a series of ornate knots that formed symbols and shapes around her limbs. Teej recognized her predicament as a form of Japanese rope bondage where her arms and hands were bound behind her back while lines from her neck and chest were tied to her ankles and legs. It forced her into a curled sitting position that was painful and strict, the slipknot around her neck tightening each time she moved. Her face was pale, and her cheeks were stained red with tears. Though her eyes remained defiant, her body was wracked with pain.

Teej struggled to contain his anger when he realized Drowden was baiting him. Closing his mind to Elise's suffering, he faced his foe. Trying to appear callous, he refused to allow Drowden leverage over him.

"I suppose you recognize *Shibari*?" drawled Drowden as he smiled at Elise's discomfort. She tried to swear at him but only made a choking noise. "I created this form, using hermetic symbols of the Gray Templars. The knots are agony on human flesh; each occult pattern increases the pain as the victim struggles. Wouldn't you agree that it is a very pretty thing?"

"No." Teej's jaw was set, the tone of his voice betraying his anger.

Drowden grinned viciously. "You'd think a boy scout would like knots. I know your real nature. You're like me. Everyone is! You just won't accept it. Deep down you know the girls are prettiest when the tears stain the cheeks."

Teej wanted to retch. Drowden reeked of sweat and filth, and he emanated cruelty. Bitter and petty, he reveled in antagonizing Teej and gloating in his apparent victory.

"This is your one and only chance, Drowden. Everyone else wants you dead, but I came to—"

"Talk?" Drowden cut him off. "That's what you do, is it not? You talk and talk. *The Diplomat.* Another name for a coward. Look at you. Pale and shaking and weak. Come now, tell me I'm wrong. Smack me down and put me in my place. Can you do that?"

Teej clenched his fists, momentarily forgetting his infirmity. His Will flared up for a second only to splutter out. He considered pulling his Periapt into the open. Even as the thought flashed through his mind, he noticed Drowden's predatory sneer. He wasn't strong enough. His hand would come back empty, and Drowden would kill him. Drowden waited until his enemies used up all their strength in order to be victorious. The cunning Dreamer had won.

"I'll fight you if I have to," Teej lied. "And who knows who would win? I've beaten you before. But if we don't have to—"

"Beaten me? Last time you nearly killed us all, you fool. This time you are alone. No Undreamer and no old man to save you. You can barely keep your eyes open. Such a pitiful excuse for a Metik."

"Like I said," Teej repeated, imbuing his words with just a tiny amount of Vig to make them more convincing, "I beat you before. Why risk this fight? Where does it get us? I know you hate me. Believe me, the feeling is mutual. All you really care about is getting away from here with your skin intact. Raguel is gone. Clearly, Rayleigh sent him to kill us *all*. Perhaps this is your chance to slip away. We are all hunted now."

"Idiot," snapped Drowden. "You have no idea what's actually going on here. You don't even know the *mechanism* of our power."

Drowden was wrong. In that moment it all came together. Teej understood.

"The blood," he said simply.

"Yes, the blood. Rayleigh shared the secret with us one by one. If we take the blood from a Muse, or even another Dreamer, we can harvest Vig from them. A simple enough concept, but one which was not always the case."

Dammit. This new rule would change everything. The Dreamers would tear each other apart for this power. They were doing so already.

Elise's moans brought Teej back to the present. Curled up in a painful position, her face was turning blue and her eyes were desperate. She was choking to death.

"I see your limited intellect struggling to comprehend," sneered Drowden. "Let me make it simple. Blood is the new currency in our economy. I suspect it was not always this way. Mayhap some Fluxa occurred which changed the rules. Perhaps it was the work that I wrought with the Apoth, Ozman, and Mott that *you* foolishly derailed. None of that matters. The only question remaining is how to secure that power with no remaining allies. Gladly, most of my enemies are also now defeated.

"Rayleigh had reasons for passing on this information, but it is pointless to guess the motivations of the master manipulator. As soon as the Doxa knew about the blood, we went to work."

"The Pilgrim used that blood. The one that killed the Apoth."

"Yes," Drowden replied, a smile on his face. Enjoying himself, he taunted Teej with his superior knowledge. The gloating gave Teej an opportunity. He just had to keep the Aesthete talking.

"The Pilgrim was powered by the blood of a great many Muses. That's why he caused you so much trouble. In the tunnels below us, John's New Motive Power was also powered with that same blood."

"*Whose* blood?" Teej asked, appalled because he already knew the answer.

"We sacrificed a Choir, of course. Oh, that shocks you! I see it in your soft eyes. Yes, indeed. What use is there in keeping Muses alive anymore? We take what we need from them with no reduction in the Vig we gain."

"Tell me you didn't," Teej said despairingly. "Tell me you didn't murder—"

"Children? The pus of man. What of it? The continuation of our community is far more important. The survival of our way of life and our *species*! No longer will we fade out. With this knowledge, we will find new ways to spread our word. I do not expect the likes of you to understand."

Teej scrambled for a way to overcome Drowden. The man was a monster and had to be stopped, but Teej had no options left. In his weakened state, Drowden could kill him at any time. Only the Dreamer's cruelty delayed Teej's death. If only he could discern some trick or desperate gambit that would at least save Elise.

"The desire for blood will change everything. Every Dreamer knows the secret now and few of them will be strong enough to resist the temptation. Even the least ambitious will eventually partake in this feast. Did you not question DeLorde's potency at the museum? Once a Dreamer realizes the power of the blood, no one can resist draining every drop.

"Do you feel even more foolish now? Facing me and sacrificing yourself to save this worthless girl? You came here to die for a *Noop*! Can you honestly tell me that you are without regrets?"

Teej tried to catch Elise's attention. Lying on her side as she struggled to ease the pain of her bindings, she looked deep into Teej's eyes with determination rather than defeat. Even as her breaths became shallow and her face drained of color, she was not ready to give up.

"No," Teej said simply.

"Then you are a fool! Once I kill you, I'll throw her into the sea and watch her struggle as she drowns. I'll think of you and laugh. You see! This is what you get when you anger me. Even after you're dead, I'll take the time to hurt everyone you care about."

"You'd better stay away from Anna."

Teej noted the change in Drowden's expression. His complex reaction combined fear, anger, and a myriad of other emotions.

"Why? I'm not afraid of her."

There was trepidation in his voice. Seeing a glimmer of opportunity, Teej continued provoking Drowden.

"You won't beat her. Why did Rayleigh want to meet her? Not to kill her, that would be easy enough. Rayleigh knows how powerful Anna can become, and he knows that she is much more useful than someone like you. He sent Raguel to kill all of us, including you. So, you better stay away from Anna because she won't stay away from you. She'll come for you."

That angered him. "That girl is nothing to me!"

"You're lying," goaded Teej. "Or you'd have no need to say it."

If he made Drowden lose focus, perhaps he might figure out an escape for Elise. Teej had to aggravate him just a little more.

"She got away from you, didn't she? Twice. The first time was on Malamun with a little help from Garret. Even after you

288

sent her to Avicimat, where no one can escape, she got out. And she got away from you *again*. You *should* be afraid of her. She will be the end of you."

Teej was on the floor before he knew what happened. Drowden brutishly backhanded him, cracking a heavy fist into his skull. His head bounced when it hit the ground. Too weak and slow to protect himself, he hurt as much from the fall as the blow.

Although Teej's body was vulnerable, his mind and his Will were sharp. This was the reaction he needed. Looking through the legs of the table and across the room, Teej fastened Elise with a glare. She noticed through her pain. As Drowden reached down and grabbed him by the back of his shirt, Teej exerted his Praxis. Flicking his fingers outward, he shot a fast current of air across the room, invisible but perfectly aimed. It neatly cut the single strand of rope that bound Elise's neck to her ankles. This freed her enough to straighten her spine, alleviating a little of her pain and allowing her to breathe. It was all he could do.

Drowden hefted Teej in the air and slammed him against the wall.

With no strength left, Teej fought back lamely. Moving automatically, he threw a punch from the elbow. It slapped weakly against Drowden's cheek. The Dreamer laughed, spat, and then slammed his forehead into the bridge of Teej's nose. For a moment, Teej's vision whited out.

"You die easier than Garret. Hell, you die easier than your Undreamer. I beat you. You see! You thought you could stop me. Even Rayleigh, the grand manipulator, thought to stop me. Well, I was the one in control this whole time. This was *my* plan! I beat you all!"

Teej spat in Drowden's face in a last act of defiance. His thoughts turned to Anna. He thought of Garret. As his fate became more certain, his mind distanced itself from his body. This was the end. What a strange life. It had its ups and downs, but this ending was very bleak. Very bleak indeed.

Drowden wasn't finished with him. The punishment continued, and fresh trauma kept him tethered to consciousness a little longer. The Dreamer punched Teej's already shattered ribs.

"Do you know what I'm doing? I'm sending you to the Black Water. The Dredges will pull you down, like they tried to pull her down. You can spend your last moments suffering, and you'll have time to realize I *won*!"

While the Dreamer pinned him against the wall with one firm hand, the other fished in his pocket for something. It took some effort to keep Teej standing, so eventually Drowden let him fall and went about his task while Teej lay broken on the ground. Finally, the Dreamer retrieved chalk from his waistcoat and sketched a wide circle on the wall. He surrounded the drawing with concentric lines and arcane symbols. A moment later, he spoke words of power, and a necrotic yellow portal opened like a wound. Teej felt the wrongness and knew he should be fighting to avoid that place—any other death would be better—but he had no strength left.

Drowden bent down and hefted Teej by the shirt to look straight into his eyes. "What does a man say when he knows all his nightmares are about to come true and he can stop none of them?"

Teej said nothing.

Moving quietly behind him, Elise plunged her knife into Drowden's back with all her strength. She held it with both hands and threw her whole weight into the attack, maximizing the damage her small body could inflict.

Well done, Elise.

Teej had given her enough slack to escape, but he had hoped she would run for safety. Instead, she'd joined the fight and put the knife hidden in her boot to use.

Roaring with rage, Drowden flailed at her. The knife punctured something vital, and his body started to wobble in a weakened state. As he spun, she ducked under his swinging arm and then simply pushed him with both arms and all her might. Getting nudged at the precise moment he was off balance, Drowden fell through his own portal. The gateway closed as it swallowed him completely.

She ran to Teej and cradled his head. He could barely believe this outcome.

"Teejay, what do I do? Will you be okay?"

He tried to say something. "Till the blood runs cold."

She didn't understand.

thirty-six

All paths had to end, and even the Moonlight Road could only twist and turn through so many worlds before a traveler reached their destination.

Before she finished her journey, Anna needed to find better clothes. If she leaned an arm over the edge of the Moonlight Road, she discovered she could pull things into her little corridor of safety. So far, she'd discovered a dusty shawl and a long piece of fabric she fastened with some rope around her waist into a *kind* of smock.

Managing to steal a little dignity back for herself, she pulled the shawl tightly around her shoulders to ward off the chill. The road faded below her feet as she approached the end of her journey. Her penultimate steps on that glistening path were pleasant, but the urgency to save her friends pushed her forward. A bright sun, a blue sky, and a sea of green grass lightened her soul and slowed her step. As she stepped through the last portal, it became clear that the Moonlight Road was fickle.

A final glimpse of sunshine flickered out as Anna stepped, once again, into the life-consuming gloom of the Sump.

"Oh no."

With mounting dread, she knew it was already too late. The Moonlight Road only went in one direction, making Anna's journey end in the worst place possible.

Anna stood close to a trickle of slick, greasy water that ran down the north rock face, creating a crevice that had led, at one time, to Ozman's cave.

She surveyed the environment. The lapping water looked just as filthy and *hungry* as the last time she'd been there, the rotted, wooden dock looked just as precarious, and the air smelled just as stale with a combination of dampness and rot. She remembered dangling her feet in that water perhaps a thousand years ago. Although everything in the Sump looked exactly the same, somehow, it was all different. She was different.

"I knew I'd come back here!" Anna cried out loud without capitulation. She felt no need to surrender to the bleakness around her. In the past, the Sump was conquered by trickery, and this time, she would walk out. Anna knew she would escape this place once more by facing her fears.

Last time she was here, Anna heard her mother's voice speak to her directly and more clearly than at any point in her life. But right now, Anna was alone. She had to face this by herself.

"Oh, this is bad comedy!" a voice suddenly broke the silence. "The fates have conspired to fill my eternal prison with the very worst company."

For a moment, Anna struggled to place the voice. *Ozman?* No, it couldn't be him. This voice had a similar pitch but was crueler and lower, more of a growl.

Drowden.

Standing close to the water's edge, she couldn't make out his ugly visage in the gloom. When he turned to face her, a flicker of moonlight reflected in his cold, blue eyes. He stiffly stood about twenty feet from her with clenched fists.

"This is my domain, and you had better—"

"Ha!" she cut him off. "This is funny!"

"There is nothing to laugh about here! You will listen to me and…what in God's name are you wearing?"

Anna pulled her makeshift robes closer to her body. For some reason, the frigid wind hadn't touched her yet. It took a while for the Sump's curious coldness to penetrate the flesh.

"I have misplaced my clothes."

He let out a short grunt before continuing. "I have brought you here—"

"No," she cut him off again. "No, you haven't. *That's* a lie."

Drowden growled like an animal and took a few angry steps forward. Anna held her ring up and declared, "Stop right there."

They both seemed surprised when he froze in his tracks. He rocked back a little on his heels. "Now, listen…"

"No, you listen," she snapped back. "Answer me. Why am I here? Why are *you* here?"

"You stupid woman!" he drawled. "You know why you are here. The Moonlight Road sent you. No doubt you sought to get back to your boyfriend, and the path would have brought you to him had he accepted defeat with grace. I beat him. Do you hear me? *I beat him*! I killed your bastard boyfriend. I killed all your friends, and I'll kill you too if you don't help me get out of here. You will show me how you got out of this place. For that, I will perhaps let you go. It is not too late to win my favor, girl."

No! Drowden's words hit her like a blow to the stomach, but she was more resilient than the first time she'd faced him. That resilience allowed her to look beyond the words to see his true motivations. He was afraid.

"I don't believe you. If you beat Teej, he'd be here. You're wrong. I know he beat you."

All his claims were lies. Even the ones she wanted to believe. Her friends might yet live, but the Moonlight Road had not made a mistake. It had not taken her to Teej; it had taken her where she needed to be.

Anna walked toward Drowden, daring herself to close the distance to the man she found so repellent and terrifying. With each step, his threat diminished. He was still massive, a gorilla bulging out of human clothes, but he looked cowed and nervous.

She wasn't afraid of him, despite his angry and threatening presence.

"The path wasn't supposed to bring me to Teej," said Anna. In a few more steps she would be close enough to touch Drowden. She didn't know what compelled her onward: a burning confidence, a desire for revenge, an unnamed rage, a willingness to use her own body and soul as a weapon?

"What are you doing, you stupid bitch? Get back or I'll hurt you. I'll cast you into the Black Water! You'd do well to beg for my mercy. Your power is weak here. If we fight each other, then we doom ourselves. Our only chance is to conserve our Vig."

Anna looked him up and down. Drowden's arms hung loose at his side. He took no action as she stepped toward him. She was expecting him to shout or strike at her, but he was limp. The architect of her recent pains, and he stood there like a puppet with cut strings. Drowden didn't even react when she grabbed the lapels of his jacket and looked deep into his eyes. In the darkness behind him, the Black Water hungered.

What was she doing? Drowden was a mountain of muscle and could snap her neck with ease, but still she held him in place.

"We have to work together," he said lamely, avoiding her gaze. There was desperation in his voice. "You're showing me you're not afraid. Fine. You're stronger than your boyfriend, I understand that, but Avicimat drains us all. There can be no fight between us here."

He almost sounded reasonable. Perhaps this was his best attempt at compromise, but Anna was not interested. She slowly shook her head.

In desperation, Drowden grabbed her slender wrists with ape-like hands. His grip was like steel. He turned her suddenly, almost yanking her arms out of their sockets. Holding her over the Black Water, he pushed her to the very brink. This was his final intimidation, the only threat he had left, and it was exactly what she had counted on.

295

His eyes were manic. Spittle flecked his dirty beard as he spoke. "You fool! You're bringing this on yourself. Why are we wasting time with this? I want to drop you, but I can't. So, let us—"

"I hardly ever think about killing myself now," Anna interrupted. "Since I met Teej."

Drowden looked at her as if she was mad.

"I'll make it out of the water," said Anna. "I always do. I'll make it out and somehow. I'll get back to Teej. But you won't."

Planting both feet on the ground, Anna pushed off as hard as she could. Drowden was heavy, but she used every ounce of her Will, not just in her hands, but in her feet too. *Maybe one day I'll actually teach you something useful.*

Teej had taught her more than he would ever know.

For a moment, it seemed like Drowden might not topple with her, but her Praxis lent her strength, and her ring glowed with Vig. As she fell deeply and completely into the Black Water, Anna pulled Drowden in with her.

I'll make it out of the water. I always do.

glossary

Aesthete (Dreamer): An artist so pre-eminent in their field that their Art can change the laws of reality and create a possibility space known as a "Haze."

Alby: A French/African Metik and brother to Pappi. He looks around eleven years old but is much older.

Ancestrals: Precursors of the Aesthetes, these ancient and powerful beings have mostly disappeared or fallen dormant. Their nature and origin are contentious theological and philosophical debating points amongst Metiks and Dreamers.

Andre DeLorde: A handsome Aesthete in his early twenties whose Art is based on performance and painting.

Apoth (John Murray Speare): A member of the Doxa and a powerful Aesthete that creates monstrosities known as Pilgrims through unnecessary surgery. Brother to Mr. Ozman.

Art, the (Mimesis): The ability held by Aesthetes to create Hazes.

August Club: A secret nightclub/brothel where every fantasy can be experienced. It is a Staid Haze that is almost impossible to find.

Banille: The pressure that Basine exerts on a Haze. Banille will cause any Haze to eventually collapse.

Basine: The "real" world. Everything outside The Realm that is not inside a Haze.

Behind the Veil: A term used to describe awareness of more than just the Basine aspect of reality. When a person is Behind the Veil, they are able to perceive Hazes and are conscious of their experiences within them.

Black Water: An expanse of malignant, hungering water located at the base of The Realm, spreading from the depths of the Sump to the silver shores of Selmetridon. The Black Water swallows "all lost things that will never be found."

Charon (the Boatman): An Ancestral that seeks out the lost and hopeless. He never provides aid, but will offer an end to suffering to the last person alive in the Sump.

Choir: A collection of Muses that produce more Vig as a group.

Corpa Haze: A Haze that is sustained by the energy of an Aesthete. A Corpa Haze is temporary, but it will influence Basine when it resolves.

Crags: Razor-beaked creatures that exist in The Realm, especially high in the caves of the Sump.

Crit Command (the Word): A verbal command issued by a Metik that compels anything within a Haze to obey. One of the four powers of the Metik (the Will, the Word, the Sight and the Sword).

Decadan: Archaic term for a Haze.

Doxa: A loose collation of Aesthetes united in their desire to bring about a theological change to Basine by creating a new deity.

Dreamer: Colloquial term for an Aesthete.

Dredges: Lost souls trapped in the Sump, these creatures are emaciated and have lost their humanity to the Black Water.

Drowden (the Occultist): A powerful, precocious Aesthete and the de facto leader of the Doxa. His Art flows from arcane symbols and occultism.

Endless Gray Sea: The sea that exists around everything in the Firmament. The end of every journey.

Etune: A living being created within a Haze. An Etune can be a person or animal, but when a Haze ends, they disappear from Basine.

Fetish: A physical object imbued with Vig, exhibiting residual behaviors from the Haze where it originated. A Fetish can seem supernatural to people in Basine.

Firmament: A term used by Aesthetes and Metik to describe "everything," including Basine, The Realm, all of the Staid Hazes, The Moonlight Road, the Endless Gray Sea and anywhere else that may exist.

Fluxa Haze: A form of Haze which is self-sustaining, pulling Vig from those who experience it and growing exponentially. Fluxa Hazes can change the nature of Basine, but they often Spiral and are always disruptive and harmful to reality. Fluxa Hazes are very rare, the most recent occurring hundreds of years ago.

Geas: (In Irish folklore) an obligation or prohibition magically imposed on a person.

Groven, The: An old museum, the Groven is also an Idyll.

Gwinn (King Gwinn, the Monarch): An Ancestral, and the unofficial ruler of the Firmament. By far the most powerful being active in The Realm, he has lapsed into apathy and torpor. His absence from Basine has loosened his influence on the world, and some now doubt whether he still resides in the holy city of Selmetridon. His nature, origins and intentions were once hotly debated amongst Aesthetes and Dreamers, but he is now rarely discussed or mentioned.

Haze: A possibility space created by an Aesthete where they use Art to change the rules of reality. Their power within the Haze is determined by their natural abilities and the amount of Vig they can retain and channel.

Idyll: A place where Vig is present in large amounts. An Idyll is often a place where people will feel inspired. Idylls are essential resources for Aesthetes and are often contested or fought over.

Kanna Island (Avalon): An ancient Staid Haze. Its origins are a mystery, and no one knows who created it. In the Firmament, it is close to—but not part of—The Realm.

Kunlun Mountain: A huge peak within the Realm from which you can see Selmetridon.

Linda: Wildey's former partner and a friend to Teej, she was killed in the Doxa's Spiraling Fluxa Haze when Wildey turned on his friends.

Malamun: A Staid Haze that appears to be located on the moon. An ancient and potent source of Vig, Malamun is currently a run-down bar and nightclub, but it has existed in different forms for as long as any Aesthetes can remember.

Maxines: A dormant Idyll, it serves as a hideout for Teej and Anna.

Metik: An individual with the ability to change the Hazes created by Dreamers. Their abilities are sometimes broken down as "The Will, the Word, the Sight and the Sword."

Moonlight Road, The (Mangata): A secret path that can only be walked by each person once. It is described as "a frozen path of Moonlight that takes you through worlds you can see, but never touch." Anyone walking the path will travel through a new location each ten steps, but they will be safe if they don't step off the path. Mangata was thought to be ruined and inaccessible.

Mott (the Midnight Man): An Aesthete and a founding member of the Doxa. His Art is based on writing, in particular macabre poetry about murdering young women.

Muse: An individual whose presence generates more Vig than normal. Muses are typically very inspiring people.

Mustaine: A sleazy Aesthete whose Art is based on rock music. He has a particular hatred for Wildey, who almost killed him.

New Motive Power, The: A malicious entity that the Doxa are trying to create with a Fluxa Haze. It is intended to be a new Dark God, but each time the Doxa attempt to create it, the Haze Spirals.

Night Collectors: Etunes created by the Midnight Man. They are large monsters that capture and suffocate their victims in constricting bags.

Noop: A derogatory term for a person who is neither a Muse nor an Aesthete, but who is nonetheless Behind the Veil and spends their time in the company of Aesthetes. A kind of groupie.

Ozman, Mr. (the Scientist): An Aesthete, formerly the proprietor of the bar on Malamun. His brother is The Apoth.

Pappi: A tall Arabic Metik. Friend to Teej, brother to Alby.

Periapt (the Sword): The weapon and tool used by a Metik within a Haze. The term "the Sword" is symbolic, and the Periapt can be any item. Often a Metik learns to produce their Periapt within a Haze, while other Metiks will retain a physical Periapt imbued with some Vig and associated with an emotional memory from their past.

Pilgrim: An Etune that has continued to exist after the resolution of its Haze. Pilgrims are anomalies and typically don't exist long as it requires large amounts of Vig to sustain them.

Pinapune: An Aesthete and old friend of Teej.

Praxis: The process by which the Art (Mimesis) is modified and co-opted by a Metik.

Provident, The: A possible precursor race to the Ancestrals, they have long since abandoned the Firmament. The one exception is Gwinn, who may be the last of their race.

Raguel (The Green Knight): An Ancestral Knight in the court of King Gwinn, he is ancient and unstoppable in combat, wielding crystal swords called the Mirror Blades.

Rayleigh (Old Grayface): A powerful and old Aesthete, and the acting leader of the community. Although Dreamers as a whole are too anarchic and disparate to universally recognize his authority, they all respect his judgments and few would contradict him.

Realm, The: The generic term given to a large, mostly empty world ruled over by King Gwinn from his throne in the Holy City of Selmetridon. Whether it is a Staid Haze, a shadow of Basine or a different reality entirely was formerly a contentious issue amongst Aesthetes and Metiks, but it is now seldom visited or discussed. No one knows exactly how big The Realm is, but it encompasses many distinct regions including the Sump, the Silver Shores, Selmetridon and many regions beyond. There are few remaining open gateways into The Realm from Basine.

Selmetridon: A sprawling, seemingly uninhabited Holy City in The Realm. Home to King Gwinn, it is now difficult to reach Selmetridon from Basine.

Spiraling: A term for when a Haze collapses, causing harm to people and damage to Basine. Fluxa Hazes are the most likely to

Spiral. Many Metiks interpret their duty to be the prevention of Spiraling Hazes.

Staid Haze: A Haze that is no longer affiliated with a particular Aesthete, and that endures far longer than a Corpa Haze.

Straight Way, The: A path through the Realm that takes the traveler through every location. It is now blocked and partially ruined.

Sump, the (Avicimat): A huge cavern and network of underground tunnels and chambers at the lowest level of The Realm. The Sump is where all lost things go that will never be found. It represents both a prison for enemies and a place of exile.

The Will, the Word, the Sight, and the Sword: The four primary abilities of Metiks. They in turn represent the willpower to change a Haze, the ability to command Etunes within a Haze, sensitivity to the flow of Vig, and the Metiks Periapt (weapon).

Torpor: A form of apathetic madness that affects the minds of very old Aesthetes and Metiks. It is characterized with a disinterest and desire to disengage from Basine, and muddled, incomplete and incorrect memory formation.

Undreamer: A rare and powerful form of Metik that has limited ability to change Hazes, but great potential to destroy them.

Vig: The fuel Aesthetes use to create their Hazes. It can only be detected by those who are already Behind the Veil, where a unique sense allows them to experience it as a kind of air current or invisible light.

Vinicaire (The Travelling Troubadour/Thespian): An Aesthete whose Art flows from acting and performance. He holds a deep love for abandoned places and hidden stages.

Wildey (The Anarchist): A Metik, he betrayed his former friend Teej and is now hiding in the August Club. He hates Aesthetes intensely, and his former partner was Linda.

acknowledgments

For everyone at Owl Hollow Press. Especially
Emma and Hannah, who always push me to be a little better
than I think possible.

To the Owl Hollow authors. What a fantastic, supportive
parliament of Owls we are!

To Amanda Evans Donnelly, Benjamin Thomas and
Sherry Ficklin. Amazing authors and friends. Buy their books!

For Nana, this time and always.

For my dear friend Lina and her wonderful family. She is a
mentor, a friend and one of the very best people I know.

And finally, for my wee niece Millie. The world will be saved
by brave little girls like you.

Thomas Welsh is the winner of the Elbow Room fiction prize and has been published in *404 Ink* and *Leicester Writes*. He received an honorable mention in *Glimmer Train's* Very Short Fiction award, and his story "Suicide Vending Machine" is featured on the *Pseudopod Podcast*.

His work has qualified him for induction into the Fellowship of BAFTA, and he has been published on major sites like *Kotaku, Unwinnable Magazine and GlitchFreeGaming*. He loves Neil Gaiman, Ursula K. Le Guin, Roger Zelazny and dark fantasy stories where women save themselves! He lives in Scotland with his wife Nana. Follow Thomas at:

calmdowntom.com

#AnnaUndreaming
#AnnaandtheMoonlightRoad

Printed in Poland
by Amazon Fulfillment
Poland Sp. z o.o., Wrocław

52343699R00183